KT-439-501

PENGUIN BOOKS

PRETTY RUDE

Northamptonshire DISCARDED Libraries

60000470347

AM I REALLY PRETTY RUDE FOR A GIRL?

REBECCA ELLIOTT

PENGUIN BOOKS

PENGUIN BOOKS

UK | USA | Canada | Ireland | Australia
India | New Zealand | South Africa

Penguin Books is part of the Penguin Random House group of companies
whose addresses can be found at global.penguinrandomhouse.com.

www.penguin.co.uk
www.puffin.co.uk
www.ladybird.co.uk

First published 2021
001

Text copyright © Rebecca Elliott, 2021
Author photo copyright © Tom Soper Photography
YouTube is a trade mark belonging to Google LLC

The moral right of the author has been asserted

Set in 10.5/15.5 pt Sabon LT Std
Typeset by Jouve (UK), Milton Keynes
Printed and bound in Great Britain by Clays Ltd, Elcograf S.p.A.

The authorized representative in the EEA is Penguin Random House Ireland,
Morrison Chambers, 32 Nassau Street, Dublin D02 YH68

A CIP catalogue record for this book is available from the British Library

ISBN: 978–0–241–37465–8

MIX
Paper from
responsible sourc
FSC
www.fsc.org   FSC® C01817

WEST NORTHAMPTONSHIRE
COUNCIL

60000470347

Askews & Holts

CC

For my little feminist boys, Toby and Benjy. Xx

ONE

Shoulders back and chin up, I manhandle my boobs into separate entities, determined as they are to lump together and form one sinister super-boob. I check myself out in the mirror on the upstairs landing. A mirror I've had – at best – a challenging relationship with over my fifteen years.

We're still hardly BFFs, and there are many days when I hate the motherflipper, but at least now she doesn't *always* stare at me with a judgemental glare. In fact, sometimes I kind of like how she looks at me now. I see myself less as an unfinished, poorly constructed primary-school project and more like I'm the real deal, not perfect by any means, but something worth looking at, something that doesn't need to be hidden.

My body hasn't changed – I still sometimes think it's like a collection of overlapping circles, like an upturned Olympics logo – but my view of it most definitely has. I like me. I like my overlapping circles – my lady lumps. And I like putting them in clothes that enhance my me-ness, like the current ensemble I'm modelling this evening – a

Princess Leia T-shirt covered by a tweed waistcoat, ripped jeans, white trainers and a red fedora hat. Good God, fashion is a lot more fun when you get over the whole 'you MUST NOT wear this if you want to look thin and normal' crap.

Thin and normal are so overrated.

Just as I'm admiring myself, like a puppy wagging its tail at the sight of its reflection in a window, I hear the whirlwind sounds of Mum manically clearing up the day's mess. I freeze. The ominous crashes move from the kitchen into the hall.

I should be in bed (or at least studying). Instead, I'm trying on outfits I *might* wear if I pluck up the courage to do my comedy stand-up routine at the local pub's open-mic night on Friday. The pub owned by the dad of Leo, the git-crush who used me for my comedy-writing skills before breaking my hopeless heart.

But, hey, his dad's pub is the only place around here you can do stand-up comedy. I mean, sure, I *could* just rock up to the corner of my street and start telling jokes to the group of sinister ten-year-olds hanging round the vandalized postbox, but something tells me they wouldn't be the most receptive audience.

The mum-tornado moves back to the living room and I breathe again.

Mum likes that I do comedy and she likes that I like my reflection these days, but she definitely does not like me 'faffing around' with these things when I should be doing something 'more important', like helping her tidy up, revising for exams or going to bed. Honestly, I love that woman, but her priorities are messed up.

As I debate whether the red fedora might be a little too much even for me, I feel the familiar buzz of a new comedy idea. I silently dance a jig of joy back into my bedroom and scribble down some notes before the idea falls out of my brain and vanishes like joke-flavoured ice cream melting on to the pavement of comedic regret. Studying can wait. I mean, there's a whole school year before my GCSE exams, so what's the rush?

I rummage around in my 'floordrobe' (the 'polite' term my delightful mother uses for the impressive landscape of clothes piled around my room) and forage for the perfect outfit to match the new idea. And eventually, after scaling Stinky Mountain and cave-diving through Pants Peak, I unearth just the right ensemble.

I strip down, put on a black strappy vest and team it with the yellow fake-fur coat I rescued from a pile of old seventies stuff my Granny Mo (or 'Grammo' as we inventively call her) was throwing out. Perfect! Then I make a run for it over to the bathroom and start slapping on Mum's make-up. I'm not aiming for sexy here – I'd say I'm going more for a look that is mad clown meets Kim Kardashian – and, when I'm finally satisfied that my face is weighed down with enough cosmetics to frighten a small child, I turn my attention to my hair. I backcomb and scrunch it up with great fistfuls of mousse, until my hair-to-face ratio is similar to a snooker ball being spooned by a poodle.

I return to the mirror. I look – well, perhaps not ridiculously fabulous, but definitely fabulously ridiculous.

Back in my bedroom, I sit in front of my phone, which is glamorously propped up on my desk against a box of Tampax Compak. I pull my mouth into a patronizing grin, press record and start a brand-new YouTube video.

'Hi, everyone! It's the PFG here. Did you know that seven out of ten teenage girls *hate* the way they look? I know, right, that is *shocking*. Just *terrible* . . . the arrogance of the other three.

'But seriously I think we should all celebrate our beauty. Now, I'm a bigger girl in case you hadn't noticed (which I'm sure you hadn't because who really cares about what girls on the internet look like, right?) and I'll tell you what really gets on my tit-end, and that's the shedloads of blogs and vlogs telling *me* what, as a plus-size girl, I *should* and *should not wear*. You know the kind of thing . . .'

Then, with a super-happy, girlie American accent, I launch into a spoof of all those 'helpful' videos.

'Hi, it's me, Stacy Beeatch, and I'm back with my latest fashion tips for the unfortunate.

'OK, this one's aimed at all you gorgeous BIG girls, all you super-sized, sexy, curvaceous fatty-boom-batties! You know who you are! And you should be proud *of who you are, while at the same time hiding it so no one else has to pretend to like it.*

'So what I'm gonna do for you today is tell you what you should NOT wear if you want to pass as a human. OK! How exciting! Let's start!

'So, first off, you need to determine what body shape you are. There's the hourglass shape, the inverted triangle, the pear shape . . . but, as this vid's for big girls, I'm gonna go ahead and presume you're potato-shaped, which just means fat all over. OK? OK!

'So here are my top five tips.

'One. Invest in some shapewear. Girls, you need something industrial-strength that will suck, tuck, punish and torture your body into some sort of recognizable girl shape. Repeat after me: I do not need full use of my internal organs. I DO need to look thinner.

'Two. Wear heels! Chances are you have stubby little legs, and who wants to see those? No one. Literally no one. But good news, jelly-bellies, alarmingly high heels are your friend! They will make you look up to three per cent sexier, and they're only thirty-five times more uncomfortable, and you just can't argue with that math. So go high or go home, ladies! Though don't attempt stairs; gravity and inelegance are against you and you'll probably end up in an ambulance. OK? OK!

'Three. Sticking with legs, do NOT wear leggings. Same goes for "skinny" jeans – I mean, the clue's in the title, dummy. These garments are made for good-looking people, not you.

'Four. Wear just one colour, preferably dark, like black. That way you can melt into the shadows like a roly-poly ninja and people won't have to endure the sight of your disgusting bulges. Remember, you won't cause a scene if you can't be seen!

'*Five. Don't wear anything tight, don't wear anything baggy, don't carry a small bag or a big bag; don't wear patterns, anything cropped, anything masculine, wide belts, thin belts, pleats, stripes, rollnecks, boat necks, anything with pockets, ruffles, fur, feathers ... basically, anything with personality or charisma. I know you're probably desperate for friends, but, trust me, these clothes are not your friends. They will ridicule you. Behind your fat back. And, really, why bother with fashion at all? You're just shoving a bargain-store sausage in Harrods wrapping paper, and that's just deceitful. OK? OK!*

'*So that's it, girls – have fun with my tips and, if in doubt, just stay at home where no one will have to see you. Bye for now!!*'

The forced grin falls from my face, back to my usual sarcastic smirk as I return from being Stacy Beeatch. I knowingly roll my eyes and shake my head at the camera.

'See you next time, beautiful people.'

As I stop recording, little excitement puppies scamper through my brain. The audience's laughter might not be there, but the high of performing feels almost the same as doing a live gig. Also, I can feel that this is funny stuff, even if it is maybe a bit rude to fashion vloggers, who probably do mean well, I guess. But I've gotta have an edge otherwise I'm never gonna be noticed.

Not that anyone's actually watching these videos. I started making them about a month ago under the handle the PFG (like BFG, but meaning Pretty Funny Girl, obvs) and so far I only have a handful of subscribers. Which is why I haven't actually told anyone, not even my best friends, Chloe and Kasia, about this – it all seems a bit too dumb-ass pathetic.

I'm mostly making these videos for my own benefit anyway. I spend so much time writing new material, but with nowhere to actually use it I needed a reason to keep writing and practising performing. So far one gig in London and one disastrous (don't ask) local open-mic gig is all my stand-up career has amounted to. But, hey, just like applying stretch-mark cream, if I keep at it, eventually something good will happen, right? (Right?!)

I grab a fistful of Mum's cleansing wipes and start mopping away the make-up, watching in the mirror as my face gradually looks less like a child's colouring book. Just as my freckly features are revealed, my phone vibrates. It's a message from Chlo, trying to persuade me again to do the open-mic on Friday, using about sixteen *pleeeeeaaaase*'s.

I reply: **Argh, I dunno. U do remember last time, when I exploded the stage with my arse, right?**

(If you don't know what this refers to, I'm not going to tell you. It's too ball-crushingly embarrassing.)

Kas joins the conversation.

K: But u were great before that happened!

C: Tho' your butt did get the biggest laugh of the set.

K: Chlo!

H: No, she's right, it did.
My booty could headline at the Apollo.

C: U doughnut, that made me laugh and smudge my nail varnish.

H: Sorry.

C: No you're not.

H: SO not.

K: Go on, Pig, it'll be fun!

C: OMG, u used the P word.

K: Fanny-farts.

Sorry, I meant Hay.

H: It's cool.

My name is Haylah, but Pig was one of the many nicknames that had been unlovingly hurled at me at school. Then, like a boss, I turned it back on the bullies by claiming it as my own and insisting everyone call me that. But in the end I totally rejected Pig, breaking away from how other people viewed me and 'coming out' as the real me. It was a sort of rebranding, a way of saying to the world, 'I'm not what you see me as – a dumpy, insignificant girl from a broken home. I'm Haylah, a big, brash, proud comedian extraordinaire, so get used to it or get the hell out of my way before I mow you down with my epic boobs.'

And, sure, I'm still on board with all that, but . . . don't tell anyone, but now that it's gone I kinda miss Pig. I'd been called it for so long by so many people – many of whom loved me – that I actually saw it as affectionate. It didn't make me think of fat, disgusting hogs. If anything, it made me think of those trendy little pet micro-pigs – cute, pink, intelligent, lovable – who grow up to be more of a handful than their owners planned for. And I kinda liked that by being happily called Pig I was shoving it to all those people who thought being big was something negative. On the other hand, I'm not sure any comedy clubs are going to book a teenage girl called Pig – so I'm sticking with Haylah for now – or PFG.

While I'm pondering this, Chlo continues to try to harass me into doing the open-mic. But I'm still not sure. I lie on my bed and shudder at the embarrassing memory of last time – which, as I HAVE SAID, I'm not going to go into, so don't even, OK? And, apart from all that, there is the fact that it's happening at Leo's dad's pub. Meaning ACTUAL LEO – ridiculously good-looking but absolute breaker of hearts and stealer of excellent comedy material – might be there. (OK, 'stealer' is a bit harsh as I did technically *give* him my jokes willingly. But he definitely didn't have any trouble taking them off me, then kissing me, then telling me he had a girlfriend.) He's not at my school any more, so thankfully I haven't seen him in a while. He's gone off to the local sixth-form college where, unlike at our crappy school, he might have a chance of getting into a top university like Cambridge. The smug git. Smug, incredibly sexy git.

Stop it, stupid brain!!

But, embarrassing memories and sexy gits aside, why *not* do the gig? I can't afford to be picky; it's not like there's any other stand-up opportunities for teenage girls around where I live. You have to get booked into the open-mic nights in London and, for that, you kind of have to have actual stand-up comedy experience and be, y'know, an *adult*. So, if I don't go to this pub gig, I'm back to desperately staring at my emails and hoping that something pings in from the impossibly cool comedy-club owner Van, who I met after I entered the London Young Comic of the Year a few months ago. I've not heard anything yet . . . which does make me worry she's forgotten about me, or realized no one's actually interested in the pathetic opinions of a teenage girl.

But the thing is, in case you can't already tell, I really *haven't* been feeling pathetic lately. I'm still on a high from absolutely blimmin' nailing that competition. I'm loving my sweet new sense of style thanks to my recent raids on Grammo's wardrobe, me and Chloe and Kas haven't had a fallout for two whole months (although they have both been off on holiday for a lot of the summer, so that's kind of helped), and I turned fifteen a month ago – though it wasn't the world's most captivating moment, as it was celebrated in a caravan in the pouring rain on a hellish trip to Norfolk with Mum, my little brother, Noah, AND Ruben, my mother's, ugh, 'boyfriend'.

OK, OK, I *do* like Ruben. At first I wasn't sure – it had been me, Mum and Noah for so long, and I didn't want to see Mum hurt again after He Who Must Not Be Named (my useless father, not Voldemort – though I think I'd prefer him . . .) walked out on her. But the truth is Ruben makes Mum happy, he makes Noah happy, and he and Mum aren't super gross and snoggy together (he hasn't ever stayed the night – thank GOD!), plus he's only here a couple of days a week so it's all fine. Truth be told, when he's not being a proper twonk, he's actually quite funny. He also gets on well with Dylan.

And remind me who Dylan is, I hear you ask . . .

Oh, *I totally forgot to say*! I HAVE A BOYFRIEND. Yay!

Yes, I, Haylah Swinton – a large, undainty, loud-mouthed non-girlie girl, who believed the world would never see her as fanciable (not that I ever quite a hundred per cent believed that cos, come on, I am pretty epic) – have a *genuine* boyfriend who chooses to be my boyfriend and so far has not chosen to un-boyfriend me. I mean, it's real happy-ending stuff, especially when I tell you the whole story. So strap yourselves in, my friends, for the, ahem, love story of the century.

TWO

OK, so here's a recap: I thought Dylan fancied m' BFF Chloe on the basis that everyone fancies m' BFF Chloe because she's really cool and beautiful AND Dylan was always looking over at us. He was a consistent git to me at school so I presumed he, like most other boys, thought I was a big fat loser and was gazing at Chloe. BUT it turns out Dylan actually liked me, like, *liked* me liked me, and wasn't trying to be a git – his badly attempted 'flirting' just sort of came out that way. Classic boy logic. I mean, when are boys going to figure out that just *maybe* the best way to let someone know you like them is by being, well, *nice* to them??

Soooooo . . . Dylan apologized and asked me out. But I haven't been force-fed feminism by my mum and my comedy heroes for nothing, and so I told him sorry wasn't really good enough. If he could prove that he could get over himself, quit the muppetry and actually be nice to me at school, then maybe we could think about going out. And that's exactly what he did. So eventually I said yes. And one trip to the park with my little brother and his little sister led to another, then another, and before you know it it's the summer holidays and everyone else has buggered off on trips with their families apart from us. So now we're hanging out more and more, at my house, at the park, the cinema, wherever. Except, for some reason, at *his* house, where I've still never actually been.

And it turns out that when Dylan is actually being himself, he's pretty cool and a laugh to hang out with. To be honest (though I would NEVER tell them this, and if you do I *will* kill you), I sometimes have more fun with Dylan than I do with Kas and Chloe. I don't have to pretend to be interested in tanning shades or some new nail bar that I know I will never set foot in (and that I genuinely thought was called Celebrity Snails). Me and Dylan mostly just hang out, watch stuff together and talk. He's persuaded me to watch all twenty-three Marvel films in order and I've got him into watching stand-up and vintage comedy series – and he seems to really get it, which I can't say has ever been the case with Chlo and Kas, much as I love 'em. He's got me into new things too – he's obsessed with music, like proper old music by David Bowie, Led Zeppelin, the Beatles. Music's never been my thing really (apart from Lizzo, who is a goddess on earth, can do NO WRONG and I have a total celeb crush on).

To be honest, my brain still thinks it's cool that any boy wants to talk to me about anything, really. Which I know is stoopid cos look at me – what's not to like, right? But I guess I thought of the girlfriend/boyfriend world as a place only for the preened, plucked, pouty and perfectly pretty people. Which definitely isn't me. So, just when I was hoping and wondering whether we were definitely a boyfriendy-and-girlfriendy thing, one night he turns to me with a mouth full of Pringles and says, 'So you *are* my girlfriend, right?' And it felt like just about the most romantic thing in the world.

So, yeah, it's nice to have a new friend. A new friend who's a boy. A BOYFRIEND – yay!

The only thing is . . . now we're back at school I've reverted to being a bit unsure about what we are. At lunch break, me, Chlo and Kas hang around on the steps to the gym with Dylan and his mates. This is a regular thing now: the boy and girl groups bridged by me and Dylan wanting to hang out. People seem to know we're a couple (I'M half of an actual SCHOOL COUPLE! POPULARITY IS MINE FOR THE TAKING!), but we're not really sure how to act like it. I know what's expected of us, but we're just not like the other show-off couples who constantly suck each other's faces off like mating leeches.

In fact . . . if I'm being really honest with you, apart from one time when he Sellotaped up one of the holes in my ripped jeans to 'save my knee from unnecessary draughts', there's been zero physical contact. We haven't even held hands, let alone kissed, which I guess is OK? I mean, is it normal if your boyfriend hasn't in any way touched you? I guess we're just doing our own thing, and we like hanging out with each other. But that doesn't mean we're just 'friends'. We're still 'boyfriend and girlfriend', right? Right?

Kas and Chlo aren't convinced. When they were away on their summer holidays, they thought me and Dylan were smooching our way through the summer. I opened up to them when we had our reunion catch-up round Kas's with a Chinese takeaway and some Polish dessert called *sernik* that Kas's mum had made, which looked exactly like the scouring sponge next to our sink, but tasted like heaven in a bowl. After listening to Chloe's tale of getting friendly down in the sand with some hunk called 'Kyle' on holiday, who's now 'totally craving for the Chloe and gonna come and stay soon', I told them about my serious lack of girlfriendy boyfriendy activities, concluding that: 'My boy experience so far amounts to Leo snogging me and then rejecting me, and Dylan not even wanting to snog me. Clearly, I'm just not girlfriend material.' I paused to shove three prawn crackers in my mouth before carrying on between crunches. 'But then girlfriend material would be something soft and smooth, like silk or satin or something, whereas I am, at best, "mate" material, like denim or corduroy – something plain and hard-wearing.'

'Rubbish,' said Kas with a swish of her hand, her normal instinct being to keep everyone in the room happy at all times by dismissing anything negative.

'Well, do you actually want to kiss him?' said Chloe, nibbling half a prawn cracker like she'd never really learned how to eat properly. 'Cos, if you don't, just dump him and move on. And, if you do, just grab the dude and stick your tongue in his mouth. Simple.'

'Urgh, Chlo! Too much,' I said. 'The contents of a snog should never be described in any detail, otherwise no one would want to partake in it at all. It's the same with sausages.'

'Is it now?' said Chloe with a saucy raised eyebrow.

We all laughed.

'Honestly, Chloe, get your mind out of the gutter,' I said. 'Clearly, when I said "sausages", I was only ever referring to *penises*.' Then I shoved two chicken balls in my mouth and they almost shot right out again as we all exploded with laughter.

But Chlo, sensing me dodging the subject, threw a prawn cracker at my head and said, 'Well? *Do* you want to kiss him?'

'I don't know, really . . . maybe? Sometimes? OK, yes.' I got flustered and started gabbling at lightning speed. 'I mean, it's not like Leo last year; it's more comfortable than that, more like seeing a really fluffy-looking pair of slippers that you think would be really cosy and warm to put on. But then, if the slippers don't want to be put on, that kind of puts you off them a bit, doesn't it?' I stopped to catch a breath as they both stared at me.

'Slippers,' said Kas, throwing down her prawn cracker in disgust.

Chloe piped up, 'Do I need to remind you, girl, that YOU SNOGGED LEO BLOODY JACKSON, Hotty McHottison who literally everyone in the school, including, I'm sure, sexless Mr Jacobs, wants to snog? YOU DID THAT. And now you're settling for a pair of *comfy slippers* that doesn't even want to look at your boobs. I mean, what the actual? No. You are worth more than that.'

'But . . . I like him. A lot.' I looked to Kas for support.

'I have to say I'm with Chloe here, babe. You also like KitKats a lot – doesn't mean you should spend *all* your time with KitKats at the expense of every other chocolate bar in the world, especially if it's a KitKat that doesn't even want you to eat it.'

'Kas!' I exclaimed with a hand over my chest in a gesture of mock shock.

She giggled. 'Yeah, OK, that came out wrong, but you know what I mean.'

'Look, it's fine if you and Dylan aren't ready for the snogging yet, that's cool, but, dude, if he's just wanting a playmate and showing you literally no signs of boyfriend-like stuff, and you're not really that fussed about him anyway, why bother?' said Chlo. 'Plus, you're acting like he's all cute and sweet when this is Dylan we're talking about. *Dy-lan*. Who once ate a stick insect in science class.'

'Allegedly,' I said.

'Yeah, but *he's* the one who alleged it,' said Kas.

'Good point,' I said. 'But . . . urgh . . . I don't wanna dump him. I mean, I do like him and I might not get another boyfriend, like, ever.'

'URGH!' said Chlo. 'I give up!'

The conversation then drifted off boys for a while, as it occasionally does, but later, when we were all hanging around in Kas's room, listening to music, it started up again. Chlo and Kas were sitting on the bed, painting one another's toenails each a different colour. I had declined to be involved, remarking that it was as pointless as painting each of your teeth a different colour. They of course rolled their eyes at me and got on with it as I messed about with Kas's mum's exercise hula hoop in the middle of the room.

'I can't believe I can actually do this – I can actually do a sporting thing!' I said, gleefully spinning the hoop round my middle.

'Dude, it's a weighted hoop. It's easy – my cat could do it,' said Chlo.

'Oh God, I'd *love* to see Ryan hula-hooping. That would be SO cute,' said Kas.

(Chloe has the only cat in the universe called Ryan Reynolds-Gosling.)

'So, tell me, apart from Ryan, who else is ringing your cuteness bell right now? I have my hot beach buddy, Kyle, and Hay has her comfy pair of Dylan slippers, but *you*, Kas, haven't crushed on anyone in, like, *ages* – so tell Auntie Chloe: who've you set your sights on at the mo, missus?'

'No one,' said Kas, concentrating intently on painting white polka dots on Chloe's multicoloured toenails.

'Oh, come on! Tell us!' said Chlo, leaning back on a mountain of cushions on the bed, her hands behind her head.

'Yeah, come on, Kas,' I said, a little out of breath with all the hula-hooping. She glanced over at me and I just caught a flash of something familiar cross her face. It was so brief it was hard to say whether it was a small frown or a huff through the nose, but whatever it was I recognized it from myself. An awkwardness, a wanting to be left alone, and yet desperation to be part of the group. I remembered when this was me, before my boy radar was woken up by Leo last year and Chlo was always teasing me about who I fancied. It used to drive me mad, as if all that mattered was boys and crushes, but at the time that whole world was as alien to me as salads still are.

Then, when I finally had my first crush, I desperately wanted to tell them, to be a part of the conversation, and yet at the same time I wanted to keep it to myself, safe in my own private world. That's exactly how Kas looked.

So I swiftly started a game of 'Would You Rather?' to change the subject. I perfectly tailored the first question to Chloe's interests to distract her from nosing around Kas's love life: 'Would you rather have an infinite shoe collection forever or be famous for only one month?' Immediately, like a magpie changing course to the next shiny thing, Chloe had forgotten all about Kas and her shocking lack of crushes.

Anyway, now that I've caught you up on my red-hot love life, let me bring you back to the present. Specifically the day after I uploaded my latest video, when I'm walking to class with Chloe and Kas.

Chlo is still trying to persuade me to do the open-mic. She's obsessed!

'I don't get it. Why are you so desperate for me to go?' I say between mouthfuls of delicious, delicious KitKat.

'OK . . .' says Chlo, stopping outside our form room and checking up and down the corridor for spies. She lowers her voice and whispers, 'Because I have the total hots for Watto!'

Her eyes widen like she's just told us world-shattering breaking news. But frankly I'm so used to Chlo telling us she has the hots for some boy or other I don't even stop chewing. Even if the 'man' in question this time is Liam Watts, a geeky, bookish, fluffy-haired friend of Dylan's, and *not* Chloe's usual type.

'Oh, he is pretty yummy,' says Kas, 'and super clever too. He's in most of my classes.'

It's still not a KitKat-stopping moment (what is?), but the thought also occurs to me that for weeks Chlo's been banging on about her 'holiday romance of the century'. And, sure, I shouldn't be surprised, because this is Chlo after all, but normally she only has the hots for one guy at a time.

I pause with one hand on the classroom door. Mrs Perkins's voice booms out over the buzz of chatter on the other side. With raised eyebrows, I turn to Chlo and ask 'Hang on, what about "Kyle", your "better-than-*Love-Island* beach hunk"?'

Chloe shrugs and gives me a smirk-pout. 'Gotta keep your options open, ladies! Kyle's totes loved-up with me, of course, but I'm not seeing him till Chrimbo. What am I supposed to do until then – become a nun?!'

'Fair point,' says Kas, nodding obediently.

I roll my eyes while inwardly giggling at the idea of Chlo as the world's worst nun.

Chloe passionately increases her pressure on me to do the gig. She explains, using her flawless Chlo logic, that if I do the gig Dylan will go, and if Dylan goes Watto will too, and then she can pounce on the poor boy like a lioness devouring her terrified prey. If, on the other hand, I *don't* do the gig, her chances with Watto, and therefore her chances of ever experiencing happiness again, will be crushed forever.

So, in the end, I agree to do the gig. I mean, what other choice do I have? It's either that or listen to Chloe dramatically explain in minute detail how I'm ruining her life.

'Yay!' she squeals, clutching her hands together in delight. 'You'll nail it, Hay. You're a whole different person to last time. There's no way the new Haylah would explode the stage with her bum.'

(Look, just pretend you didn't hear that, OK? I told you, I am NOT going into the grisly details of my last gig there.) But Chlo's so right – I AM a different person now. I am the new and improved Haylah 2.0, right?! And, although she may have slightly dodgy motives, I love that Chlo sees that.

I puff up with pride. 'I bloody am, aren't I? I *am* gonna nail it. Oh, it is so on!'

'Yay, Hay!' says Kas, clapping her palms together in her delicate fairy-princess way as we walk into the classroom.

Mrs Perkins, our spindly, angular form teacher with a voice like a cannon, sarcastically tells us 'Take your time, girls,' as we make our way past our chattering classmates.

'Sorry, miss,' says Kas, flashing Mrs Perkins her most innocent smile.

Mrs Perkins smiles sweetly back at Kas, before pointing her sharp features in the direction of me and Chlo and scowling. All the teachers love Kas. I think they're bewildered by her association with Chlo and me; you can see it in their eyes as they try to fathom why a sweet kitten is hanging out with a ridiculous pug and a vain poodle.

As I walk past his desk, Dylan gently grabs my arm – he actually touches my arm! – and asks quietly, 'Still all right if I come over laters?'

My heart cartwheels at the contact as I reply, 'Yep. Sure.'

I know it seems pathetic, but give me a break – he's my first boyfriend! And also, to give me some credit, Dylan is pretty HOT. Not in an obvious, boring boy-bandy kind of way, more in a James Corden meets Gaten Matarazzo kind of way.

Neanderthal dumb-nut Greg at the back of the class over-enthusiastically wolf-whistles at us before loudly snorting like a pig. Greg's friends snigger as the whole classroom quietens and stares at us. I'm just about to tell Greg where to shove it, but I stop when I notice Dylan quickly dropping his hand away from my arm and his cheeks flashing red.

Why did he do that? Is he embarrassed to be seen touching me?

'Shut it, knobhead,' Dylan shoots back at Greg.

As my man loudly and proudly defends me, my doubts are replaced by a warm glow. Yes, the response could have been a *little* more devastatingly witty, but the sentiment was heroic.

'Oh, don't be too harsh,' I dramatically say to Dylan as I strut my stuff over to Chlo and Kas at our usual table at the back of the room, making them and a few others laugh as I turn a ridiculously undainty pirouette. 'He's just jealous, and frankly who wouldn't be?' This gets a further flutter of giggles that lights up my laugh-hungry brain and spurs me on to more. 'After all, the only girl who's ever come close to Greg is his mum, and that's only when she's helping him into his big-boy training pants.'

The room explodes into throaty laughs and whoops and I take a bow before I sit down, my brain greedily lapping up every drop of that delicious laughter.

Later on I pick up Noah from his after-school club, and on the way home he does his very best to drag my excited thoughts away from seeing Dylan later by asking incessant and ridiculous questions. He's obviously the best five-year-old brother who has ever existed, but also, O.M.Geeesus, that boy can talk.

'Why don't cats have belly buttons?'

'Is a sheep without legs a cloud?'

'Why do cakes go hard in the oven, but when I put that plastic cup in there it went soft and melty and Mummy got angry?'

After what feels like a lifetime, he moves on from the bonkers questions to telling me every detail of every kid in his class, including the breaking news that his friend Kyson has just got to 'reading level 5', but when I ask what level Noah's on he bafflingly replies, 'Purple.' Then, as he starts telling me about a new superhero he's invented called 'Gareth Deeds' who does 'one good deed every two days', and I start losing the will to live, I joyously remember I have some illicit chocolate buttons stashed in my bag. I dig out the distraction candy and they immediately have the desired effect of shutting up his nonsense and restoring my desire to exist. I've always known it to be true. Chocolate saves lives.

The new-found peace leaves me free to go back to wondering about Dylan and what we might get up to when he comes round later. Will there be more hot arm-grabbing action? Who knows. The day is young and literally anything is possible.

We get into the house and from the kitchen I hear Mum and Ruben laughing; his is a ridiculous ho-ho-ing Santa roar and hers is a cheeky, throaty cackle that always makes me smile. It's a proper dirty laugh. Mum could be watching *Hey Duggee* on CBeebies and she'd still shriek like she's just heard the filthiest joke in the world.

Noah disappears into the kitchen as I collapse on the sofa and check my phone to see if Dylan's messaged me. He hasn't, which doesn't mean much . . . but my heart thuds when I think of how he dropped my arm in class. God, I hope he isn't going to cancel.

At that moment, Noah bursts back into the room, wielding a spoon. 'We're playing "Spoon Balloon"!' he says, and begins drumming the teaspoon on my boobs.

'Ow!' I yell, wrenching my gaze away from my phone. 'Noah, you do know "Spoon Balloon's" not an actual thing, right?'

'It's an epic and noble sport, Haylah, and you know it!' booms Ruben as he prances into the room armed with a balloon and a teaspoon. 'It's also a game I happen to be very good at. I believe I won our last game seven – five, Noah, isn't that right? Come on then, fella, your serve. Underarm only, please, no kickbacks and first to ten gets to progress to the final quadrant.'

I do like Ruben, I really do, but, and I'm sure you'll agree here, sometimes he makes it very hard to think of him as anything other than a complete numpty.

As I prop myself up on the sofa, Noah giggles, picks up the balloon and 'serves' it by hitting it over the coffee table with his teaspoon. Ruben dramatically dives on to an armchair to hit it back, his legs flying up in the air behind him, and he *still* manages to miss the balloon. I brace myself, fully expecting to be hit by the familiar yet obscene image of Ruben's sockless ankles, *even though he's wearing shoes*. Disgusting. But to my surprise there's a pair of actual socks covering his feet and ankles! Mum must have finally got him to see sense! I feel a rush of warmth towards him, almost like I'm proud of him.

Then, before he serves the balloon back, Ruben starts holding his spoon like a guitar and shaking his head while loudly 'singing' the guitar solo from 'Bohemian Rhapsody'. The warm feeling quickly fades.

As the 'game' resumes, I sigh and leave the sofa to go and join Mum in the kitchen.

'Good day, babe?' she says as she peels potatoes at the kitchen table, the sound of *Woman's Hour* chuntering out of the Alexa behind us.

'My day *was* good until Ruben and Noah started playing that deranged cutlery-based sport,' I say as I scan the cupboard shelves for anything snackable.

Mum snorts. 'They're guys, hun. They can't sit still for too long without trying to beat each other at something.'

'Uh-huh. But seriously, Mum, is it normal for a sixty-year-old to want to beat a five-year-old at a game he made up? And which, in fact, isn't even a game so much as an exercise in self-humiliation?' I say, now elbow deep in the fridge and mid-rummage.

Mum's tone becomes exasperated. 'They're just having fun, Haylah. Ruben's a Play Specialist, for goodness' sake! It's what he's good at, plus he's keeping Noah entertained, meaning you don't have to, so don't be such an old grouch –'

'Yes, yes, I know, it's all good,' I say, cutting her off as I shut the fridge door and present her with my finds: a can of Diet Coke, a tube of yoghurt with a cartoon character on it and a small red cheese. 'Can I have these?'

She sighs. 'Well, they were for Noah's lunchbox, but, yes, whatever, fine. And also, by the way, Ruben is NOT sixty – he's forty-two!' She points the potato peeler at me as if it's a sword and she's challenging me to a duel.

26

Smirking and leaning back against the sink, I wave my own weapon of choice – the tube of yoghurt – right back at her. 'Forty-two, sixty . . . really, what's the difference? It's like people making a fuss about the difference between African and Asian elephants – they're *both* elephants.'

Duel won, I give Mum a wink and triumphantly tear open the yoghurt tube.

'Cheeky mare,' she shoots back with a grin, before reaching out and grabbing my sides right where she knows I'm the most ticklish.

I yelp. 'Get off me, woman!' I wriggle away to escape her clutches.

She lets out an evil cackle and gets back to peeling her potatoes as my mouth opens up for a massive yawn. Never one to do something subtly, it is, of course, the biggest and loudest yawn anyone has ever done. 'Uh . . . uh . . . uh . . . uh . . .'

'You sound like you're about to sing "Staying Alive",' says Mum with a chuckle.

'Uh, uh, uh . . . uh, staying awake, staying awake.'

Mum laughs some more. 'Nice. Write that one down for your funnies. Why are you so tired anyway? You've only been back at school for a couple of weeks.'

Instantly, I feel the air in the room change from fun time to nag time. Which means it's time for some major evasion on my behalf. I try to look casual.

'Yeah, erm, I know, but the homework is already insane, y'know? It being the big exam year and all that.' I speed up, my words trying to outrun the nag train. 'I've been staying up to get it all done and actually I ought to go and do some now, before Dylan comes over later.'

Dammit.

That was stupid. I know the mere mention of my boyfriend will really spark off Mum's meddling, so I swiftly stuff the yoghurt, can of Coke and the small cheese into my pockets, like a hamster stuffing its cheeks with snacks for later consumption, before quickly beginning the retreat towards my bedroom.

'You and Dylan still good then?' Mum calls after me as I head out of the kitchen and climb the stairs.

'Yep. All good,' I call back.

'Are you *actually* doing homework, Hay, or are you just watching and writing comedy?'

'Yep. All good,' I call back again, pretending not to have heard her. Then I firmly shut my door behind me so that she can't follow up with any more passive-aggressive questions.

Heaving a sigh (that was close!), I sit at my desk and swivel round on the chair a few times before looking through my latest notebook to see if anything I came up with last night is good enough for tomorrow's open-mic comedy set.

Truth is, Mum's Spidey sense was bang on as always, but for God's sake don't tell her that. I *am* tired because I keep staying up and either watching comedy or recording YouTube vids that she has no idea about. I'm still writing my comedy diary every day, which is so much more fun than an actual diary – I mean, who would ever want to read about what happened back in the day and what they felt about it and blah-blah-blah, when you can ignore all the serious stuff and just write the funny bits instead?

I read back through this week's entries, what had made me laugh that day, some one-liners and a few longer ranty comedy bits. I smile as I see things I might be able to make something of for tomorrow's set, so I start writing. And, before I know it, Dylan's knocking on the door.

THREE

Even though he's been here loads of times, the sound of Dylan at my door still makes my heart bounce around my chest like an ADHD rabbit on a pogo stick. I run down the stairs to get to the door first, but Noah beats me to it, of course. For a chunky little dude, he's surprisingly nimble.

'Hey, Dylan!' he shouts as Dylan appears in the doorway, almost filling it. Dylan's a big guy, over six feet tall, and kind of wide and solid with a big square face. Like a life-sized Minecraft character, except, y'know, a bit more sexy.

Dylan looks slightly confused and dazed, as he always does, like he's not really sure how he ended up standing at my front door.

'Noah!' he says, like it's just coming back to him where he is and who we all are. Then he puts on a fake, over-the-top posh accent as he bends down, one hand behind his back, the other outstretched to shake Noah's hand. 'Old chap, how the devil are you?!'

Noah looks up at him blankly and then laughs. 'Why didn't you bring Ruby?'

We sometimes meet Dylan and his little sister, Ruby, and Noah has now decided that the two of them are 'in love like Woody and Buzz', destined to spend infinity and beyond together.

'Yeah, sorry, mate, Ruby's at home today. Maybe next time?'

'And when can we come to your house?'

I clear my throat, look down and twist my foot a little against the bottom step I'm standing on. *Oh fanny-farts. Super awkward. Nice one, Noah.*

Although I kinda want to be cool and breezy about the whole thing, the fact is it does bother me that Dylan, in case you've forgotten, has *never* invited me to his house. And, OK, yes, it might just be that he hasn't got around to asking me yet, or maybe his parents are satanists, or maybe he's poorer than us and lives in a shoebox by the side of the road or something, but I'm presuming it's because he's embarrassed about me. I just haven't had the courage to ask him yet. Cos what if I don't like the answer?

'Soon, Noah, yep. Need to sort that out,' Dylan awkwardly replies. 'When are *you* getting your own place anyway, mate? Isn't it about time you moved out, then you can invite me over to yours? I can bring a couple of beers; we can just chill, right?'

Noah stares at him with a 'yeah, I don't know what to do with that' look on his face, like a cat who's just been handed an iPhone. Then he chuckles, turns and runs off back to Ruben in the living room.

Dylan grins at me. 'He's a strange little man.' He runs his fingers through his persistently dishevelled hair. 'So, yeah, erm, I've brought you something . . .' He's still standing on the doormat with one hand behind his back.

'You have?' I say, wondering if this is it, this is where our 'relationship' takes its next step and he gives me flowers and maybe even kisses me, and already I'm imagining telling Chlo and Kas, and I can see their jealous faces as they realize *I* am actually the one who's in the romance of the century.

'Here you go,' he says, proudly walking towards me and placing something in my hand.

As I take it from him, my fingertips brush his, which is weird – not that I touched them, just weird that I noticed. I mean, if that happens when the postman hands me his package, I don't notice it.

(OK, so the word 'package' there was not well thought-out.)

I turn it over in my palm and see that it's a pink-and-black plastic key ring that says 'Bitch'.

'I saw it and thought of you,' he says in a fake gushing voice with his hands over his heart.

I burst out laughing and clutch the key ring to my chest. 'Wow,' I say through snorts of laughter. 'This is the most beautiful thing I have ever seen. I will treasure it forever.'

He laughs. Although I was being sarcastic, I'm surprised to find that I do actually prefer this to him bringing me some boring flowers. The thing is, although I know I *should* like the 'romancey' stuff, cos that's what the world tells us girls we should want, some flowers would actually have been easy, obvious and a bit, well, boring. Instead, he bought me something that he knew would make me smile. And now we're both standing here, laughing together. That's way better than anything else.

He follows me into the living room.

'Hey, Dylan,' says Mum brightly.

'Sup? I mean . . . hello,' he says like a proper doughnut.

He settles on the sofa, I get him a Coke, and then we watch some crappy early-evening TV game show, both of us merrily slagging off everyone on the TV with sarky comments, while Noah and Ruben play board games on the floor and Mum makes a shepherd's pie.

I like that Dylan's relaxed with my family (plus Ruben). I mean, he's not nearly as confident as Leo around them, but then Leo was an overconfident arse. Instead, Dylan is surprisingly polite, although occasionally inappropriate, which always makes me laugh. It's like he can't quite keep the real him hidden for too long – it just kind of seeps out. Like when he swears in front of Noah or he laughs loudly at some accidental euphemism (like when Ruben exclaimed that he'd lost two of his balls – KerPlunk ones, that is) or when Dylan was rearranging the contents of his trousers at the dinner table, noticed Mum shooting him a questioning look and said, 'Just doing some junk-modelling.'

There's this moment afterwards, when he realizes he shouldn't have done or said what he just did or said, and he gives me a little private look with a grimace and one raised eyebrow, and it's the funniest thing ever. He's such a dork.

Mum lets us go back to my room after dinner. 'AS LONG AS YOU KEEP THE DOOR OPEN, HAY!' she mortifyingly shouts up after us.

Like we would be doing anything that required the door to be shut anyway.

We both awkwardly glance at each other with a forced grin before quickly breaking eye contact again and silently climbing the stairs.

I think back to earlier at school when he touched my arm, but immediately let go when he realized other people were looking. And, yeah, it's clear he likes me, but you've gotta wonder whether he would have done that if I'd looked like Chloe. *Ugh*.

'Oooh, I've gotta show you these; they're hilarious,' he says, thankfully breaking the silence as he flops down on my bed.

I sit back next to him and he shows me some funny shred videos on his phone of one of his favourite bands, the Beach Boys, and one of our shared least favourite bands, One Direction. The sound on the videos has been replaced by a convincing bad version of what they're playing, and it has us both in stitches.

When the videos finish, I tell him about Ruben's butt-clenchingly embarrassing air-guitar habit. 'He even does the pained rock-star facial expressions. Honestly, he looks less like he's playing guitar and more like he's doing a poo while hoovering the curtains. He's all right really though,'

I add. 'And he keeps Noah entertained, what with them having the same mental age and everything.'

Dylan laughs, then says, 'So he's not Noah's dad?'

There's another slightly awkward mini silence as I figure out how to answer. We've never really spoken about anything deeper than movies, comedy and music. This is new and, well, fine. Good even, I guess. Though it catches me off guard. Like any thought of my actual dad does.

'Sorry,' Dylan says, sensing the awkwardness and looking down at his hands as he taps a beat on his legs, like he always does. I haven't decided yet whether it's cute or annoying. 'I get it, none of my business.' He smiles kindly at me. 'Let's watch something else.'

He goes to grab the iPad, which is propped up against a pillow between us.

'No, no, it's cool. There's no great secret or anything!' I say.

He leaves the iPad where it is and shifts his weight a little to face me. I clear my throat and continue. 'No, Ruben's not his dad. Thank God, cos Noah really wouldn't look great with one of those monstrous beards sprouting out of his face.'

Dylan snorts out a laugh. 'Yeah, I think beards *tend* to come through when you're a bit older than five.'

'Well, ordinarily, yes, but I'm pretty sure Ruben's half Wookiee so . . .'

He laughs some more, which spurs me on. 'C'mon, that dude's chin-rug has a life force of its own. It's sentient. It has its own personality. I swear I saw it walking into town the other day without Ruben. I tell you, any child of that man's would also be a child of that beard.'

While I'm talking, Dylan is laughing so hard he bends forward, holds his belly and shakes. It makes me smile. I'm tempted to leave it there. I've done what I always do and diffused an awkward, way-too-'real' subject with humour. But this is the first time Dylan's ever talked to me about anything that actually matters. So it feels like I ought to say something proper back.

I take a deep breath and twirl some of my hair round my fingers. He feels the change of atmosphere and looks at me expectantly, with his head cocked to the side like a giant puppy.

'Truth is, I'd take Ruben and his beard over my dad any day. My dad's a total jerk. Left me, Mum and Noah over four years ago, for his, urgh, secretary. I mean, the guy's a walking cartoon of a midlife cliché. He visited us for a bit at the start and then just didn't bother.' I stop myself from saying any more. 'Sorry,' I add, before reaching for the iPad, 'it's not funny or anything, just tragic really. C'mon, let's watch something hilarious.'

Dylan awkwardly smiles and nods. 'OK,' he says.

We start watching some Amy Schumer stand-up on Netflix, both of us lying on our stomachs with bent legs flailing around in the air behind us. I laugh when I'm supposed to, but inside I'm not laughing. As much as I'm trying not to, I'm thinking about Dad. But why the hell should I waste a thought on that arse-wipe? God knows, he barely thinks about us.

After months of fighting with Mum, lying and sneaking around behind her back with his secretary, he told Mum he was leaving her, or perhaps she told him to go. I'm not sure it even matters.

He left when Noah was three months old and I was ten. A few days after all the initial battling and slamming of doors, he and Mum sat me down and gave me all the normal crappy twaddle that, 'Mummy and Daddy aren't going to live together any more . . . but it's nothing you've done wrong –' which frankly I didn't ever think it was – 'and nothing will really change. Daddy will still come and see us all the time.' Blah-blah-bloody-blah.

For the first few weeks, Dad saw us once or twice a week, then every fortnight, then hardly ever.

It's like seeing us was some good-intentioned, though ill thought-out, New Year's resolution to go to the theatre more often or something.

About four years ago he moved up north somewhere with *her* and we literally never saw him again. We'd occasionally get a phone call out of the blue – I'm guessing when the guilt got too much for him – but Mum would tell him to get stuffed and that was it. Then she'd get depressed and angry for a few days, and it would be like all her soft, mumsy qualities were turned down and all her crazy, hyper, evil-mum powers were turned up to maximum. Her nagging and irritability levels would increase along with the volume of her cooking, as she took out all her grievances on the contents of the kitchen, slam-dunking saucepans into cupboards and plates on to tables, each crash sending a shiver of dread through me and Noah.

Sometimes I think the whole idea of the happy 'family' is kinda like Noah's SodaStream-based idea for 'fizzy milk'. Sounds good on paper, but in reality it just doesn't work and inevitably separates, leaving everyone involved feeling a bit sick and depressed.

Dylan's foot brushes mine and my thoughts come back to the present.

My heart does a small leap. *Was that an accident?*

'Sorry,' he says, sounding utterly embarrassed and shuffling his whole body away from mine.

Definitely an accident then. *Oh God, does he actually find me physically repulsive?*

He clears his throat as if to say something and then Noah bounds in through the door, making us both jump, swing our legs round and sit up, as if we were practising synchronized sitting, or indeed *had* actually been up to something.

'Mum said I should come up and see what you're doing,' says Noah, climbing up and sitting on the bed between us.

'Did she now?' I say, folding my arms across my chest in angry defiance, even though Mum's not actually here to see it, and after only a few seconds my arms spring apart again anyway under the pressure of my massive norks.

He grabs the iPad. 'Noah!' I protest.

'What? I just wanted to show Dylan my new game.'

38

Noah pulls up some colourful, noisy app and I get up to stretch my legs before sitting on my desk chair and slowly spinning it round.

My head is still in a funk about Dad and after Dylan has spent a few minutes pretending to be interested in Noah's nonsense, I make some excuse about needing to write the rest of tomorrow's set.

Dylan gets up, burps, scratches himself and says, 'I ought to be going anyway. Meeting Filch, Watto, Ginger Dan and Belge in the park. Sure you don't wanna come? Watto says he's bringing some of his grandad's homemade cider, though Ginger Dan says it's actually just a big bottle of something yellow Watto found in his grandad's shed. Could be anything. Should be a laugh though.'

'Tempting, but no,' I say.

Dylan shrugs and pulls up another YouTube video on his phone for us to watch before he leaves: a monkey throwing its poo at a toddler.

'Just before I go, you gotta watch this. It'll make you laugh your tits off,' he says.

Ah, what did I ever do to deserve such enchanting romance?

After he leaves, I try to chase away the dad thoughts by writing my set for tomorrow night. I look up at my Comedy Wall of Hilarity and Greatness for inspiration. The wall next to my bed is covered with photos I've cut out from magazines and newspapers, and I add to it all the time when a new funny person grabs my attention. All the greats are up there, from the old to the new, from sketch comedians to stand-up, from inspirational funny women I want to be friends with to hot, funny men I want to snog (those pics are stuck nearer to my pillow, obvs). I scan down the wall, looking for inspiration. *Help me, Gods of Comedy. What should I do?* But they all just grin at me inanely.

I pick up my notebook and try to think of jokes or anything funny that happened today. But nothing comes to me. I mean, what am I gonna write?

'Knock knock.'

'Who's there?'

'Absent father.'

'Absent father who . . .? Hello . . .? Absent father who . . .?! Oh fine, I see, so you've gone again, have you? You HEARTLESS SACK OF ARSE GRAVY!'

FOUR

Ah, Friday, the queen of all weekdays.

Tonight is the open-mic night at Leo's dad's pub. Ugh. My stomach has been a big bag of vomiting butterflies all day, my mind filled with disturbing memories of the last time I was there. Then there's the possibility of seeing Leo, and I'm just not sure how I feel about that. I mean, on the one hand, Dylan will be there and it'll be nice to show Leo I've moved on, but, on the other hand, me and Dylan don't exactly look like a couple; we're hardly all over each other. Not even lightly sprinkled over each other. And then there's the fact that I might just melt when I see Leo. Which is bat-crap crazy because he was a git-crush who stomped on my heart, but Jeez, he's a good-looking git-crush. And he snogged me once. Like, totally, beautifully, stomach-tinglingly snogged me. Which Dylan's shown literally zero signs of even coming close to. And, even if he did, what if it doesn't have the same heart-skipping effect as snogging Leo?

What if I'm doomed to live under the spell of Leo Jackson's git-charms for evermore? What if I see him and, like a complete turd brain, jump on him and start snogging him, which will be unsettling for all involved? Plus, him batting me away will not exactly put me in the right mental place for doing a stand-up set.

After school, all I want to do is disappear to my room and start going through what I'm going to say this evening. But Grammo comes round, and what with Mum still being at work I don't think it's really fair to leave her alone downstairs with Noah, who doesn't really get that the woman is seventy and way past playing 'Horsies' on all fours. We've been seeing a lot more of Grammo, my mum's mum, since Uncle Terry finally died in the summer. And, yes, I know that sounds harsh, but he wasn't my actual grandad, who died before I was born, and honestly Uncle Terry had barely said anything for around five years anyway. When he did say something it was either grumpy, aggressive or wildly inappropriate bordering on lecherous – or when he was on top form all three – so really it's a blessed relief all round.

Grammo is definitely so much happier now. After decades sitting in a beige living room with a barely conscious Donald-Trump-in-a-stained-cardigan for company, she's now bought herself a whole new wardrobe with the life-insurance payout, got her hair cut into a chic old-woman pixie cut, and she's paired up with June, who she met at some widows' club at the church. The two of them have a new lease of life, going to the cinema, theatre, out dancing, you name it. Celestially speaking, I'm not sure, but in this instance there definitely is life after death.

As I make Grammo a cup of tea, I hear Noah forcing her to play with him. Us Swinton women aren't known for having a natural, doting, patient way with children. I mean, we all love Noah and think he's the cutest thing since someone dressed a kitten as a pirate, but still that doesn't mean that when he asks you to play some game with him that you *know* will go on for an hour and a half, your insides don't sink into a pit of despair.

I purposely take my time as I stifle my laughter, listening to Grammo battle on with a game of 'Shops' that Noah is fiercely directing.

'Haylah!' Grammo screeches almost hysterically. 'Is that tea ready?!'

I try to erase the smirk from my face as I walk through with her tea, which was actually ready several minutes ago.

After handing Grammo her tea, I flump down on the sofa. 'Let's stop with the shops now, Noah. Why don't you draw a picture for Grammo on the iPad?'

'OK,' he replies brightly before digging out the iPad and sitting cross-legged on the floor with it.

Grammo shoots me a thankful look as she sits on the sofa next to me, and under her breath she says, 'God bless technology.'

While Noah draws, we talk about Grammo's latest plans with her BFF, June. First to see a burlesque show in London then, in a couple of weeks' time, to go salsa dancing with some local instructor called Brad Sizzle (if June's hip replacement holds out).

'Wow, Grammo, you guys are really living it up. Good for you.'

'I know,' she says with a cheeky grin. 'We're so busy these days, running around like a couple of headless horsemen!'

I suppress a laugh and plan to write that one down in my notebook of funny later. Grammo is known for getting her phrases and metaphors mixed up. 'I mean, of course I miss your Uncle Terry, but, OH MY GOODNESS, I'm having so much fun now he's gone.' She squeals with excitement. 'I have something for you – wait here.'

Grammo shuffles off excitedly to her car and brings back a bin bag full of clothes. It's more stuff she's cleared out and even some of Uncle Terry's, some of which, when I've got over the 'these are the clothes of a dead guy' chills, are actually pretty cool. I thank her and take them up to my room, where I play about with different combinations with my existing wardrobe to find something for tonight.

I try on around thirty thousand outfits, using Grammo and Noah as my test audience. I pouty-catwalk past them, hand on swaying hips, head followed by body turn at the end of the living room, making Noah laugh hysterically every time.

Then at the bottom of the bag I find the best thing ever – one of Uncle Terry's old pipes. It still smells of tobacco and Uncle Terry, which is pretty gross so I wash it with industrial-strength antibacterial soap, and boil the crap out of it in a pan, until I'm satisfied that it has been well and truly exorcized of Uncle Terry. Building my final outfit round the pipe, I eventually decide on DMs, black tights, some old jeans that I take a pair of scissors to to make into shorts, and an old orange shirt of Grammo's with one of Uncle Terry's tank tops over it, closely hugging my chest.

Looking at myself in the mirror, puffing on my pipe, I nod as if to say 'my work here is done' – characterful without being a caricature. It looks and feels like me. Which is exactly what I'm after for the gig. I practise some pipe stances, and find that cupping it in my left hand, with the sucky bit of it in the corner of my mouth, while my right hand holds my pipe-smoking elbow, looks just awesome, especially with my chin up and a single raised eyebrow. I look wonderfully formidable and dignified. Or maybe I look like a sophisticated orangutan pondering the daily news, but, either way, I'm happy.

Mum comes home and we have tea together. She's being all funny and sweet, which makes me feel horribly guilty. The thing is, I haven't told her I'm actually going to a pub tonight; she thinks I'm going round to Chloe's. Which, yeah, I guess is just your bog-standard fifteen-year-old white lie that wouldn't bother most teens. But, however much she drives me insane with her constant nagging and interfering, the fact is it's been just me, my mum and Noah for so long that it's never really felt like it's kids vs parents in this house; it's more like it's me and Mum parenting Noah together. When Dad left, me and Mum had to trust and rely on each other more than most mums and daughters. Which is maybe why it feels super crappy when

I lie to her. With Grammo here as a safety airbag, I decide to go for it. I wait for the opportune moment, when she's just stuffed a forkful of spaghetti in her mouth, take a deep breath and quickly garble where I'm actually going before she has a chance to swallow. I make sure I get in that it's a family pub, that the owner is a friend's dad (OK, so it's *Leo's* dad and Leo's hardly a *friend*, but, come on, one little fib's OK, right?), that there will be no drinking, that we're only going because it's a fun open-mic thing and I can do a set, and that we'll be there with Chloe's sister and boyfriend who are both totally responsible types (also a stretch). As Mum continues to scowl at me and chew thoughtfully (or is that angrily?) on her spaghetti, I keep garbling and quickly grab my phone to AirDrop her their phone numbers and the pub's phone number. I tell her I'll be back by ten thirty and that I'm sorry I lied about going to Chlo's, and that I won't do that again and I love her and she's the best mum ever.

When I'm done, I hold my breath, rest my head in my hands and offer her some apologetic raised eyebrows while I await the 'How dare you lie to me?' backlash. Sure enough, her cheeks go red and I brace myself for the impending explosion, but Grammo senses it too and defuses the bomb like a boss.

Grammo puts down her fork, leans over, rubs Mum's back and gently says, 'Oh, Dawny, let the girl go and have some fun. You only live twice.'

'*Once*, Mum. *You Only Live Twice* is a Bond film,' Mum shoots back.

'Well, whatever, you know what I mean; she's a good girl that one, look at her.'

I clasp my hands together under my chin, dip my head to one side and flutter my eyelashes at Mum. The only thing more innocent-looking than me right now would be a unicorn in a nun's outfit collecting for charity.

Still frowning, Mum lets out a long sigh.

Oblivious to the tension in the room, Noah holds his fork above his head with the spaghetti hanging from it and squeals, 'Here, wormy wormy!' as he slurps it into his mouth.

Mum ignores him, still focusing her glare on me until she finally gives her verdict. 'Haylah Swinton, there will be a *forensic* examination of you on your return home, which *will* be at precisely ten thirty, and, if I even smell *one drop* of alcohol on your breath, you will be grounded until you graduate. From university. As a postgraduate student with a doctorate. Do I make myself clear?'

'How am I going to get to university if I'm grounded?'

'*Haylah*,' she growls.

I beam at her. 'Crystal clear, Mum. Thanks.'

I keep up the sensible, grateful girl act and quickly help tidy up the kitchen (while secretly dancing a jig of joy in my head). Then I ask Mum if I can leave early as I'm meeting Chlo and Kas first and wanna run through my set with them before we have to go.

Mum agrees and follows me out to the front door. After saying all those classic contradictory mum things to me, which basically amount to 'have fun, but don't have too much fun', she smiles and adds, 'So you're really doing a set tonight? So proud, Hay – you'll be amazing. Shoulders back, tits forward, go knock 'em dead, girl.' Then she whacks me round the butt as I step outside.

'Aw, Mum! Boundaries!' I laugh. 'You really think I'll be OK?'

'You'll be GREAT!' she yells to the whole street.

'Shh! Mum, seriously, don't yell like that tomorrow morning because, what with my massive hangover and everything, that's really gonna sting.'

'Cheeky cow,' she says with a smile as she closes the door.

As I start the walk to Chlo's, I pull out my phone and in my excitement post everywhere that I'll be doing a set tonight at the East Street pub. Hell, yeah, I'm a gigging comedian and frankly I want the world to know it. I put on my headphones, turn Lizzo up to the max and strut all the way to Chloe's, feeling pretty damned confident for once. Then my phone shivers with an 'emergency' message from Kas.

K: At Chloe's.
   We need you.
   Like NOW, DUDE!
H: Jeez.
   Quit your fanny-flapping, I'm on my way.
   What's the prob?
K: Oh God, she's crying again . . .
   Just get over here now, yeah.

On the way, I pass a group of boys, all under ten. They take one look at my waistcoat outfit and start sniggering.

Since deciding to dress how I want to dress, I've almost got used to this now. And it's not just the little kids, it's all ages, staring at you as you walk past, daring not to blend into the bland.

One of the boys points and shouts, 'LESBIAN!' as I pass by.

I turn back to them, point at their faces and shout, 'STRAIGHT!' and they stop laughing and look confused.

Pleased with my comeback, I continue on my journey.

I know I should perhaps be acting with a little bit more urgency and concern about Chloe, but the girl's a drama queen, although obviously I'd never tell her that. So it's difficult to sustain any real concern for her when, based on past experience, this could genuinely be anything from a realization of her own mortality to a notification that L'Oréal aren't making her favourite 'naked blush' lipstick colour any more.

At Chloe's house, her sister's boyfriend, Alarmingly-Good-looking-But-Painfully-Dull Jake, opens the door to me and immediately starts walking back to the living room, his pants more than half on view above the waistband of his jogging bottoms. He waves his arm loosely towards the stairs, grumbling, 'They're up there.'

This is so often the way with super-good-looking people. They don't have to put in the effort like the rest of us; the world will love them whatever they say or do.

At the top of the stairs, the smell of ammonia assaults my nose and eyes. I begin to get an inkling of what might be causing the 'drama'. Kas beckons me into Chloe's room.

Chloe is sitting on her bed with her hair up in a towel and her face wet with tears.

So this is a hair-related 'emergency' then.

'Well, what the Garnier Nutrisse happened here?' I ask.

Chloe slowly unravels her turban of towel and for a moment I wonder if I have underestimated the situation and she's actually going to reveal Voldemort's face underneath it, but instead a mop of very wet and very green hair falls down. And I'm not talking Billie-Eilish-cool-grunge-girl green, not that that would be Chlo's vibe anyway; I'm very much talking clown-fancy-dress-costume green.

Turns out Chloe had dragged Kas round after school to help her dye her hair from blonde to brown in an attempt to 'look more intelligent', if you can believe that. The brown dye mixed with the bleach already on her hair (no one actually knows what colour Chlo's hair really is; it's a closely guarded government secret) and created not the mid-chestnut colour one might expect, but a putrid, watery-swamp green instead.

After calming Chlo down and stopping Kas from apologizing for literally *everything*, from her part in the hair-dye incident to global warming, I ask whether Chloe has asked for her sister's help, seeing as Freya's training to be a beauty therapist and is just downstairs and all that.

'She and Jake'll just take the piss out of me,' Chloe whimpers.

'Still, better that than, you know, looking like the Joker, right?' I offer, rubbing her foot a little to comfort her, though inside I'm very much rolling my eyes. I do feel sorry for her, but tonight *I'm* the one getting up onstage, which *she* wanted me to do, and now instead of thinking about my set I've gotta worry about this crap. 'And who the hell said brunettes are more intelligent than blondes anyway? And *why* do you want to look more intelligent? Is it because Batman keeps outwitting you?'

Chloe gives a snotty laugh, then explains that this was for the sake of attracting Watto, who, she believes, is a genius, and who, she believes, thinks she's an idiot. We of course tell her that there's no way he'd think that, and she reveals that if he didn't before today's history lesson he really does now after she asked him if 'Irish troubles' meant a girl's period.

At this point I truly try to keep up the sympathetic, understanding friend act, but, c'mon, that's bloody hilarious. An explosive laugh escapes through my nose.

Chlo pulls her knees up to her chest and hugs them tight as she rests her forehead on them. 'Oh *God*, he does think I'm an airhead, doesn't he? Why does this stuff always happen to me?'

I get my laughter under control as Kas shoots me a look. I shrug back at her with a guilty smirk.

'C'mon, Chlo, stupid stuff happens to *me* all the time!' I say. 'You remember the other day when I came back into art class with my skirt tucked in my knickers?'

'Yeah,' she says, laughing, 'that was pretty stupid. You never do anything stupid though, Kas; you've got it all sorted. How do you do that?'

'Oh, come on, that's crap.'

'It's not, Kas,' I say. 'You seem to be the only one of us who really knows what they're doing. You're clever, you're calm, you work hard, you're focused on your exams, you're pretty, you –'

'Crapped myself at school on Tuesday,' she says, going red and staring at the floor.

'What?' I say, unable to keep the delighted expression off my face.

'Seriously?!' shouts Chlo. 'That's brilliant! I mean, poor you, but –'

Then me and Chlo can't hold it in and fall back on the bed, exploding into laughter.

'I'm sorry, Kas, please tell us what happened,' I say, sitting back up and trying to pull my expression down into seriousness, but failing.

'You can't tell ANYONE,' she says, covering her face with her hands.

'Of course,' says Chlo through her grin.

'You have my turd, SORRY, word.'

'Hay!' says Kas.

Red-faced and looking at us only through her fingers, Kas explains that after stealing one of her mum's protein shakes she had an explosive 'sharting' incident in PE. Turns out the difference between 'squats' and 'squits' doesn't just involve vowels but bowels too.

'Luckily,' Kas says, her hands falling from her face and toying with the corner of the duvet, 'Lola was there. Lola, y'know, from geography.'

'The one with the teeth?' says Chlo.

'Most humans have teeth, Chlo,' snaps Kas. She rolls her eyes at me in a 'can you believe her' look. Which is fair but surprising, as Kas is not normally one to show even the mildest amount of disagreement with anyone, especially Chlo. Maybe Kas is growing some balls. Good for her.

'Lola's cool, and I think her . . . *powerful* teeth give her a distinguished look,' I say to Kas, and she smiles and carries on with her delightful story.

'Anyway, while I shuffled off to the toilet and flushed my knickers and dignity down it, Lola went and told Mr Bolton that I had to go home because I'd had a "women's event".'

'Isn't that a charity bake sale?' I say.

They laugh. And then we all agree that we're big fat losers together.

After a quick Google and raiding of Chlo's kitchen, Kas and I give Chloe moral support as she alternates between shampooing with ketchup, lemon juice and mayonnaise. Actually, if you just slung some crustaceans into the remnants at the bottom of the sink, you would have a half-decent prawn cocktail.

'There, you look fab!' says Kas rather overenthusiastically.

With still-wet hair, Chloe settles on to her bed with crossed legs, examines herself in a small mirror and nods appreciatively. She produces a wipe and starts removing the remains of her half-cried-off make-up before applying a bewildering array of moisturisers, toners and primers in preparation for the re-installation of her face.

Relieved that Chlo seems OK with her hair now, Kas and I give each other a brief 'phew' expression as we sit on her giant double bed with her. In a certain light, it looks like Chloe's hair is still a bit green, but mostly it's now just a washed-out browny-grey. If her current colour was ever bottled and sold, which it wouldn't be, it would be called 'nude sloth'. Obviously I don't tell her that because I value my life.

It's a rare thing these days to see Chloe without her make-up on, and she catches me giving her a weird look.

'What?' she says. 'Oh God, it still looks bad, doesn't it?'

'No, no, it looks fine, really. I'm not used to seeing you without your face on,' I say, turning a fluffy purple cushion around on my lap.

'Oh, I know. I look awful without make-up,' says Chlo matter-of-factly.

'No!' I say, and of course she doesn't – she's naturally beautiful, but, boy, does she look different. Like her face has half disappeared. And, yes, I know that sounds mean, but it's just that your eyes get so used to the faces they see every day, and Chlo's face normally has these big, cat-like, dark smoky eyes, pouty lips and cheekbones you could crack an egg on. Now all that's been turned down to zero, I look at her and see a pretty face that looks only a *bit* like a vague impression of Chloe.

Equally, I know that I'd look terrible if I *did* wear that much make-up, like a bad drawing of a drag queen. I guess some people just suit wearing make-up and some don't. It's not better or worse to wear it or not wear it, just

54

different, suited to different personalities more than different faces perhaps.

Kas grabs Chlo's foot to make her point firmly. 'You look chuffin' *gorgeous*, Chlo.'

Chlo glimpses herself in one of her many mirrors and sighs. Her hair's half-dry now and it's clear that the green still remains. Me and Kas look on as Chlo forlornly walks over to the mirror, raking her fingers through her hair as she goes. She winces at her reflection, though she can't tear herself away from the grisly image before her, like some disfigured soldier catching sight of himself for the first time after the bandages have come off.

'Dude, don't worry about it. You really do look good,' I say with a teeth-sucking smile.

And it's not fake sympathy. I do feel sorry for Chlo, because, underneath all that perfect skin, toughness and sloth-green hair, she's just as insecure as the rest of us really. Her confidence just as fragile. Her need to be looked at approvingly by this dumb-ass world that seems to value beauty over everything else just as strong.

'You're right!' she says, shaking off her mood, pulling her shoulders back and standing side-on, one hand on her hip in full red-carpet pose and pouting at her reflection. 'I would still totally hit that,' she says before blowing a flirty kiss at her reflection.

OK, maybe not *quite* as insecure as the rest of us.

'You really do. Now can we all just agree on one thing? Come close, this is important . . .' I grab one of the many cushions on Chlo's bed and start pounding them both to drive my point home. 'THAT WE ALL *STOP* TRYING TO *CHANGE* OURSELVES FOR *BOYS*! WE ARE *ALL* FRICKIN' *AWESOME* AS WE ARE, YA BIG … *DOUGHNUTS*!!'

This soon evolves into a huge pillow fight. And not in that soft-focus boy fantasy, but rather in a brutal 'grab your mate in a headlock and smack a cushion in her face until she pisses herself laughing' kind of way. Then the two of them drag me into the centre of the room and take their seats on the bed, insisting I practise my set.

I do, and then before we know it Jake and Freya shout up that it's time to go. And weirdly I don't feel too nervous. I'm actually excited. Oh God, I hope I get some laughs.

FIVE

As we walk from the car to the pub, the nerves that I thought I had under control break free and are now charging round my insides like hyperactive kids in a soft-play centre. I know I'm only going onstage for a few minutes to tell some jokes, but, on the other hand, I'M GOING ONSTAGE FOR A FEW MINUTES TO TELL SOME JOKES.

I walk behind the others who are all politely pretending to listen to Jake prattle on about his day at work. He's a car mechanic and quite wrongly believes his 'anecdotes' about fixing the squeaky brakes on a Ford Mondeo are as hilarious as they are fascinating.

I take a deep breath and internally grab my nerves out of the manic ball pit of my stomach, strap them down at the cafe highchair of tranquillity and tell them to calm the hell down and drink a slushy.

When we get to the pub, I see Dylan and his mates standing out front, hands in pockets, kicking at the pavement and trying to look cool, but actually looking awkward as hell. They're just as new to this going-out-to-the-pub-with-your-mates thing as we are.

The sight of Dylan actually calms my nerves. I'm excited to see him, sure, and even a bit heart-fluttery, but instead of those insane monkeys-doing-cartwheels-in-my-stomach feelings that seeing Leo did to my insides last year, I look at Dylan and feel warm, comfortable, happy. I guess I really *do* see him as a comfortable pair of slippers. Which, as Kas and Chlo pointed out, isn't exactly sexy.

'Hey,' they mumble as we approach.

'They with you?' asks Jake.

Chloe, her green hair well hidden inside a black velvet cap, nods towards Dylan. He looks the most laid-back of the bunch, but then that's just Dylan's regular look, like an old man who's just woken up from a nap and can't quite recall who or where he is.

'Yeah, that big dude's Haylah's.'

My cheeks flash red, but I can't help liking the sound of some 'big dude' belonging to me.

'It's all right, guys. Just stick with me and Kingston won't chuck you out – we're tight,' says Jake, like a total spanner.

'Sup?' I say as I move a little closer to Dylan, producing my old-man pipe from my waistcoat pocket and pretending to puff on it.

'All right?' He glances down at the pipe in my hand and grins. 'I like ya pipe.'

I follow the group into the warmth of the dimly lit pub and we make our way to the bar. Like last time, it all feels a bit new and a bit grown-up and a bit delicious because of it.

'Don't think he's here, dude,' whispers Kas to me as she notices me scanning the room for any sign of Leo.

Which, yes, I know is stupid, because that dude is totally OLD NEWS that I am in no way interested in revisiting. Honestly. But, I dunno, this is his dad's pub, and as I step inside my thoughts are drawn to him. Like moths to a flame. Or flies to poo.

'What? Who? Why?' I stammer, but she gives me a knowing look.

'Yeah, all right, busted. I couldn't help it. You're right though – he's not, which is a *good* thing. Definitely a good thing.'

'*Dylan's* here though,' she purrs.

The pub's already pretty busy, but we manage to grab a table big enough for us all that still has a good view of the stage area while Jake gets a round of Cokes for us. Kas and Chloe sit on one side of the table, Chloe making sure she's also sitting next to Watto, and me and Dylan are squashed together on a bench on the other side.

I love that we're hanging out with boys now too. The conversation can't just be *about* boys any more, so it naturally widens out to heated yet flirty (if Chloe's involved) debates about TV shows, films, music and which teachers are the biggest losers, and then ends with a big gossip-fest about who's recently been caught snogging who.

As everyone chats and laughs and Belge waffles on about how many times he's been in this and apparently *every* other pub in town with his older brother, Dylan is uncharacteristically quiet. Our thighs are squashed together under the table and I wonder if, like me, he can't get his mind away from the fact that this is the closest our bodies have ever been. To be fair, my other thigh is touching Belge as I'm sandwiched between them, but somehow that thigh action barely registers on my radar, whereas my left thigh is radiating electricity throughout my whole body. Which is SO not how I feel when I put on a pair of slippers. And I DEFINITELY don't imagine snogging a pair of slippers. But snogging Dylan is exactly what I'm imagining right now . . .

STOP IT, BRAIN!

The thing is, as soon as I start thinking about these things, I'm immediately slapped out of it by the knowledge that he has had every chance to do this exact thing and has never shown the slightest interest in it. I can't let my mind go down that road. I need to focus on the gig. But my brain continues speeding off in the wrong direction.

He probably just doesn't see me like that. Maybe I don't see him like that? But then there's the electricity in my leg. Maybe it's just pins and needles. Or maybe he's realized he doesn't actually fancy me, but doesn't know how to dump me. I mean, he still hasn't invited me to his house. Maybe I'm just not fanciable. ARGH! I smack myself on the forehead.

And now I've whacked myself in the face in front of Dylan like an absolute nutter. *Good going, Haylah, now he's really gonna fancy you.*

The whole table, having of course noticed the random forehead slap, stop their chattering and turn to stare at me before falling about laughing.

I laugh along with them – what else can I do? 'Ha! Just practising a new stand-up technique – if in doubt, bash yourself in the face!'

The table sniggers before returning to their chattering. But Dylan looks at me with a concerned frown. 'You all right?' he asks.

'What? Oh yep, yep, yep, all good,' I say defensively, quickly looking away from him as if he can peer into my eyes and see my deranged thoughts.

Sucking nervously on my pipe, I tune back into the conversation the others are having, which has somehow moved from Ginger Dan's disappointingly dull new pet iguana to the injustice of why you can get pick 'n' mix sweets, but not pick 'n' mix crisps.

When Chlo thinks no one is looking, she carefully takes off her hat. And her still-slightly-green hair falls round her face.

The boys look at it and there's a beat of silence before they explode with snorts of laughter. Especially Belge.

Dylan starts laughing too until I nudge him with my foot. The last thing I want is Chlo and Dylan not getting on, but he looks at me with a confused frown.

'You got something to say, then say it to my face, Belge!' says Chlo.

'You'll find it under that piece of turf,' says Dylan and, although you've gotta admit it was a good line, I proper kick him under the table.

Trying to deflect the attention from her hair, I say, 'I don't know, Chlo, the whole "just say it to my face" thing,

I've always thought that expression was a load of bobbins. I mean, frankly, if someone's saying something horrible about me, I'd much *rather* they say it behind my back. I mean, *I* don't wanna hear that. I'm quite happy if you just say nice things to my face and keep all the bad stuff out of earshot. Tell it like it *isn't*, I say, not like it is.'

'Why'd you dye it green anyway?' says Belge.

Even under all the make-up, you can see Chlo's face burning red before she explodes with, 'I DIDN'T DYE IT GREEN! IT JUST WENT GREEN!'

'All right, all right!' says Belge, his hands up in the air defensively.

'She's right, it isn't *green*,' jokes Dylan. 'Green would've at least been a colour. This is an anti-colour; this is the shade of despair and nothingness.'

And, yes, another good line, but I kick him under the table again. Although, as I'm wearing DMs, I kinda hurt him more than I mean to.

'Ow! Jeez! What did you do that for?' he says with a playful smirk.

I roll my eyes at him. 'OK, for future reference, dude, if I kick you under the table, it's because I'm trying to find a more subtle way of saying, "Shut up, Dylan, you're being a prick."'

He laughs. 'You're not normally worried about being subtle, Hay. You're wearing an old man's waistcoat and puffing on an unlit pipe!'

And, although it might sound like we're arguing, if I'm honest, I am LOVING this attention.

'I think you'll find,' I say, taking a long drag on the pipe, 'that it's a look that *subtly* says, "if you're mean to my friends, I *will* kick you".'

We all laugh and thankfully Chlo seems OK and doesn't take offence at Dylan's cack-handedness.

Dylan leans back in his chair, still smiling. 'Well, thank God I wasn't mean to *you* too. What would be your subtle way of warning me off that – knifing me in the throat?'

'You're always mean to me. How would I possibly tell the difference?' I say with a grin.

'Honestly, you two bicker more than my mum and dad,' says Kas.

Dylan clears his throat and shuffles awkwardly, making the bench wobble. Then, thankfully changing the subject, he turns and looks down at me. Even when sitting, he's a full head height above me. 'So you gonna put your name down then, woman?' he says, nodding his head towards the board on which Jake is busy scrawling his own name.

I look at the board and get hit with a bolt of reality. The memories of last time's catastrophic, bum-based embarrassment (DON'T ASK, OK?!), coupled with the fact that all my mates are here, is pulling my confidence down through my feet and on to the sticky pub floor.

'I don't know . . . I mean, now we're here, I could just sit and enjoy the other acts with the rest of you guys, right? Right?'

I grab my Coke with both hands and take a shaky slurp as everyone around the table looks at me. Chloe shakes her head and Kas rests her chin in her hands and gives me an exaggeratedly disappointed look.

'C'mon, Hay, we wanna see you do your thang, that's why we're here,' says Chlo.

I know they're right. I need to do this; I need to overwrite the humiliating memory of last time and replace it with a new shiny one.

'Fine!' I say, throwing my hands in the air. 'I'll do it. Move your arse then, Dylan, and let me go put my name down on the list of doom.'

They all cheer. Which makes my insides glow.

As I'm finishing writing my name, I hear behind me, 'Good to see you, Hay.'

My heart flies up into my throat as I realize it's Leo.

He *is* here.

Just be cool. Just be cool.

I fake what I hope is a convincing impression of confidence and turn to him. 'Yes, it must be.'

He smiles at me with that glint in his eye that draws you in and makes you believe there's no one else in the room but you. All my intentions of coolness bugger off through the window as he laughs. Good God, that laugh. That face. That face that once kissed my face.

Stop it.

I yammer something about it being nice to see him too. I mean, yes, he was a bit of a prick, but that was months ago – we can move past that now, right? Just like I've totally moved past him sending desperate butterflies of longing through my insides when I see him. I *have* TOTALLY moved past that. There's Dylan-shaped proof sitting just over there that I have well and truly moved past that! Except that the Dylan-shaped thing has never shown much of an interest in the Haylah-shaped thing other than in a matey way, whereas the Leo-shaped thing is even now looking at me like I'm the most delicious dessert on the menu.

Oh, get a HOLD of yourself, woman!

'So are you doing a set tonight? Still comedy-ing?' I ask, doing my best impression of someone who doesn't really care about the answer.

'I am, but, nah, not tonight. Me and my mates are moving on somewhere a bit, well, somewhere a bit less Dad-owned soon. I'll stick around for your set though, *Haylag.*' With a smirk, he nods towards the board.

I look and see that, because of my mortifying jump of excitement when he turned up, the final letter of my name looks like a 'g'. *Dammit.*

I shrug and give out an 'oh, what am I like!' laugh, which I intend as a girlie giggle, but actually comes out as a throaty cackle. 'Erm, thanks. Hopefully, my butt won't be the star of my set this time.'

'Oh, it always will be to me,' he says with a smirk and raised eyebrow. He knows that line was as cheesy as hell. But he also knows it was more than a bit sexy.

My cheeks heat up as I laugh in a slightly over-the-top way, attempting to cover up my embarrassed excitement at what he just said.

Oh, why is he flirting with me and making my insides feel like they're filled with monkeys on a trampoline?

I clear my throat with a mortifying squeaky sound. 'Right, better get back to that lot.'

'Yeah, see ya later, Hay.'

I return to the table, my cheeks still hot with added nerves now that I know Leo will be watching and guilt that that matters.

Dylan looks at me. 'You look like a slapped beetroot. Nervous much?'

Oh God, his sympathetic concern is only increasing my sense of guilt.

I nod.

Dylan picks up a beer mat and twiddles it around in his huge hands. He balances it halfway off the table, then flips it up with his hand and catches it mid-air. He gives it to me. 'Bet you can't do it.'

OK, so he's *not* actually all that concerned about me. Which is good, although at the same time not good.

God, how are boys supposed to know what we want from them when we don't even know?

I roll my eyes and play along.

'All right, here goes.'

I try and fail. I flip it up way too high and instead of catching it I hit it in mid-air and fire it hard into Watto's face.

'Oi!' he says, though it seems he and Chlo are both relieved to have something jump up and pull them away from what looks like an awkward moment. (Later she will confirm this and tell me that she had stupidly decided to talk to him about history again in an attempt to persuade him that she wasn't, in fact, an airhead, and had somehow

66

ended up suggesting that the First World War started because of the assassination of JFK.)

Everyone laughs and before long we are all seeing who can flip and catch the most beer mats. Me and Dylan take the pee out of each other, me, pipe in mouth, suggesting that his hands are so massive it's like watching a bear try to pick up a postage stamp.

Kas wins, of course. There's seriously nothing that girl's not good at, except perhaps owning her brilliance. She spends the next ten minutes apologizing for winning and suggesting she probably had an advantage over the rest of us as her 'bit of the table was less sticky than the rest'.

The brilliant thing is, I actually do forget about my nerves for a while. I wonder if that's what Dylan intended all along.

Then, just as I'm thinking maybe he can be sensitive in his own way, he loudly farts and the boys around the table laugh. (Us girls mouth-breathe and pretend to be disgusted, but obviously under our nose-pinching hands we're laughing too. I've said it before and I'll say it again: there's nothing funnier than a well-timed fart.)

My nerves return as soon as the first act is announced by Kingston (Leo's dad, who, like his son, is cooler than cool. He's the only dad I know who can legitimately and convincingly rock a dreadlocks-and-leather-waistcoat look).

There are eleven acts and I'm on sixth. I just hope the five before me aren't too good. I needn't have worried though, as what follows onstage is a whole bag of awful.

Bad, mumbly musicians spending far longer tuning their guitars than playing; a shouty 'poet' who swears a lot; an old woman with a weird instrument that she blows into, looking, and indeed sounding, like she is doing something obscene to a tortoise; and Jake with his guitar, singing songs about love and cars, at one point ambitiously rhyming 'dirty carburettor' with 'the day I met her'.

And then. *Gulp.* I'm up.

'Next up we have the comedy stylings of Ms Haylah Swinton,' announces Kingston into the mic.

'Good luck, Hay,' says Chlo.

'You'll be great, Hay,' adds Kas, chewing her fingernails and looking, if it's possible, *more* anxious than I feel.

Dylan gets up to let me out and looks at me with a teeth-sucking, sombre grin.

While everyone, I know, is trying to be supportive, their reactions just add to the already all-encompassing feeling that I'm now taking my last lonely walk to the gallows before a rope is slung round my neck. Although, frankly, death might be preferable to what I am about to face.

Musicians can play and even if people only politely clap at the end of their set their work is still done; they did what they came to do – play music. But comedians are setting themselves up for the potential living nightmare of standing onstage, with all lights and eyes on them, as they try to make people *laugh*, which of course can't be faked like applause. People only laugh if you're funny. And, if you fail, there's silence. The audience knows it, you know it: if there's no laughter, you are publicly shamed as a complete and total loser.

These thoughts aren't really helping me right now.

I am a comedian. *I am* funny. *People* will *laugh*.

I get to the 'stage' area, the corner of the room that is hemmed in by two tall stacks of speakers, and pick my way through the various bits of equipment: stands, guitars, mixing desks and the complex network of leads and wires snaking round the floor that links everything together.

Kingston passes me the mic and sits back down on a chair near the stage. Taking the mic into my shaking hand, I nod my thanks to him. And, as soon as I'm gripping the mic, I feel like I'm home. The nerves go. The high of performing replaces them.

'Thanks, Kingston,' I say. 'I'll try not to explode your pub this time around.'

A few titters of laughter from those who remember what will from now on only be referred to as 'the incident'. Kingston smiles at me, a warm, welcoming grin just like his son's, and says, 'I'd appreciate that.'

Then I swallow hard and go for it.

'Hi, everyone, my name's Haylah. You all having a good night so far?'

Everyone cheers, especially my table of friends. Though there's also a definite hollering from Leo standing with his mates at the back.

God, this feels good.

I proudly take a puff from the pipe in my non-mic hand. 'Yeah, I'm trying to bring pipes back. I mean, what's not to like? Gives you something to do with your hand, good for pointing at things, and it wins any argument. I'll show you. Someone give me an opinion on something.'

'Avocados are rubbish!' yells Chlo. I told her to say this earlier and she's come in right on cue. I put on my best posh-English-bloke voice; it's basically my impression of General Melchett in *Blackadder*. 'I think you'll find –' puff – 'that your argument's invalid.'

The audience laughs.

'Next?'

'You suck!' Kas shouts. *Well done, Kas*.

'I think you'll find –' puff – '*Mum*, that your argument's –' puff – 'invalid.'

Another surge of laughter. I am *really* enjoying this.

'You see? You just can't argue with a pipe. If women had all been issued pipes a hundred years ago, there would never have been any need for feminism. Argh, who am I kidding? Blokes would have started smoking didgeridoos or something just so they could make bigger, louder, more ridiculous arguments.'

I go into a few one-liners to get everyone going, wafting the pipe around expressively to punctuate my jokes.

'Watched a documentary the other day on the most important technique in rock-climbing . . . Gripping.

'What else have I been doing? Oh yeah, went to London the other day to see the sights. Went up the Gherkin. But the lift got stuck. I thought, *Oh God, we are in a pickle.*

'I have a friend who thinks I'm immature and delusional. What the hell does she know though? She's only an *imaginary* friend.

'I've also been going to the *gym*. Yeah, I like to work out . . . Work out how many KitKats I can give myself as a reward for actually turning up to PE.'

It's all going great, the room is loving me, and I'm soaking the laughter up into my bones. It fills me with a lightness, like I could literally float up any second. My confidence soaring, I go into a longer ranty bit about people who insist on social-media-sharing their gym achievements. I point out that going to the gym is important for self-care, but it's also a private thing. Like washing yourself. And similarly no one wants to hear you showing off about how clean you got yourself in the shower that morning. 'Pushed myself further than ever in the shower today. Hashtag exfoliationmotivation.'

Suddenly my balloon-like floatiness is brutally burst and comes crashing down with an almighty bang. Because, as I'm taking a moment to scan the laughing faces around the room and soak up what is a beautiful feeling, my eyes stop dead on a familiar face at the back of the pub.

Propped up against the bar and watching me through his round glasses.

Oh God.

It's my frickin' dad.

SIX

I drop the pipe, which lands with a loud clang on the floor, and I lose my train of thought as it hurtles through the brain station before derailing and killing several commuter thoughts in its path of destruction.

My dad. My actual human dad. Is here. Now.

My hands start to shake and I don't know how to deal with the weight of the confused emotions running rampage through my brain. Should I scream? Run? Vomit? Faint? Throw things? Cry? Violently explode? All of the above? I can't do any of those things because I'm onstage.

Oh crap, I'm onstage. And there are lots of clueless faces still beaming at me, waiting for me to continue. And wondering why the hell I just dropped my pipe.

'So, yeah, erm . . . if you do a five-k run, don't social-media it because . . . because . . .'

As I stumble over my words and lose the joke entirely, the confused faces of strangers, wondering if somehow this is all part of the act, and the concerned faces of friends, who know it isn't, stare back at me.

I barely see them though, as my frowning eyes are now fixed on the bad impression of a dad standing at the back of the room. He's daring to give me a tentative grin and raised eyebrows as if he's a normal dad, encouraging his daughter, rather than someone who I've literally spoken to less than my dentist in the last five years.

I mean, WHAT the . . . How DARE he? How *dare* he come into my life again, unannounced, and when I'm onstage, for God's sake? The fecking, cacking, dumb-nut excuse for a father – stinkhole! I mean, can you BELIEVE this douchebag?! My confusion has swiftly turned to rage.

Oh, OK, 'Dad', you wanna come in here, into my life, and mess things up for me? Well, I'll show you how little you being in the room matters to me, and make you wish you'd never dared set foot in here, arse-wipe.

'Yeah, not sure where that was going, but, yeah, dads are funny things, aren't they? I don't know my dad; he left years ago. I've never tried to find him or anything, but Mum says I look just like him, so I guess I should be looking out for a guy with massive boobs.

'I don't know, I just think, for me at least, having a dad is like weekday afternoon telly . . . It's all just pathetic dramas and *Pointless*.'

The jokes get laughs, but they're uneasy ones. I don't care. My anger has overtaken my pride and currently wants to launch itself at my dad's chest and rip his heart out.

I stare right at him as I fire my jokes straight into his face. Only I can't see his face any more because he's dropped his head down while one of his hands rubs his forehead.

Oh, he's upset, is he? Good.

The fire is running out of me now though, and hot on its heels is the strong feeling that I just need to get away from him. Pretend he doesn't exist again.

So I put the mic back in its stand and half-heartedly say into it, 'Thanks, you've all, mostly, been awesome.'

The room applauds and my friends whoop as I race off the stage. I can't sit back down with them though. I can feel the back of my throat tightening and I fear if I stay in everyone's gaze much longer I will totally start crying, which would just be one humiliation too far.

So instead, swallowing back the tears and rage, I walk past my table of friends, only vaguely aware that they're all shouting their congratulations at me. Then when I've passed them I turn swiftly on my heel and power-walk out of the back door. And then I run.

Where I'm running to, I don't know. Just away. From these thoughts. From him.

I'm not very good at running though, and as soon as my boobs start to hurt I slow to a determined walk up the street, the air around me purple as the sun spreads itself thin, preparing to melt away.

'Haylah!' I hear behind me. It's Dylan's voice.

I stop in my tracks. He must have followed me out of the pub. Which is kind of sweet, I guess, but there's very little room in my brain to process this right now. And I don't know what I'll say to him. OK, so I've spoken with him a tiny bit about Dad, but otherwise the deepest conversations we've had together have been about superheroes and farting. Sometimes at the same time (those latex costumes do not look breathable). The point is, we have just the beginning sparks of a relationship at the moment and the last thing that spark needs is a bucketload of cold daddy-issue dung dumped on top of it.

Before I respond to Dylan, I also hear Kas's and Chloe's voices behind me.

'Hay!'

'Dude, wait up!'

I take a deep breath and turn round. The tightness in my throat is now growing to a lump, but I'm still determined not to cry. Kas, Chloe and Dylan half jog up the pavement towards me and stop, concerned expressions on their faces as they see that I'm frowning, red-faced and close to tears. Like I've just gone twelve rounds with Tyson Fury.

'You were excellent. What's the matter?' says Dylan.

'Was it cos you dropped the pipe? Cos that was nothing. I think some people thought it was part of the act. You were epic!' offers Kas.

Chloe pushes the other two aside and throws her arms round me, and though I'm not much of a hugger it feels good. I hug her back and bury my head into her bony shoulder. Though, as with any hug when your head's in turmoil, it pushes me over the edge and squeezes out the last morsel of dignity I had in me. I can't hold on any more and feel the tears filling my eyes. And I just want to tell them all that I need to go. Now. But I can't get any words out.

'Oh, sweetie,' Chloe says gently as I sob into her hair. 'I'm sorry. I saw him, that man, at the bar – it was your dad, right?'

I let out a 'unnnhgg' in response.

Kas says, 'Oh God. I didn't see him. Hay, I'm so sorry.'

'Bloody hell,' Dylan offers.

In films, they always get crying wrong, like it's all in the eyes, but crying consumes your whole body. There's a dark rumbling behind my ears, a strangling of the throat, then my heart bangs against my chest and my whole body shakes. My mouth pulls into an absurdly unattractive grimace and my breathing erupts from me in fits and starts as snot starts to fill my nose. This is definitely not a delicate Hollywood cry. This is an animalistic release of all the emotional crap that seeing my dad has brought to the surface, forcing me to remember that his leaving ripped my world's limbs off. It smashed the rock that was my mum and dad and their love for me to bits. I had loved him so much and felt so safe in the knowledge that he loved me too, and then it was all gone. *He* was gone. And then all my life lived up to that point was rewritten, my memories revised. Cos now it was clear that all that time he had really wanted to be elsewhere. He was simply playing the part of a loving dad until he finally had the guts to get the hell away from us and the dull life that we had forced him to live.

'Sorry, Chlo,' I manage to splutter. (And why is it that your mouth fills up with disgusting mucus crap when you cry? Seriously, crying is disgusting.) I pull away from her and wipe my face with both hands in a fight to grab a hold of myself. 'I think I got snot in your hair.'

'That's OK, no one would notice a bit of extra green in there at the moment anyway.'

I respond with a short, snotty snort of a laugh.

'Do you want me to tell him to eff off?' asks Kas, reaching out a hand to my shoulder.

'Haylah,' says a deep voice from behind us, and we all turn to see my dad standing a little way down the street.

He holds his head to one side and slowly walks closer, like he's approaching a wounded animal and doesn't want to make any sudden moves in case it runs or attacks. Which isn't far from the truth of the situation.

Chloe and Kas, standing either side of me, instinctively move closer and link their arms through mine to protect me from the enemy in front of us.

Dylan, standing a little closer to my dad with his hands in his pockets, shifts his weight uneasily from one foot to the other. He turns to me, chewing his bottom lip, clearly at a loss as to what to do.

'That's your dad?' he whispers.

I nod silently before pointing my frowny red 'just go away now, you bastard, or I'm going to cry again' face back at Dad.

Dylan steps towards 'Dad' and offers his hand to shake.

Can you believe that?! I mean, I know it's good to be polite when you meet your girlfriend's parents, but surely he gets that this is a slightly different situation?

'Erm, nice to meet you, Mr Swinton. I'm Dylan.'

'He's not Mr Swinton,' I spit, wiping my sob-snot on my sleeve and managing to regain control of myself. Then I revert back to simply feeling pissed off again. 'He's Mr Taylor. Him and his name have nothing to do with me. And it's *not* nice to meet him.'

'Oh. Right,' says Dylan, lowering his hand and taking a step back. 'Wait, your name was Haylah Taylor?'

Kas leans forward and whacks Dylan on the arm.

'We thought it was cute,' 'Dad' says with a nervous smile, 'like she was a TV character, Tinky Winky or whatever.'

Dylan, Kas and Chloe laugh a little.

I dramatically unlink myself from Chlo and Kas and they both mumble an apology for laughing before staring at the ground like puppies who've just been caught pooping in slippers.

'Shut up, everyone! And *you* –' I aim a finger at my dad. Dylan sheepishly hands me my pipe; he must have rescued it from the stage – 'Thank you, Dylan. *You,*' I say again, pointing the pipe handle directly at my dad's face, wishing it was a functioning wand so I could Avada Kedavra his arse, 'don't you *dare* use your charm on my friends.'

'Sorry,' he says. And although he says it with meaning it's about five years too late and roughly a thousand times not enough.

'Sorry, Hay,' says everyone else.

'I think I'll just, y'know, go back inside,' says Dylan, taking a tentative step away.

'No you won't,' I say firmly, grabbing the back of his T-shirt and dragging him towards us.

I know this is awkward as hell for him, but having him here at least means it's four against one.

'Fair enough,' he says, bowing his head and kicking at the ground.

'If anyone leaves, it's him.' I point the pipe at my dad again, but its powers don't seem to be working as he takes a step towards me, his handsome, if weathered, face looking full of warmth and apology. *Manipulative git.*

'I'm so sorry my coming here upset you. I just want to talk, Haylah. I owe you that.'

Seriously?! Years of pain, heartache, neglect, rejection, but, hey, a brief chitty-chat will surely square things!? Is *that* what he thinks?

'Oh, you owe me *way* more than that, but I don't want it, any of it. If you're suddenly feeling guilty, great, but go and take it somewhere else. I don't wanna know.'

'How did you know she'd be here anyway?' says Chlo.

I scowl at Dad as he answers, looking directly at me. 'I found you on Twitter and saw that you were doing this tonight and . . . Look, I'm really sorry, I just didn't know where else to find you.'

Damn that treacherous blue bird.

'Well, you know where I live! You remember,' I say in a faux-chirpy voice, 'it's the green house with the white door *that you SLAMMED when you ran out on us five years ago!*'

Dad winces. *Good.*

'Yeah, I really think I should be going inside now,' mumbles Dylan with his head still low and his hands in his pockets.

'No, you're fine *here*. *He's* going,' I spit.

'Yeah, that's fair, and I do know where you live,' says Dad sadly as if he's talking to the pavement. Then he looks up at me. 'But I didn't want to just spring on Noah like that, and your mum won't let me phone you and –'

'Well, that's a lie for starters,' I scoff.

He looks confused. 'It's not, Haylah.' Then he waves away the confusion with his hand. 'It doesn't matter though. Look, can we go and talk somewhere? As much as I'm sure your friends are loving this live episode of *EastEnders* being played out before them, perhaps we could just go and have a quiet chat and . . .'

I feel the tears rising in me again as Chlo and Kas step forward to fill the gap between me and my dad.

'No. She's asked you to leave,' says Chlo firmly, her arms crossed.

'And I think you need to respect that,' adds Kas in a shaky voice.

'Erm . . . yeah,' adds Dylan, still looking down at his shoes, but nodding with a serious frown.

'Of course, I . . .' says my dad in a sad, low voice. He looks at Chlo and Kas. 'You're good friends. I'm glad she's got you.' Then he looks at me. 'You were great onstage and . . . it's so good to . . . see you, Hay.' His voice cracks as he wipes his nose on his sleeve, just like I do.

Oh God.

My anger starts fading into sadness and I don't want it to. There's strength in the anger. There's only patheticness in the heartache.

'Haylah,' he says as we both look at each other through tear-filled eyes, 'I'll go and it's fine if you don't want to, but I'll be in town on Sunday, at, say, twelve in Costa, so if you want to . . . I'll just be there, OK?'

Then he gulps hard, turns and walks away.

And Kas and Chlo hold me as I cry some more. In fact, a lot more.

'You can . . . go . . . in . . . now . . . Dylan . . .' I say between sobs.

'Right, erm, if you're sure? OK then. I'll see you back inside. You sure you're OK? OK. I'm just going then. Just . . . going back into the pub.'

'Oh, sod off, Dylan!' says Chlo.

'Cool, yeah,' he says and leaves.

SEVEN

Back in the pub toilets, Chloe sorts my face out, wiping away the mascara that's run like spiders' legs down my cheeks and putting concealer under my eyes so it doesn't look *too much* like I've been crying.

'So what are you going to do, Hay?' asks Kas from behind a cubicle door as we all ignore the sound of the massive wee she's doing.

As Chlo dabs at my face with a small sponge, I take a sideways look in the mirror and, in an attempt to steady my still-pounding heart, I put my shoulders back and take a deep breath. *I'm a Swinton. I'm a strong, independent, fabulous female. I am not gonna let this ball-bag of a man screw up my life.*

'Simple,' I answer. 'I'm gonna forget I ever saw his stupid face here tonight and never see him again. Then everything will go back to normal.'

'You sure, babe?' asks Chlo as she steps back from my face with her head to one side, admiring her handiwork.

'Yeah. Totally. I'm better off without him,' I say. Which of us am I trying to convince?

I'm a Swinton, I think again proudly. Then my thoughts race to my mum. Half my brain wants to tell her about Dad showing up. Kas and Chlo are being gorgeous about the whole thing, but Mum's the only one who'll truly understand what I've been through. I imagine the hug she'll give me, the way she'll stroke my hair and tell me I was so brave for dealing with that hunk of junk. Then the other half of my brain kicks in with thoughts of how upset she'll be. She'll be angry, sure, but she'll also cry. Hard. And there's nothing worse than the sound of your mum crying. I won't tell her. I *can't* tell her.

Kas's disembodied voice adds, 'I can't believe he just showed up like that.'

'I know, right?' agrees Chlo. 'You did really well though, Hay. Even with him there, you still nailed that set.'

'Really, you think? Was I OK?' I say, clinging on to the opportunity to think about something else.

'Totally,' says Chlo. 'It was hilarious, although I do think me and Kas stole the show with our lines.'

'Oh, I agree,' I say, glad to be off the subject of Dad. 'Kas, how can you *still* be going? Honestly, it's like War Horse taking a piss.'

They laugh as Kas finally emerges from the cubicle and washes her hands.

'You OK, babe?' asks Chlo.

'I really am. Thank you, guys. This is the only way to go: just ignore the tosspot and crack on, right?' I say, before pouting at myself in the mirror and shimmying my shoulders with my fists up in the air in an exaggerated

I'm-a-funky-sex-goddess-and-I got-this way. After all, if in doubt, just do what Lizzo would do, right?

'Abso-frickin'-lutely,' says Chlo, giggling as she packs away her make-up.

'Totally the right decision,' agrees Kas with a smile.

And, yeah, a big part of me just wants to go home and wallow under my duvet, mulling over the immense crap mountain I've had to confront today, but, on the other hand, I really need my brain to be swept away from it. So I stride as confidently as I can back towards the bar.

Chlo holds the door open for me and Kas, then she squeezes between us, linking her arms through ours so we're like a set of freaky conjoined triplets.

'Now, there's some boys out there that need flirting with. Ladies? Shall we?' she says.

Me and Kas look at each other.

'What?' Chlo says, noticing our rolling eyes. She lowers her voice to a whisper as we make our way past the bar and back to our table. 'Hay needs to think about something ELSE and boys are JUST the thing. So, Kas, listen up . . . Hay has Dylan and I'm aiming for a bit of Watto-love, so how about you? Belge and Ginger Dan are both up for grabs?' She giggles.

'I . . . er . . . well, I don't really fancy either of them, to be honest,' says Kas.

'What? Why? Gingers are hot and Belge, well, yeah, he's a bit of a plank, but there's one definite way of shutting his mouth up!' She makes an exaggerated kissing sound.

'Chlo!' Kas almost shouts.

'What?' says Chlo in her most innocent voice, like a cartoon cat in a bib holding a knife and fork who's responding to the accusing look of the mouse tied to the plate in front of him.

And I see it again: that weary look from Kas whenever Chlo gets full-on about this stuff.

I quickly step in to rescue Kas and steer Chlo back in her favourite direction – herself. 'So what's your next genius move with Watto then, Chlo? Gonna tell him that 1914 was a strange time to start a war; they should have at least waited until bang on quarter past?'

'Oh, shut up,' whispers Chlo with a snort of laughter.

Kas gives me a thankful look. And I get it. Maybe Kas has got her eye on someone else, which she might want to keep totally her business. It's fair enough that snogging Ginger Dan or Belge just because they're going spare isn't exactly high up on her priority list right now.

Back at the table there's a fresh round of Diet Cokes and a brief interlude between acts where we can talk. Everyone tells me it was a great set, and even a few strangers tap me on the shoulder to tell me they thought it was good, which is encouraging, but doesn't get my mind away from churning over what happened earlier. My dad. *Dad*. Was actually here.

While Belge is showing off his new phone and warbling on about all the 'totally awesome' selfie modes on the camera, not picking up on the fact that nobody cares, Dylan whispers to me, 'You OK?'

'Yep. Fine,' I say with a half-smile.

And, I mean, what else can I say? I'm sure Dylan doesn't really want to know what's going on in my head, and frankly I don't really know what's going on in my head anyway. He's just saying what he thinks he should say. I try to change the subject to let him off the hook.

'So did you catch some of Jake's lyrics earlier? I found the one about "her eyelashes cascade like wiper blades" particularly moving.'

But surprisingly he doesn't take the easy way out I've offered him.

'Yeah, so dumb.' He lowers his voice. 'But are you going to see him? Your dad? On Sunday?'

I've made my decision to forget about the whole thing and it's kind of peeing me off that Dylan's making me revisit it. And doubt it.

'Erm . . . no. He's basically a bastard and I'm better off without him, so . . . no.'

'And that's it then?'

He almost seems *offended* that I'm not seeing my dad again. Which pisses me off some more. I mean, what the hell does he know? He barely knows me, really, and he certainly knows nothing about the way Dad treated us and left.

'Yes. That's it,' I say sharply before taking a noisy slurp of my Coke, signifying the end of the discussion. It doesn't work though.

'OK, but . . . for what it's worth . . .' He gulps. 'I think you're wrong.'

'*What?*' I say rather too loudly, as the whole table stops and stares at us.

Then their attention is redirected as Kingston introduces the next act, a band called Strange Reckoning.

Dylan breathes loudly through his nose, sits back in his chair and faces the stage. My snapping at him seems to have stopped his interfering, but, really, is it too much to ask for a little support from him? He's supposed to be my boyfriend, after all, so isn't it his job to agree with me?

It turns out that Strange Reckoning are so shockingly terrible they actually do a pretty great job of dragging me out of my mood. The band consists of a man wearing a balaclava simply pressing a button on a keyboard that starts playing drum and bass, and another man, who looks exactly like a garden gnome, frantically shaking maracas and half rapping, half yodelling over the top of it. Nothing, *nothing* could *ever* be as bad as *this* 'music'.

We all watch with open mouths, and then I make the mistake of catching Dylan's eye, widening in disbelief, and we both have to simultaneously lower our heads as laughter shoots out of our noses. And, yes, I know it's weird to be laughing so soon after the major, upsetting Dad incident, but God do I need it – and isn't that what laughter is for anyway? The positive release of balled-up tension and emotion, however inappropriate the timing?

The rest of the table notices us and their eyes light up as infectious laughter spreads round the table. The pressure building behind Watto's face is so much that his eyes actually start watering. Once Chloe notices his face, it's too much for her and she's gone, desperately trying to cover it up by coughing, but it just comes out as a stuttering, breathy cackle, which in turn forces my laughter to once again explosively escape through my nose. Ginger Dan shoves his T-shirt into his mouth, Kas's hand is clasped over her creased-up face while her body silently convulses, and I can see Belge pinching his own leg hard and locking his eyes shut, but it still doesn't stop the grimace spreading across his face.

Then suddenly we're all snapped out of it as Jake slams his hands down on the table, leans over us and angrily whisper-shouts, 'Yeah, all right, *kids*. I think it's time to go now.'

I look at my phone. It's ten fifteen already and, although the laughter has helped, the thought of going home and closing my bedroom door on everything actually sounds pretty good right now.

We shuffle out of our seats, heads held low though still smirking, and file out of the pub.

As I'm following the others, now audibly laughing and giggling, through the back door and out into the car park, I feel Dylan's hand on my arm tugging me back.

I stop and turn to him as the others walk ahead. 'What? Are you going to tell me I'm wrong again?' I say, realizing as I say it that I'm still annoyed with him (though weirdly pleased that he just touched me, even if it wasn't in any way romantically intended).

'Yeah, sorry if all that came out wrong,' he says.

'Whatever, it's fine,' I say and turn to leave.

'Wait.'

'What?' I turn back to him with a sigh as I'm starting to feel totally done in, and the post-crying headache is kicking in hard.

He looks down at the ground, then stares up at me with his head to one side. 'Look, I get why you wouldn't want to see your dad, but I just think you should maybe give him a chance, hear him out? Otherwise you might regret it.'

I mean, *seriously*? For someone who up to this point has seemed to have the emotional depth of a brick, what the hell makes him think he can give me advice on my family? And after I've made it bloody clear that I don't want it. Annoyance, combined with tiredness and Dad-anger, now take over my brain and I snap back at him. 'Well, what the hell do you know about it, Dylan? I mean, this is *my dad* we're talking about, who walked out and left us five years ago and only turned up again *tonight*. Have you any idea how that feels?'

'You're right, you're right, I'm sorry,' he says, his hands held up as if showing me he's unarmed.

But I'm in mid flow now so I continue my assault, which, yes, OK, might be a little on the harsh side. 'And who the hell are you to give me advice anyway? I don't even know if you've *got* a mum and dad. You've never even invited me round your house – what the *hell* is that about?' I step towards him, my arms becoming more expressive as I go on, like an anger-powered puppet. 'If you want to start giving me advice on my life, you at least need to let me into yours a bit. Argh, forget it, I just –'

'So come round then,' he blurts out.

Did he really just say that?

'You don't mean it. Let's just go. It's been a turd storm of an evening and I just want it done.' I turn to leave, but he puts a hand on my arm.

'I do mean it.'

'No, you don't. No one's ever been round to your house.'

'Apart from tomorrow, when you're going to come round,' he says in a tone that indicates he's trying to convince himself as much as me.

'Really?' I ask.

'Yeah,' he says with a nod, and then he leaves his mouth open, like he is giving it a chance to come up with a reason why I shouldn't actually come round. So he ends up looking like a fish.

'Well . . . OK then,' I say.

I'm still not really sure if he actually wants me there, or if he just came up with the first thing he knew would stop me ranting at him.

'We'd better catch up with the others,' I say, and as we walk together he tells me his address, a street I've never heard of before, but I just nod because otherwise you get into that awkward thing when you ask for directions and the person says, 'It's near such-and-such,' and you say, 'Well, I've never heard of that either,' and this is repeated a couple of times so by the third time around, even though you still haven't heard of the place it's near, you go, 'Oh yeah! Of course, yeah I know it,', but actually you're just going to look it up on your phone.

And just like that it's settled. I'm going round Dylan's tomorrow. Which wasn't my idea at all, and yet somehow it feels like I pushed him into it.

'One thing though,' he adds before we reach the others. 'Don't tell anyone. I mean, not in a sinister way or anything, tell your mum or whatever, just don't tell any of that lot. I haven't had anyone round in years and . . .' He shuffles his feet awkwardly on the pavement.

'Erm, yeah, OK,' I say, confused, but too knackered to probe further.

Sweet baby cheeses, what an evening.

EIGHT

At home, I find Mum and Ruben sitting on the sofa, several empty curry cartons and broken bits of poppadom sitting between them.

'Good food?' I ask.

'The best,' says Ruben. 'I had this new dish, samosas in a spicy sauce – can't remember what it was called . . .'

'Kevin?' I offer as I go to get some water.

'Erm, no . . .' he says, not getting the joke.

Mum joins me in the kitchen and I pass her smell test and interrogation about the evening, and I tell her the gig went well. She picks up that something's not right, but I shrug it off and tell her I'm just tired. As much as part of me wants to offload some of this brain ache, I'm still determined not to mention the Dad thing to her. There's no point in us both being in emotional turmoil, especially as I'm not going to see him again anyway.

'Ruben's here late tonight,' I say as I leave the kitchen. He normally leaves at around nine because when Mum's not working shifts she likes her sleep.

Mum follows and then inhales sharply.

I turn back to her. 'What?' I ask, maybe a bit too bitchily.

'Oh . . . nothing,' she says and saunters back to the sofa.

Honestly, she can be such a freak sometimes.

Then I say goodnight to both of them, go up to my room and collapse on my bed, not even bothering to get undressed, hoping that sleep will quickly drag me under and away from the dad storm that is still swishing round my throbbing head.

But sleep is being a tease – flirting, but playing hard to get. After about half an hour I give up and start pacing round my room, which, as it isn't a very big room, feels more like I'm doing some sort of deranged, old-fashioned box-step dance.

I slump on to my desk chair with a massive grunty sigh. My brain is fighting to stay online when all I want is for it to power down. It's insisting on rerunning the evening and, though I try to make it settle on the good bits of the set and the laughs I got, it keeps fast-forwarding those and focusing in on the teary, crappy bits instead.

Bloody brain.

And I don't want to go there. I can't begin to dive fully into my anger with Dad as it's just too much. But I *can* dip my toe into my much milder frustrations with Dylan. So, as a way to keep my brain otherwise occupied until sleep gets lonely and asks me to join it again, I start writing about Dylan in my notebook of funny. It's actually pretty good stuff, so I decide to make it into another YouTube vid – I'll put it out there, see what happens.

I switch the video on my phone on and start ranting. Dylan says he likes my rants so I'm sure he would approve. *Then again maybe not.*

'So, boyfriends . . . they're a tricky bunch, right?

'Can't live with them . . . because I still live with my mum and go to school.

'But, yeah, I've got a boyfriend. I know, go me, right? And it's official and everything. He asked me if we could be girlfriend and boyfriend, and I said yeah, as long as I get to be the girlfriend.

'I dunno, maybe I made the wrong decision there though. I mean, boys have it a bit easier, don't they? They don't get interrogated by their mates for one. When girls tell their mates they have a boyfriend, they ask, "Is he caring? Is he sweet? Is he sensitive? Is he romantic?" Boys tell their mates and they just ask, "Is she hot?"

'Anyway, I've come to realize that there's a very big difference between what we tell our mates about our boyfriends and the truth. For example, "My boyfriend's so sensitive!" actually means: "When I told him my grandad died, he shrugged, but he cried for an hour after Iron Man died."

'"My boyfriend's so dreamy" actually means sometimes he falls asleep when I'm talking. "My boyfriend's so romantic" actually means he once held in a fart for me for so long he crapped himself. And then told me all about it in graphic detail.

'I dunno, I think getting your first boyfriend is like getting a pet iguana. It seems like a great idea – it'll make you more interesting, keep you company, look good in selfies. Then you finally get one. And the reality sets in. Turns out owning one isn't as interesting as you thought it would be. It smells weird, barely moves unless it's eating, doesn't seem all that interested in you, and you get the feeling you're never gonna be hot enough for it.

'Nah, I'm kidding though. My boyfriend's great. I mean, it's not a classic fairy-tale relationship. He's not the boyfriend of your dreams, who, oh, I don't know, *doesn't* throw pens at your head in geography class and *doesn't* rearrange the contents of his trousers when he's having dinner with you ... and your mum. Still, he buys me presents though. Yeah, I know, really romantic. The last thing he bought me was pretty special ... it's a key ring that simply says "bitch". Which is actually super thoughtful, cos how did he know that was my dad's pet name for me when I was little, right? So that's, yeah, that's my boyfriend. Back off, ladies, he's mine. See ya next time.'

After I turn off the video, I feel better, like I've released some pent-up frustrations or something. And, yeah, maybe I was a *bit* rude about Dylan, but seeing that my last videos still have a pathetic number of views I figure what the hell and upload it under the title 'Boyfriends Are Idiots'.

Then I get my pyjamas on and climb into bed. Luckily I don't have to wait long before sleep feels sorry for me and climbs in with me.

NINE

I sleep on in the morning until Noah bashes my door open and prances round my room in just his pants, singing loudly. Although he doesn't really understand singing so it's more like prolonged shouting.

I turn towards the wall and drag the duvet over my head. You know when you wake up and at first there's that delicious moment when you're only half awake and the weight of the world hasn't quite fallen on you yet? Then it does and you feel crushed by the memories of your bumhole of a dad turning up last night.

I really need a bit of quiet before I face the day, but Noah's not nearly done yet. He jumps on the bed and climbs over me until his head is just above mine, then he lies there quietly for as long as he can keep still, around thirty seconds, then peels back the duvet.

'BOOO!' he shouts.

'Aww! Dude, I knew you were there – you're lying on me!'

'I have a question! I have a question!'

'But it can wait till later, right?'

'No.'

'Yes it can, Noah. I'm asleep. Go and ask Mum.'

'She's busy.'

'Doing what?'

'Having breakfookst with Ruben.'

'Ruben's here already?'

'Yep.'

'Jeez, the guy was only here last night.'

'Him and Mummy had a sleepover.'

I sit bolt upright, knocking Noah backwards. 'WHAT??'

He slept OVER – actually slept OVER – in my mum's actual, ugh, BED, which is just the other side of the wall next to MY BED!

'Can I ask my question now?' says Noah, pulling himself back up to sit on my legs.

'No,' I say, trying to sit up and get past him so I can go and ask Mum what the *hell* is going on.

'But you always say I can ask you anything!'

'Fine, go on. But make it a simple one,' I snap, knowing from previous experience that there's no way out of this bed until the question is asked and answered.

I lie back down and he clambers up and straddles my belly. 'You know God?'

'Ye-ah,' I say through gritted teeth. This doesn't sound like the beginning of a simple question.

'He is Jesus-es-es dad, right?'

'Yeah!' I say brightly, relieved that it was a simple question after all, until I realize he's not finished – that was merely his opening statement.

'And Joseph is Jesus-es-es dad too, right?'

'R . . . ight.'

'So how does that work?'

'Seriously? Holy Trinity, Noah! You're asking me theological questions?! I can't get my head round that this early in the morning. Why are you even asking this?'

'At school, we're going to do the Nanivity.'

'The Nativity? It's September, Noah, that's months away!'

He just shrugs at me. The boy doesn't even understand the days of the week; the concept of months is as alien to him as the concept of 'avoiding carbs' is to me.

(Sure, in an ideal world, I'd want buns of steel, but not if that requires giving up buns of Starbucks.)

'OK,' I say, trying to work out how the hell I'm supposed to explain the Holy Trinity to a dude who finds the plot of *The Emoji Movie* hard to follow.

'Well, Joseph is Jesus-es –' *he's right, that* is *hard to say* – 'erm . . . earth-dad. And God is Jesus's . . . space-dad.'

I feel pretty pleased with this and try to wriggle out from under him.

'And who's the Holy Ferret?'

'Do you mean Spirit?'

'OK. My friend Izzy's the Holy "Spirit" in the Nanivity.'

Jeez, I think, *that is one advanced Nativity.*

'OK, so the Holy Spirit is, erm . . . Jesus's . . . space . . . stepmum.'

Happy with that, Noah finally releases me from my duvet shackles.

I storm downstairs to confront my mother about Ruben staying over in *her* bed and . . . urgh . . . Sorry, a little vom just came up.

Then, with Noah following me, I stop halfway down the stairs. Mum and Ruben have been together for months. I like Ruben. He makes Mum happy. And they're adults. This was inevitable. So what the hell is my problem? I guess it just never crossed my mind that they would be – *ugh, here comes the vom again* – sleeping together. In Mum's bed. Which sort of feels like the family bed, the same bed that me and Noah sit on to open our Christmas presents or curl up on with Mum to watch *Strictly Come Dancing*. The same bed that she used to sleep in with . . . Dad.

I mean, Mum doing anything else in there, especially with that bearded lump, is too gross to comprehend, but it's happening. It's . . . urgh . . . happened . . .

Just don't think about it.

Noah prods his podgy finger into my back. 'What you doing? I want breakfookst!'

We carry on down the stairs and into the kitchen. Mum and Ruben are sitting opposite each other at the table and drinking steamy cups of tea.

Note to self: never use the word 'steamy' in the same sentence as Mum and Ruben again.

Ruben's looking all bright-eyed and bushy-bearded and Mum's looking a little flushed and embarrassed when I walk in and nod a good morning in their direction. She stares intently at her tea, not making eye contact, as I head to the fridge to grab some juice.

Just don't think about it . . . Just don't think about it . . .

'I've made porridge. There's some left over if you want it?' says Ruben.

You disgusting pervert, I think. *Stop it. Just don't think about it.*

'Erm, no thanks, just gonna have some toast,' I say, pouring out juice for me and then Noah after he punches me on the bum to signal that he also wants in. Then I flop a bit of bread into the toaster and stare at it while it does its job.

'I want toast too!' shouts Noah, punching me on the other other buttock.

'Mum, can't you do his breakfast?'

'Haylah! You're standing *right* next to the toaster!'

'Fine,' I scoff, shoving another bit of bread down with an exaggerated sigh. I've always been a firm believer that if a job's worth doing, it's worth doing reluctantly.

'That curry last night was amazing,' says Ruben.

'I know, right, although my stomach's suffering today,' says Mum.

'You know, last night I farted so loudly and for so long I actually woke myself up. It was almost comic, really,' says Ruben.

'While also being tragic,' says Mum in fake disapproval.

Ruben laughs. 'Yeah, like a tragicomedy.'

'Are you saying your farts are Shakespearean classics?' Mum says, and they both fall about laughing.

Good God, could this conversation be any more offensive to my ears?

In a desperate bid to change the conversation, I announce, 'Oh, and I'm going round Dylan's house later, Mum. I'll message you his address if you want.'

To be honest, I half hope she'll say no as I'm not all that sure I want to go round Dylan's with my mind still churning around the Dad thing, and knowing Dylan's not overly keen on me being there anyway. But, clearly sensing the awkwardness in the room after Ruben stayed the night and probably feeling pangs of guilt, she doesn't.

'Oh wow. First time you've been over his. Well, yeah, OK, love,' she says. 'Will his parents be there?'

'Yeah, totally,' I say with hopefully convincing confidence. I actually have absolutely no idea if he even has human parents.

I smother the toast with butter and 'Nutello', covering all three major food groups – carbs, fat *and* sugar – then slump down at the table opposite Mum, who's still looking super shifty.

'Hey, Noah, you wanna come watch *Hey Duggee* with me?' says Ruben before whisking Noah and Noah's breakfast out of the room.

Elbows on the table, I swallow the last of my toast down, rest my head on one hand and give Mum a raised eyebrow. 'OK, what's going on?'

'Well, love, so Ruben, erm, stayed round last night.'

'Yeah, I kinda noticed, and I've chosen to deal with that by in no way mentioning it ever, is that OK?'

She nods with a smirk, then her face goes all frowny and serious. Which does not look good. 'Yeah, that's fine, but . . .'

'There's more?' I ask.

Oh God, does she somehow know about Dad turning up last night?

'Well, Hay –' she stops to take a sip of tea – 'it's not a big deal, really . . .'

Obviously, as soon as someone says that, it becomes very clear that it is, in fact, a very big deal.

'What's not a big deal?' I say, sitting up and getting worried that, if it's not Dad, she's ill or something.

She laughs nervously. 'Don't look like that, Hay. It's nothing serious, honest; it's just, erm . . .'

'Spit it out, woman.'

'Right, yes, you know Ruben?'

'Who?' I say, just to wind her up.

'Ruben!'

'Yes, Mum, I believe I know of whom you speak,' I say, actually starting to enjoy the rare feeling of being in control of a conversation with Mum.

'Right, yes.' She takes a deep breath before her normal fast-paced talking resumes. 'Well, obviously we've been together, y'know, for a number of months now, and his lease is up on his house, and he wondered – well, *I* wondered, no, *we* wondered – if you wouldn't mind, I mean, if you think it might be OK or even a good idea if he, maybe just temporarily, we'll see how it goes . . . well . . . moved in with us.'

As soon as the word 'us' is out of her mouth, she downs the rest of her boiling-hot tea like a proper lad on a stag do chugging down a pint.

So Ruben's moving in. And, this morning's knee-jerk 'urgh' reaction about him staying the night aside, on some level I knew this would happen. It's not really coming as a surprise. What *is* coming as a surprise, however, is that I'm *not* upset about it. Or angry, or feeling like I'm losing Mum to him or worried he'll leave and hurt Noah or anything like that. In fact, if anything, it kind of feels right. I mean, he's clearly into Mum (and, let's face it, he's not going to leave her; I mean, the guy looks like *prehistoric man* – he is punching *well* above his weight) and he gets on super well with Noah, because he's basically the same mental age, plus he's here a lot anyway, and it's kind of nice that I feel like Noah's sister again rather than his second parent. And he keeps Mum happy and dilutes her nagging so it's spread between the three of us, not just me and Noah. And, because of our sorry excuse for a father, Noah kinda needs a dad and frankly, well, he could do a lot worse than Ruben.

Wow. I am impressed with myself. I mean, I have really *emotionally matured.*

Obviously the beardo's still a total flump nugget and I'd rather chew my own elbows off than ever call him 'Dad', but, well, all in all, *why not*?

Doesn't mean I can't wind Mum up a little bit more now though. I'll never be too emotionally mature for that.

'In *this* house?' I say with a frown.

'Yes,' she splutters, replacing her now-empty cup on the table.

'With us . . .?'

'Yes.'

'Living here at the same time?'

'Yes!'

'Hmm ...' I say, my eyes rolling around as if deeply considering my next move. 'That guy in there?'

'YES!' she says, throwing her hands in the air. 'Shetland Islands, Haylah!' (Sometimes Mum makes up swear words.) 'Seriously, girl, *could* you just *try* to make this a *little* bit easier on me?'

I laugh. 'I'm just messin' with ya, Mum. Of course it's fine.'

She looks at me, stunned for a moment, then smiles broadly and claps her hands together. 'What? Seriously? Oh, Haylah. Thank you, sweetie!'

She gets up, trots round the table and embraces me in a full-on-faceful-of-boobs Mum-hug.

'Finding it a little hard to breathe in here, Mum,' I whimper.

'Right, sorry, love,' she says, releasing me and sitting in the chair next to me. 'It won't be for a couple of months, but he might start moving a few things in before then, OK?'

'Yep, that's cool.'

'You are *the* best daughter ever, you know that?'

'Yeah, I'm pretty awesome.'

'You are a little minx though, Hay. I believe you quite enjoyed winding me up there.'

'Never,' I say, shaking my head. 'That tea must have been pretty hot when you downed it though. Burn yourself much?' I ask with a smirk.

'*Cannot* feel my tongue,' she says and we both laugh.

Noah and Ruben return to the kitchen to play some deranged game with a grape and a spatula so I retreat to the sofa in the living room.

I remain pleased with my new-found emotional maturity, although my chilled reaction may have partly been because of my relief that Mum doesn't know about Dad's appearance last night, and my brain is so busy with Dad and Dylan thoughts that it has little room for anti-Mum-and-Ruben thoughts.

Faffing about on my phone, I send Dylan a message asking if he still wants me over today.

Yeah, why not? Nothin' else on.

Well, with such lukewarm sentiments, how can I resist?

I don't even notice Mum stealth-advancing on me until she plops down next to me, her hand landing firmly on my knee.

'Look, babe, I mean, you going round Dylan's, just the two of you, you know, well, you are being *careful*, right?'

Classic. Ruben stays over for one night and now she can only think about one thing. Get your mind out of the gutter, woman!

'Mum! It's not even like that. We don't even kiss.'

'Oh,' she says with a look of relief. 'Right, well, that's great. I mean, you're *way* too young for any of that stuff anyway, but look, if that changes, you can always talk to me about anything, OK? I should have known my Haylah's always careful.'

'Yeah, but are *you*?' I look at her with a judging smirk and a raised eyebrow.

'What?' she asks with wide, 'innocent' eyes.

'Nothing, Mum, honestly. I'm glad you have Ruben.'

I think about seeing Dad last night and all the times Mum cried over him.

She studies my face and for a moment I worry that somehow she'll be able to tell that I saw Dad at the club. And I really don't want her freaking out about that.

'Haylah, you're so often sarcastic that it's difficult to know when you're being genuine and when you're not.'

'I'm really sorry. I'll try to get some kind of sarcasm alarm fitted.'

'And what would that sound like?'

'Ooooh, I'm a sarcasm alarm; aren't I a fantastic idea?' I half sing in my most sarcastic voice.

We both laugh and she gets up, kisses my cheek and goes back into the kitchen. To Ruben. Her bed buddy. *Ugh. I'm just gonna have to get used to it.*

Looking back at my phone, I check my videos and weirdly last night's 'Boyfriends Are Idiots' video has had a ton of views, even more than the Stacy Beeatch one and way more than all the rest. Which is still not a lot, but hey. Maybe I'm on to something here. Maybe I needed to be rantier, sassier, ruder. Maybe *that's* my comedy persona. Feeling like a superhero realizing the true purpose of their power, I run upstairs and upload a new video: 'Dads Are Idiots'.

I use some of the jokes from my stand-up last night and make light of Dad's affair, saying, 'My dad had an affair with his secretary – can you believe that? So clichéd.

'And what is it about secretaries that drives men wild anyway, and why haven't us women picked up on that? I mean, for an evening out on the pull, why are we wasting our time getting our hair and nails done when all we really need to do is pitch up in the corner of the club with a filing cabinet and crack on with some light admin work – the guys would come flocking!'

And I rant on about how a 'good' dad is supposed to be someone who teaches his daughter about the world and, to be fair, he did: he taught me that it sucks . . .

'Oh, and if you find a pair of knickers that are way too small for your mum in your dad's car don't presume they're a present for you and put them on.' (This didn't actually happen to me, thank God, but who cares if it's funny, right?)

As I rant on, the anger at Dad builds, but as I hit upload it fades.

And my thoughts migrate to seeing Dylan later as I try on a few outfits before my magical mystery tour to visit his house.

Oh God, I'm going to Dylan's house.

TEN

After I've settled on a Primark Rolling Stones T-shirt under one of Uncle Terry's tweed jackets, a pair of cut-off denim shorts, red tights and my old trusty Adidas Stan Smith trainers (Oh, I am so rocking that rock-chick look), the realization that I'm going to Dylan's actual house hits me again. Does he really want me there or did he offer out of pity and as a way of shutting me up?

Just before I leave, I check my video views and see that the 'Dads Are Idiots' video is doing really well too. *And* there are a few lovely comments beneath, like, Hilarious and heartbreaking – stay strong, girl.

Ha! I owe my dad nothing; this video is staying out there. It's my closure.

As I walk to Dylan's house, I'm excited about seeing him, but unsure what I'm going to find. Seeing Leo last night made me remember how wanted he made me feel when we kissed. My only kiss. Cos, in case you need a recap, Dylan hasn't come anywhere near me. There's been NO kissing. None. Or even hand-holding. Or arms round shoulders. Or anything resembling a boyfriend-girlfriend thing. In fact, when you lay it out in full, here's my idea of a boyfriend-girlfriend relationship, as acquired through watching films, listening to pop songs and Chloe and Kas's constant droning on, versus my *reality* with Dylan. In chart form. That's what this relationship has driven me to – voluntarily drawing up charts in my brain.

REAL COUPLE	ME AND DYLAN
Show affection, often physically through kissing, etc.	The only time he has ever touched me was when he once 'fixed' my ripped jeans by Sellotaping up the knee.
Give gifts to express their feelings.	My only gift has been a plastic 'Bitch' key ring.
Admire and compliment the way the other looks.	He has never said one single nice thing about the way I look. Even when I've clearly made the effort and, y'know, washed my hair or cut my fingernails or whatever. And I've never once caught him looking at or anywhere near my boobs. And they often fall into a natural line of sight, so he must be making quite an effort NOT to look at them.

After a walk that takes forever into a part of town I've never been to before, I finally find Dylan's street. And it's not at all what I expected.

I thought that the most likely reason I've never been round his house is that it is a crappy house in a crappy street and he is embarrassed about it. I mean, that's normally the reason I don't invite people over to mine. But this is a proper nice street, wide and quiet with leafy trees down either side. Then there's the houses: all different, but all huge great beasts with drives longer than my road and fancy cars parked on them that probably cost more than my house.

A classy young couple walk past me, pushing a baby in one of those huge old-fashioned prams that looks like Cinderella's carriage. The woman's eyes flicker over my clothes, making me reassess them through her eyes – an old man's jacket, ripped shorts and a pair of trainers that look like I found them in a bin. She offers me a patronizing smile. The man keeps looking ahead, his chin held high, refusing to acknowledge that he shares the world with someone like me. I feel like a knackered old pigeon that's somehow flown into a rare bird enclosure at the zoo.

How on earth does dopey, bumbling, loud-mouthed Dylan live on a road like this?

I get to his house and stand on the pavement for quite a while, looking at it with my mouth hanging open. His house is not like the others on the road. It's just as big, but this thing is modern – lots of glass and wooden cladding. Like a barn-style spaceship. It looks like something off one of those home-design TV shows about people we're supposed to feel sorry for because their million-pound dream mansion is taking a bit longer to build than they expected.

So now that I know he's totally *not* poor, I'm left wondering if the reason I haven't been invited round is the same reason Leo didn't like talking to me at school, because he's embarrassed about me. I'm probably going to find super-posh, marathon-running, intelligent, go-getting parents in there, and they'll take one look at me – a fat weirdo wearing an old tramp's outfit – and ban Dylan from ever spending time with me again.

But then what do I care if they and, more to the point, *he* thinks that? Sure, I like the guy a bit. Well, OK, a lot. But it's hardly bluebirds-singing-around-us-Disneyesque-true-love here, is it? So, if he doesn't want me around any more, what's the problem? Screw him and his posh family. I'm *Haylah*. Take me as I am or jog on, losers.

Then I remember the electricity I felt when his leg was touching mine last night. And the way he makes me laugh. Oh God, I really, *really* do like him. I just don't know if he likes me the same way.

As I get closer to his massive front door, my hand shakes a little and my heart thunders in my chest. I press the bell.

Half expecting a butler or the Queen herself to answer, I'm relieved when Dylan finally opens it. It doesn't open like a normal door; instead, it swivels open.

My hand stops shaking and my insides calm at seeing his face. We offer each other an awkward nod of hello as a pug bursts through the door and starts swirling round my legs, snuffling with great excitement.

'That's Brian,' Dylan says with a smirk.

'Hi, Brian,' I say.

I walk into the house, and Dylan catches my raised eyebrows as I watch the door do its thing.

'Yeah, sorry, it's a weird door.'

'Yeah,' I say, stepping into a vast hall that opens out into a huge open-plan living space the size of a school gym, 'this whole place is a craphole.'

He gives a low, awkward laugh. 'Anyway, erm, hello,' he says in his usual confused manner. So it's still kinda difficult to tell if he's happy to see me here or not. The dog is overcome with emotion at my arrival though, and is urgently jumping up at my legs. 'Brian, stop being such a needy knob! Sorry, he's just desperate to know he's wanted.'

He's not the only one, I think.

'Hi,' I say to Dylan, before stooping to give the dog some much-needed attention. 'And don't listen to him, Brian. I get this excited when new people come round to my house.'

Brian does a small wee on the floor near my feet.

'Well, maybe not *that* excited,' I say.

Dylan laughs a little, then clears up the wee with some kitchen roll as I stand there awkwardly.

'Right, that's done,' he says. 'So, did you wanna ... What do you wanna do? Go watch a Marvel movie or something?'

Is he kidding?! He's seen the actual craphole I live in; he must get how frickin' amazing this place is. I don't wanna finally come here only to watch good-looking people with superpowers complain about how they have to save the world *again*.

'Screw that, dude. I wanna look round this dump of yours. It's chuffin' awesome!'

He looks relieved somehow that I'm excited about it.

He starts showing me around. Brian follows on behind us, his little claws clicking on the polished wooden floor. We begin in the kitchen, which is off the main living area and is a mix of shiny surfaces and old (or, at least, made to look old) benches and shelves.

'Do you want something to eat? I'm not sure we've got a lot in though.' He idly picks up a potato from the top of a tall vegetable rack and turns it round in his huge hand. 'I guess I could . . . make you something?'

'Seriously –' I smile – 'you're going to *make* me something, out of proper ingredients and everything?'

'What?' He grins, leaning back on the kitchen worktop. 'It can't be that hard. Most food is just the same old ingredients squished into a new shape.'

I laugh. 'Yeah, I don't think you've *quite* got the right idea about cooking. On the other hand, you might have a point.' I start walking round the kitchen, expressively using my hands as I talk, almost like I'm onstage and he's the only audience member. He hangs his head a little, but his eyes are very much on me. 'I mean, no food has done that quite so successfully as the potato. Mash, chips, waffles, they each hold a separate place in our hearts, but I guess it is all just the same thing squished into a new shape.'

We agree not to have anything to eat, but I think we're both feeling more relaxed now that we've made each other laugh.

When we're out in the big open-plan bit, Dylan and Brian slump down on to a massive worn corner sofa in the centre of the space, and Dylan lazily points up to a balcony thing that has doors leading off it. 'So those are, like, bedrooms,' he says, then he swings his pointing finger to other corners of the room. 'And there's a toilet over there, and my dad's office out there and stuff, and . . . that's it really.'

The fact that he's so super awkward about living in this gorgeous place is really kinda cute.

'Dude, don't ever become an estate agent cos that was *seriously* deficient.'

I'm still standing in the middle of the room, slowly rotating and drinking it all in. The house is big. It isn't a mansion or anything, but it's so frickin' . . . cool.

He smiles at me. 'Well, what do you want me to say? It's just a house. Have a look around if you want. Go nuts.'

So I start wandering about as he puts a TV the size of a billboard on, though I get the weird feeling that he might be watching me not the TV.

Could it be that he's looking at me in *that* way? A fancying way? As a proud feminist, I don't want guys to look at me that way, but as a girlfriend I TOTALLY want my boyfriend to look at me in that way!

Shut up, brain and just be cool!

Everywhere you look in this house there's incredibly cool stuff – old carpets, guitars, a big modern-art statue (which from some angles looks like an angel and from others a misshapen root vegetable, but, whatever, it's still cool), and loads of mismatched armchairs, all interesting shapes and colours. On all the walls between the floor-to-ceiling windows there are huge artworks, weird, swirly shelves full of books, a wooden stag's head with a dapper moustache drawn on it and displays of stuff that don't normally get displayed, like colourful skateboards all in a row and loads of Chinese fans in a massive circle.

'Oh my *God*,' I say, wandering around behind where Dylan's sitting and taking it all in. 'This place! What do your parents *do*? Are you guys like *royalty* or something?!'

He turns the volume down on the TV and leans over the back of the sofa. 'Oh, shut up,' he says with a sheepish grin. 'I know, I know, it's all a bit *much*. It's why I don't often have people round. Don't want everyone thinking I'm some spoiled rich brat, you know?'

'But you are, right?' I say, shooting him a cheeky smile.

'No! I'm just, I mean, it's not ... Well, OK, maybe I am.' He gives a half-laugh.

'Dude, I'm kidding!' I say. 'It's a great house! Why the hell shouldn't you live in it – and enjoy it? God, I'd love to live in a house like this. So, seriously, what do your parents do, and where are they by the way? And Ruby?'

'Ruby's at my aunt's for the day. And my dad's in his office out in the garden, and . . .'

'And your mum?'

'Yeah, she's, erm, well, she died like . . .'

Wait, what? A jolt of shock and sadness runs through me. I stop my wandering and turn to look at him as he squints off to the side and counts on his fingers.

'. . . seven, no, eight years ago.'

'Bloody hell,' I say, walking over to him. And of course anything I say now won't come close to cutting it. 'That sucks. I'm so sorry.' See?

I slump down on the sofa near him, feeling pretty terrible that not only has he gone through this, but that I've been so wrapped up in my own life crap and his interest, or not, in it that I've hardly asked him any questions about his.

'Sorry,' I say again.

'Why? Did you do it?' he says with a grin.

'Jeez! Dude, you can't joke about that!'

'Sorry. And you can actually. That's one of the things you find out when someone dies. Joking helps.' He notices my intensely sad expression as I imagine what it must be like to have your mum die. 'Look, it was cancer. It was rough, but it was a long time ago, Hay. Don't worry about it.'

'I know but still.'

Then there's a prolonged silence between us, more thoughtful than awkward, but still borderline. And I get that me giving him sad looks is probably really unhelpful and making him feel pants about it all over again. So I change to our default mode of communication: mild faux anger.

'And why the *hell* didn't you tell me about that, or this,' I say, waving my arm around the room, 'ya big doofus? I'm supposed to be your, y'know . . .' I pause before awkwardly whispering 'girlfriend' as if it's the rudest word I've ever said. I know we officially *are* boyfriend and girlfriend, but we've never used these words in front of each other and somehow the terms seem to imply a proper hands-on, loved-up relationship. My eyes dart away from his as I wait for him to awkwardly recoil from the word. But amazingly he doesn't.

'Well, now you know, *girlfriend*.'

And I have to admit my heart dances a pathetic jig of joy.

'If you're *so* interested, come out to Dad's office and I'll show you what he does.'

'Come on then, rich boy.'

'Oh, shut up, you knob.'

We get up and start walking to the big slidey glass door to the garden. On the wall next to the door there's a gallery of black-and-white pictures. I pause to take a look.

'Is that your mum?' I ask, pointing to a photo of a beautiful woman with a severe fringe and a kind face.

'Yeah,' he says with a soft smile.

'She's beautiful.'

I look at the rest of the photos, mostly arty pics of Dylan and Ruby from babies to now. In the centre is a picture of a naked baby Dylan lying on his back on a sheepskin rug chewing on one of those teething rings. Dylan notices the picture I'm looking and smirking at and he covers it with his hand.

'*God.* Yeah, my dad thinks he's a bit of a photographer and insists on putting these up no matter how much I beg him to at least take *that* one down, but *please* don't feel you have to look.'

'Can I at least Instagram it?' I say, fake-reaching for the phone in my pocket.

He laughs. 'Don't you frickin' dare!'

We walk out of the back door along a path through an overgrown but beautiful back garden with actual trees and flowers and stuff, unlike the small square of concrete and weeds at my house.

'So Ruby is your –'

'Half-sister,' he says.

And, yeah, obviously I'd noticed that Ruby doesn't look all that much like Dylan, but I knew one of his parents was Chinese and one wasn't so I guess I hadn't put that much thought into it.

'Right. And Ruby's mum?'

'Yeah, Suzy. She's cool. She lives here, but she's away at the mo. She's a TV producer and works in London a lot. The house, getting it built and decorated and everything, that's all her.'

'Was it weird when she first started staying over?'

'A bit, why?'

'Oh, it's just that Ruben's moving in soon and he stayed over for the first time last night and, *urgh*, it really grossed me out is all.'

And it actually feels great to share that with him. Look at the two of us having proper grown-up conversations about actual stuff!

'He is? That's cool. Oh, you'll get used to it – just always, *always* knock before you go into their room. Believe me, I learned that the gross way.'

I laugh. 'You poor thing.'

Then we take the last few steps towards the 'studio', which weirdly doesn't seem to have any windows, and he pulls open a big heavy door.

The dull *thud-thud-thud* of a drumbeat and *ba-doom boom-boom-boom* of a bassline hits us when we enter, soon joined by the muffled sound of a wailing guitar solo.

Be cool.

'HOLY FUDGE NUGGETS, THIS IS AMAZING!'

Dammit!

'Shh!' Dylan whispers with a grin.

In front of us is the back of a massive tall man wearing headphones, hunched over a huge desk with loads of slidey switches and knobs, like the mixing desk at the open-mic night, but about a thousand times the size. On the other side of the desk, through a wall of glass, is a vast room with a big black grand piano, towers of amplifiers and guitars hanging on every wall and, in the middle of it all, a band playing. Underneath them a patchwork of old rugs and a spaghetti-tangle of leads covers the floor.

'So your dad's an accountant then,' I whisper to Dylan, making him laugh.

Two gorgeous backing singers, huddled round a microphone, but currently patiently waiting for the guitar solo to finish, wave at Dylan and he waves back. This alerts a man who I presume to be Dylan's dad to us being here, and he sits up, his sitting height being about the same as my standing one, and swivels in his chair to face us.

Dylan's dad's face looks just like Dylan's, although far more rugged, and he has long black hair tied back in an untidy ponytail. But it's the same square shape, the same broad nose, the same laid-back, half-asleep expression on the same wide mouth.

He smiles at us and raises a long finger, mouthing, 'Just one min.'

Dylan sticks a thumb up to him in reply and we watch the band finish their song, which is loud and kind of rocky and funky and isn't half bad. And I can't believe Dylan has this really cool house and cool dad and cool life and hasn't told anyone – I mean, if this was my life, this would be the *first* thing I would tell everyone.

When the song stops, Dylan's his dad presses a few buttons, takes his headphones off, then gets up and walks over to us.

'Dylan, who have you got there, old boy?' he says in an impossibly deep and slightly slurred voice, smiling at the both of us.

'Dad, this is my mate Haylah.'

'Hey, Haylah,' he says, reaching down to shake my hand. 'How d'ya do. I'm Peter, but everyone calls me Two-meat.'

'Two-metre Peter,' Dylan explains.

'Yeah, I think she could have worked that one out, son,' he says with a wink.

'Probably not. I would've presumed it was something to do with a bacon-and-chicken sandwich you'd invented,' I reply.

He lets go of my hand and laughs in a low, slow, grumbling way. Like how you'd imagine a hippo would laugh.

'You kids all right then?' he says, still looking at me as he slumps back down into his chair and slings the headphones round his neck. 'Dylan being his normal cool self?'

'Yes, *thanks,* Dad,' says Dylan with a snort of a laugh. 'We're fine. Just showing Hay what you get up to in your little garden shed.'

'Yeah, probably not the best day up here for that.' He leans in towards us, shielding his mouth from the band who are milling around on the other side of the glass. 'Between you and me, the girls are just about saving this, but the rest of this lot wouldn't know a good song if it bit them on the balls, though they think they're the bloody Rolling Stones. Nice T-shirt by the way.' He nods towards my shirt before turning back to the band.

I glow a little at the compliment. Hope he doesn't ask me anything about the Rolling Stones though, as I literally know zero about them.

'Yeah, we can hear you, you know,' a small angry voice says from the headphones.

We all look through the glass as the band stares back at us awkwardly, the spiky-haired lead singer who just spoke frowning back at us, microphone in hand.

Dylan's dad leans down to a small microphone jutting out of the mixing desk. 'I was only winding you up. Love your work.'

He switches a switch and swivels in his chair away from the glass and towards us again. 'Whoops. Oh well, 'bout time they heard it from someone. Let's just check they can't hear us now. YOU'RE A BUNCH OF TALENTLESS ARSE CRACKS! Anything?' he asks me with a grin.

I laugh as I slowly peer round him to see the lead singer silently throwing his mic stand on the floor and shouting, the rest of the band angrily arguing among themselves, and the backing singers looking smug with hands on hips.

'No, it, er, all looks very calm.'

'Does it?'

'Yeah, y'know, like a really calm . . . Third World War.'

He laughs again and sits back in his chair, turning to Dylan. 'Cool *and* funny – you lucked out there, boy!' He looks at me again. 'You got a good one there too – you won't find a kinder dude than my Dylan. Underneath all that teenage stink, hormones and bravado there's a heart of frickin' gold.'

I laugh and Dylan puts his head in his hands as his dad continues. 'Oh, I could tell you some stories though. Next time you're round ask me to tell you about the time he shat himself at the top of the Blackpool roller coaster and they had to shut it for an hour to clean it up.'

Dylan emerges from behind his hands, laughing, looks at me and rolls his eyes before saying, 'Yeah, thanks, Dad. We'll leave you to it then!'

'Love you, son. See ya later.'

We leave, both of us laughing, and Dylan shakes his head as he walks back to the house. 'I was four, OK?' he says.

I laugh. 'If you say so.'

We go back to the kitchen and he pulls a couple of Cokes out of a giant silver fridge that looks like it was designed by NASA to transport an entire family to Mars.

'And he's the other reason I don't have people around much,' Dad says, laughing.

'Ah, come on, he's like the coolest dad ever – and chuffin' funny too!'

'Yeah, I know. I'm kidding. God, he's *such* a knob sometimes though.'

'That's parents,' I say, taking a Coke from him, ridiculously aware that our hands almost touched. 'They're there to embarrass us; it's evolution's way of making us want to turn out better.'

We go up to Dylan's room (I'm actually in Dylan's room!), which is big with a wooden floor and large windows like the rest of the house, and posters of bands, most of which I haven't heard of.

There's a drum kit in one corner and a record player in another and lots of vinyl records stacked everywhere. As I'm nosing around everything, Dylan he sits on a gaming chair in the middle of the room and tells me more about his dad's job, that he used to be a session musician, which apparently means you play guitar or whatever on lots of famous songs, even though you're not actually in the band, and now he still does that, but also produces a lot of bands' albums. No one hugely famous, well, I hadn't heard of them anyway, but sort of semi-famous bands, bands on their way up.

'And you play the drums?' I ask. 'I didn't know that.'

'I'm not in a band or anything yet, but, yeah, I'm pretty good. The drummer is always known as the stupidest guy in the band though. Wanna hear some drummer jokes?'

'Of course.'

'How do you know the drum riser is balanced?'

'Hang on, what's a drum riser?'

'Oh right, yeah, that's the little stage thing the drums sit on.'

'Cool, continue.'

'OK, so how do you know the drum riser is straight? Because the drummer drools out of both sides of his mouth.'

I laugh and as he tells more jokes, I go to sit on the bed, leaning up against the wall. Then my face turns a little red when I realize I'm now actually sitting on a real boy's actual bed, in fact, my *boyfriend's* bed. It feels different to sitting in my room with him somehow. This is an unfamiliar place, *his* place, *his* room; *he* decides what happens here. I look down at his pillow next to me, an indentation still there from where his face rests when he sleeps. *Why am I fixating on that? Everyone's face rests on a pillow when they sleep! STOP LOOKING AT HIS PILLOW, YOU FREAK!*

'What do you call a drummer with half a brain? Gifted.'

I laugh again.

When he gets up from his chair and moves towards me, I start to get nervous, though also a tiny bit excited that maybe the reason he asked me here today is because he's planning on finally kissing me, which I think I'd maybe – well, OK, I'd *definitely* – be up for.

He settles back on the bed next to me. Oh, holy crapballs, is this it?! Is this when he finally kisses me? But then he starts up an episode of *Flight of the Conchords* on a big TV opposite the bed and we sit and watch that instead. Dammit. It's a great episode, but . . . I don't know, I guess I'm disappointed again. Why won't he make a move?

After the episode, we continue our Marvel-movie marathon, but then he twigs from my not-so-subtle sigh that I'm a bit bored, so he turns the TV off, gets up and asks how the comedy is going. And I love that he genuinely seems interested. This turns into a discussion of why I like comedy and comedians so much. I tell him it's because they're life's misfits, daring to rebel and laugh in the face of life's stupidity, unlike so many films and songs that take things too seriously.

This immediately gets a rise out of Dylan, as he feels his precious music obsession is under fire, but I tell him I don't *get* the music thing. But then that might have something to do with the fact that, apart from Lizzo, my experience of the world of rock and pop is limited to Mum's Radio-2-on-in-the-kitchen-every-Saturday and Chloe and Kas's pop divas and boy-band love-ins. I explain that I think I've never got into music like I have comedy because the music world doesn't seem to represent the loud-mouthed, unconventional-looking and thinking, fun, strong women I want to identify with.

He starts to actually look a bit angry when I say this, his full cheeks burning red as he shakes his head. I continue winding him up. 'You know, it's all songs *about* or sung by hot, "perfect" women. I mean, good for them and all that, but I don't really see myself in any of it. I get it: these people are sexy and they fancy each other and wanna sing about it, but what's that got to do with me?'

He glares at me in disbelief. 'Oh my God, shut up, woman. What are you talking about?!'

He smiles as he says it, so it's not 'real' anger, but still, I've never seen the boy so animated before. 'Where to even start with this BULL CRAP? I mean, *firstly,* music is about more than the words; it's the, you know, *actual music* that moves you and makes you want to dance or cry or whatever. The lyrics and pop videos are just the icing on the cake –'

'Mmmm, cake,' I interrupt dreamily, then pretend to snap out of it, sitting up cross-legged on the bed and giving him my 'serious' voice. 'Sorry, please continue telling me how stupid I am.'

He shakes his head in mock despair and I can't help but let out a laugh.

He ignores it and continues, '*Secondly,* you have clearly been listening to the wrong stuff – you want strong, gobby, unconventional women? POP MUSIC IS FULL OF THEM!'

'Oh yeah, sure, up to a point. I mean, you've got your Beyoncés and your Pinks and your Taylor Swifts and your Lady Gagas, and they are all great, strong women, but still the overriding thing about them all? SEXY HOT STUFFS. Not something I can identify with.'

I only, at most, half believe all this, of course. I'm just enjoying the heated debate. I mean, it's about time *something* was heated between us. I do genuinely think those women are awesome, but at the same time, yeah, they do pretty much seem to have come from a different planet to me, unlike, say, Melissa McCarthy, who could've been a sister by another mister.

'Right,' he says. 'I'm gonna put together a killer Spotify playlist for you, so check your account later because, urgh, you need to be educated, woman. This is . . . You're just . . . You've gone wrong. YOU'VE GOT IT ALL WRONG.'

He flails his arms around during this last sentence and at this point I keel over on the bed, laughing at him really quite a lot. He looks at me, mortified for a moment, and then he's unable to stop a smile forming as he realizes that we're actually having fun here, and that, while I kinda mean what I say, I am largely just enjoying him going mental over something so trivial. For once, there isn't awkwardness between us.

He points at me in faux anger. 'To be continued, woman.'

And after a couple of hours I tell him I ought to be getting home, do some homework, that kind of thing. It's not exactly true as I don't ever do much homework until about half an hour before it's due, but it just kind of feels like we're done here. And it's been great, and we've had fun and it's kept my mind off the whole Dad thing, but I'm finding the 'does he or doesn't he *like*-me like me?' questions continually racing round my brain a bit exhausting. I need to go away and process it all somewhere where he's not.

Then at the front door, right before he opens it, Dylan turns and says, 'So last night, er, what I said about your dad and how you should see him . . .'

'Yeah?' I say sternly, immediately feeling defensive.

He looks at the ground and frowns like a toddler being told off, but keeps talking.

'I dunno, I just . . . I know it's totally different, but I'd do anything to see my mum again, if I could. I know your dad screwed up, but, well, he's here now. He seemed to really want, I don't know, to make it good again? It's up to you, I know, but . . . life is short. Maybe give it a chance?'

He winces as if bracing for my retaliation. But I'm not angry – his way of looking at parents is different from mine; he lost his mum, for God's sake. I get that now. Doesn't mean I wanna see Dad, but I get that he's just trying to help.

He's still looking at the floor, his eyebrows raised, a questioning smile lurking at the side of his mouth.

'Thanks,' I say gently.

And I lift my hand to touch the side of his arm to stress that I'm not pissed off with him. Only, when I do, he raises the arm I'm aiming for, softly grabs my hand in mid-air, firmly interlaces his fingers into mine and holds on tightly as our joined hands gently fall and sway together.

And, OH MY GOD, my eyes widen as a hot jolt of electricity shoots up my arm and courses through my insides, making my heart gallop like a pony that's just been kicked up the butt, and I bite my bottom lip as it's all I can do not to let out a small squeal of excitement.

It's only holding hands. Get a grip, idiot! We stand there for a moment, our arms outstretched and our fingers linked together like a bridge between us, me looking to the side, still biting my lip, and him casually looking down at his shoes. Then he slowly rubs his thumb up and down the side of mine, as if he's hoping to get away with this tiny movement without me noticing it, as if it's for his benefit, not mine. And I'm frightened for a moment that I'm going to bite my bottom lip clean off if this tension keeps up. Then he raises my hand up to his mouth and ACTUALLY KISSES IT.

But, just as I'm trying to stop myself from squealing with excitement, he loosens his grip and lets my hand fall away. 'Right, see ya then,' he says, swinging his hand away and over to open the door in one swift motion.

'Yeah, OK, see ya,' I say, a little breathless.

Then I'm suddenly outside and the door is shut behind me and after a few shaky steps I almost skip home, ignoring the confused looks from strangers as they pass by the crazy girl with the inane grin plastered all over her face.

At home, over the sights and sounds of annoyingly overenthusiastic Saturday-evening TV, my conversations and time with Dylan play out over and over again in my head.

I mostly, of course, think about the holding-hands bit. And the kissing-my-hand bit! Who would have thought that Dylan, who normally resembles a lethargic Snorlax Pokémon, could be such a fiery ball of romance and passion? And, I mean, I *know* holding hands is just your very basic kiddie form of expressing that you like someone, or that you want to help them cross the road safely, or that you're happy to meet them. It's just . . . it felt like so much more than any other hand-holding I'd previously experienced. It was everything at once: surprising yet comforting, gentle yet strong, shy yet confident, which, yes, all sound like advertising slogans for loo paper, but more importantly, and all things considered, it was a surprising move.

I mean, he must really be into me, right? Perhaps I read it wrong though. When you put it back into context, maybe he just needed comforting after talking about his mum. I mean, God, *his mum's dead*, and shouldn't *that* be the real shocker of the day, Haylah, *you selfish, hand-holding-obsessed hussy*?

I can't imagine what it must be like to lose your mum forever. I mean, it's your *mum*. How would you ever get over that? The thought of losing my mum is just too horrific to bear. And then I think about what he said, and maybe he has got a point about Dad. I still have two parents, which is luckier than a lot of people. And, even if one of them has undoubtedly been an absolute tosser, if he wants to see me now, shouldn't I at least give him that chance, not for his sake, but for mine?

So I make the shaky, scary decision to be brave and see my dad tomorrow.

I message Chlo and Kas to tell them about my Dylan adventures, though not about how awesome his house is or that his mum's dead. I think he trusted me with that stuff and, if he doesn't want people to know, then it's not my place to say. Obviously I told them about the picture of him with his tackle out as a baby and the whole holding/kissing hands bit though.

'Dude, that's amazing!' says Kas.

'Holding hands? Wow, I'll alert the media,' says Chloe, then she sends me a GIF of two pathetic little kids holding hands and skipping.

I also tell them I've changed my mind about seeing Dad and they both say something along the lines of, 'Well, if you think it's for the best, Hay, then go for it, but don't take any crap from him.' We agree I'll go round Chlo's afterwards so I can rant and rave about him, cos I can't do it at home. I can't ever tell Mum I'm seeing the git; she'd be distraught, and I couldn't do that to her. Plus, she might be really pissed off and go proper mental at me, and I couldn't do that to me.

I'm lying on my bed, staring at the ceiling, when my phone pings. It's Dylan sending me a Spotify playlist of twenty-five songs all by female artists, including Janis Joplin, Macy Gray, Aretha Franklin, Kirsty MacColl, Rickie Lee Jones, Joan Armatrading, Dolly Parton, Joni Mitchell and Haim, and to be fair *none* of them sing about being sexy or thinking someone else was sexy. Dylan called the playlist 'Haylah is Stoopid', which makes me laugh. And my insides also turn warm knowing he's spent time putting this together for me.

I lie back on my bed and listen to the playlist three times in a row, the music totally blowing my brains out, making me spiral through every emotion from teary nostalgia to joyous, heart-pumping elation. As it's playing, I look up each of the artists and read about their extraordinary lives and humour, how they went against the grain, wore whatever they wanted to wear, said whatever they wanted to say, dated whoever they wanted to date. These women have balls. I mean, not lit– You know what I mean.

H: O.M.Girlie Rock GOD. I am in love with each and every one of these women and these songs.

D: Told ya.

H: Smug git.

D: Basic girl x

See the 'x' at the end of the message??

So it turns out Dylan, big bumbling *Dylan*, has not only made me bite my lip with passion today and introduced me to a whole new world of musical awesomeness, but he has also managed to change my mind, not an easy task, on a big life decision.

I *am* going to see my dad again tomorrow.

Oh God.

ELEVEN

As soon as I step into the coffee shop and see my dad staring at me from a table in the corner, I start to regret the decision.

Bloody Dylan.

My heart hammers in my chest as I walk towards him. Literally nothing he could say will make me any less angry with him or make it all fine. Plus, lying to Mum about where I was going this morning has made me feel like I'm cheating on her or something, which is just plain wrong. And disturbing. And anyway *he's* the cheater, not me.

As I walk over to Dad, he gives me a half-smile and stands up.

If he even tries to hug me, I'm going to kick him in the balls.

I sit opposite him, looking across the table where there's a drained coffee cup the size of a bathroom basin. I'm not late, but he must have been here for some time already. Maybe he was nervous about this too. Good. He bloody should be; this is hardly a loving family reunion.

'Thanks for coming, Hay. I –'

'Whatever. Get me a Diet Coke,' I demand as I cross my arms and refuse to make eye contact. My heart is still bouncing around like an angry kangaroo in a lift, and all I want to do is get up and leave. But I'm here now. I'll give him two minutes.

'Yeah, sure. You want anything to eat?'

'No, I won't be here long,' I snap.

'Right,' he says sadly and walks off to the counter.

I inwardly fume. *Did he honestly think I was going to make this easy on him?*

I message Kas and Chlo while I'm waiting for the Coke, telling them I'm here and he's here and, holy hell, I want to slap his tosspot face.

Dad returns to the table with a Coke and another bucket of coffee and sits down.

After a slurp of the Coke and an awkward moment of silence, I say, 'Well? Why are you here? What do you want, "Dad"?' I even air-quote the word 'Dad', which may be a little bit overdramatic, but I don't care.

He sighs. 'Look, I'm sorry it's difficult –'

That ARSE-WIPE! What does he want – my bloody SYMPATHY?!

'Oh, is it? Oh, poor you – that must be terrible for you. Why don't you go and cry into your girlfriend's massive cleavage?'

'We've split up, OK? Six months ago. Happy?'

So is this why he's come back? He's got nothing better to do these days as his bit on the side has also realized he's a prick and left him?

'Good. But no, I'm not "happy". Why the hell would any of this make me "happy"?'

He holds his hands up in front of his chest.

'I know. I'm sorry. Look, it's all coming out wrong. I'm not good at . . . stuff like this.'

'Being a dad, you mean? You got that right.'

He half smiles at me. 'God, you've really got your mum's brutal, quick-fire wit. Yeah, I deserve that. I deserve anything you throw at me.'

Oh, he's got that right, I think as I start eyeing up the surrounding ammunition.

'Anything? So, if I throw that massive coffee cup at your head, you would be cool with that as you know you deserve it, right?'

'Right . . . Could I . . . just take my glasses off first though? They're new, so . . .'

A small treacherous laugh escapes through my nose. Dammit. And then his face brightens again and he laughs a little and then I remember again that he's a bastard.

'Stop being charming – that's not fair.'

'Sorry,' he says, and takes a sip of his coffee. 'I don't know where to begin. God, this is impossible. I love you, Hay. You're my daughter, and I've missed you, and –'

Red mist starts to creep into my brain. '*Balls*,' I say, slapping the table to make my point. 'You don't *love* me. You don't even *know* me. You left when I was ten, still a little kid, and if you'd *missed* me, and Noah – you remember Noah? Your *son*?' I see tears in his eyes as I continue, my own throat tightening and my voice cracking, but I have to say this stuff; I have to get it out of my head otherwise my brain might explode with anger. 'Noah, who was a *baby* when you left and couldn't even talk and now won't bloody shut up, but he's brilliant and weird and funny, and you don't even know that because you're not there. Because you left us, you absolute . . . stinking . . . *arsehole*.'

I look down as my tears drop into my glass of Coke and I hear his fractured breathing as he tries to respond.

What am I doing here? This is all a waste of time.

I slam my hands down on the table to push myself up and get the hell out of here, but he puts a hand on top of mine.

'Please,' he rasps. 'Just . . . stay for a moment . . . Let me speak.'

I think about it, then sigh and decide that if I've come this far I may as well hear him out. I yank my hand from under his and sit back, glaring at him.

Let him see my tears. Let him get what he's done.

'Well?'

He clings on to the handle of his cup and wipes his face with the back of his hand, his eyes still filled with tears. But they're tears of guilt, not pain like mine.

He opens his mouth, but nothing comes out. *God, he's so pathetic.*

'Look,' I snap, 'if you don't know where to start, how about I ask the questions? But you *have* to answer them. Honestly.'

I mean, while I've got him here, I may as well get some answers, right?

'Yeah, OK,' he says.

I swallow hard. 'Why did you leave us?'

He looks shocked. I mean, what did he expect me to kick off with? 'What's the capital of France?'

'Dawn – I mean, *Mum*, told me to.'

Oh, that is so not true. He left us, that's what it comes down to, and, if he's not even going to bother being honest with me, really what is the point?

'You're a liar,' I spit.

'No, well, yeah, sometimes, but not about this, I swear. Don't think badly of her though. I totally understand now why she did it.'

'Oh, believe me, I don't think badly of *her* in this situation, but OK, let's presume you are breaking the habit of a lifetime and telling the truth here. Why did she tell you to leave?'

He sighs heavily. 'Because we were yelling at each other all the time and it wasn't good for you and Noah. I don't blame her, Hay. You must remember all the fighting?'

My mind shoots back to one particularly explosive Saturday afternoon a few days before Dad left, when I took a tiny Noah up to my room and sang that God-awful kids' song, 'Wind the Bobbin Up', about a trillion times to him very loudly to try to disguise the sound of insults and crockery being thrown around downstairs. OK, so maybe she did tell him to leave, but it's hardly like he hadn't given her another massive reason to dump his sorry ass.

'That wasn't the only reason though, was it? There was also the fact that you were knobbing your secretary, Tits McGee.'

He sighs and looks down at the table. 'Julie – it doesn't matter. Look, I know. I was . . . lonely . . .'

I give him a look like '*Really?*'

'I'm not giving you excuses, Hay. I'm just telling you what happened.'

He goes on to tell me his sob story of how things at work and home were bad and that after Noah was born it was like Mum hated him. He says he 'loved' me and Noah, but home life was pretty crappy and then Tits McGee came along who was 'gentle and wanted to spend time with him'. (*What is he, a frickin' puppy?*) He says he thought it was love, but it was probably a midlife crisis.

To which I reply, 'Duh.'

He sighs again, takes a gulp of his coffee then continues. 'Instead of fixing stuff with your mum, I took the easy option and backed away from it all. Told myself that you'd all be better off without me.'

'And why did you stop seeing us altogether? You get bored of us?' I say, scrunching up my fists under the table, determined not to cry again.

'No. Of course not,' he says softly. 'But I was moving up north where there were more work opportunities anyway, and every time I wanted to see you I ended up having a massive row with your mum. I knew she'd be depressed for days afterwards, which was no good for you and Noah – or her. I thought the best thing was to step away and let you get on without me. I thought I was doing the right thing.'

'You weren't.'

'*I know that now*,' he says through gritted teeth, his head in his hands. After a moment, he shakes off the frustration and sits back up, his face red, his eyes sad. 'I'm sorry. I'm just angry at myself and you shouldn't have to deal with that.'

He's right. I bloody shouldn't. But I don't say anything. I'm worried that if I try to it'll come out as a pathetic sob and I don't want to be the pathetic one here. So I stare at him coldly and let him continue.

'I kept trying to get in touch, just a few times a year, on your birthdays and stuff, and your mum would answer the phone and tell me to sod off, which was fair enough.'

I nod in firm agreement with my mum.

'Yeah,' he goes on, 'I know this all sounds like a crappy list of excuses, Hay, and I guess it is, but please believe me when I say I thought about you guys *every* single day.'

I'm not sure I do believe that, but right now I'm not sure what to think. I try to take it all in. I didn't know Mum had been so against him seeing us, but I totally get why – the git had cheated on her and then gave up trying to see us because it was a little bit like hard work. I think about Noah missing out on a father because his was too chicken to make an effort. The anger builds in me.

I take a deep breath and put my fists on the table, no longer clenched to stop the tears, but because I kinda want to punch him in the face. 'Every single day? Really? Cos

139

you could put a brick wall round Noah and throw knives at my head every time I tried to get near him, but nothing, *nothing*, would stop me from seeing that boy. And you . . . just gave up. Because, aww, diddums, it was a bit tricky. You absolute arsehole.'

He rests his elbows on the table and buries his face in his hands, his breath coming out short and stunted, his shoulders silently bobbing up and down.

I keep my arms firmly folded. I'm not falling for this crap. On the other hand, although this is totally what I was aiming for, seeing an adult, especially a parent, however absent, proper cry, is just weird and upsetting. It's not the normal order of things. It's like seeing the Queen do a poo.

He shakes off the tears and carries on, going on about how Tits McGee left him for someone who wanted kids (boo-frickin'-hoo), how he was sad but relieved that he was free to move back down here, which he has, so he could try to fix the relationships that should have been the important ones all along, with me and Noah.

'I'm not asking you to forgive me, Hay, really I'm not. I'm just asking if you'll give me a chance to be what I should have been all along, something good in your life, someone who's there for you. Let me get to know you again, maybe see you again . . . but only as often as you want.'

As he slurps his coffee nervously, I keep the frown fixed on my face and think about all he's said. It's hardly like everything's OK now he's come back and explained *why* he's an arse. I mean, he's *still* an arse. Although he does seem genuinely sorry, and the fact that he's moved down here suggests he's serious and really does want to try to build some sort of 'relationship' again. But do I actually want that?

We drink in silence as I think things over. It's just so weird sitting down and talking to my dad again. Weird-bad in so many ways as it's reminding me of him leaving, but also, I have to admit, almost weird-good in that, well, I've missed him. He doesn't deserve my missing him, but I have. I wouldn't be so upset about all this if I hadn't. I mean, he's my dad. He was the centre of my world for ten years. It feels comforting to see his face again, and makes me feel nostalgic for when I was little. He'd been a good dad up until he wasn't.

Maybe I've punished him enough, at least for today. Maybe it's time for an olive branch. (A very small, measly, withered one.)

'Do you remember that day when we went to the beach?' I say.

His face lights up a little in the glow of the first slightly warm thing I've said to him.

He gives me an apologetic grimace. 'We went to the seaside a lot. Which time?'

'Seaside?' I laugh a little. 'Who calls it the "seaside"? Apart from, like, little girls in the nineteenth century.'

'Yeah, OK, fine,' he says with a smirk. 'Which *beach*, when?'

'It was cold. I think it was a New Year's Day. I was probably about eight?'

'OK, yeah. Probably Felixstowe?'

'I'd had food poisoning or something for a few days before and still felt dodgy.'

'God, yeah, I remember the food poisoning. You stood at the top of the stairs and yelled, "Mum, Dad, I feel a bit weird!" And when I got to the bottom of the stairs you hurled chunks and it sprayed out at all angles, all over the walls, the stairs and me. Like something from a horror film.'

I laugh. Not a proper laugh, my brain's not in the right place to do that, but a half-laugh. 'I'm not sorry. I totally did that on purpose. Anyway, back at the beach, I –'

'Fell off the slide! Of course I remember,' he says, his face really coming to life as if the memory is replaying behind his eyes. It's nice seeing his face like that, more as I remember it.

'Yep. It was in the park next to the beach. I stood up at the top of the slide and I remember looking out to the sea, then I started swaying and I saw you and Mum slow-motion running towards me as everything went blurry and then –'

'You just dropped like a stone, and I didn't get there in time to catch you. God, I felt awful.' He shakes his head with a smile.

'Mum made you pay for that one for weeks; she'd be, like, chucking apples at you in the kitchen and yelling, "Catch! Oh no, I forgot – you can't catch."'

He laughs, though it's a sad laugh.

'After I landed –'

'We took you to the hospital. We thought you'd broken your arm. Turns out it was only sprained.'

'You say "only" – still hurt like hell.'

'Oh God, right, no, it was a *tragic* injury, one of the worst I've ever seen, almost fatal,' he says with mock sincerity.

I smile. 'Right! Anyway, when we were in the A & E waiting room, and we were –'

'Putting those cardboard piss bowls on our heads and pretending to be cowboys!' he excitedly adds, and I kinda love that he remembers this stuff. I'd convinced myself he'd only put up with playing the role of Dad and had been relieved to find an excuse to forget it all. Maybe I was wrong about that.

'Right! Jeez, Mum was so embarrassed. "Can you two behave, please? You know I have to work with these people!" And then we went to see the doctor and then get an –'

'X-ray, that's right. I came in with you. We had to put on those metal bib things.'

'Yep. They wanted me to straighten out my arm and it hurt like a bitch. I was really freaking out. And I remember . . .' I gulp and hope my voice holds out. His face falls as he notices mine do the same. 'I remember you held my other hand really tight and said, "Don't worry, Hay, honey. I'm here. I'll never leave you."'

I look down at the table as we sit in silence for a moment.

'I'm so sorry,' he says gently.

I inhale a ragged breath over the large lump in my throat and wipe my eyes on the back of my sleeve. This is all getting too much. I sniff heavily, grab my phone off the table, scrape my chair back and get up.

'I can't do this. I gotta go,' I say quietly.

'Wait! Hay!' he says as I sweep past him.

But it's too late. I'm out of the door.

TWELVE

Swallowing back the tears, I walk to Chloe's. I need to empty my mind of this confusing swirl of emotions: anger, sadness and yet somehow *excitement*, which I know I shouldn't feel, but I can't help it. I feel like a traitor to Mum for even thinking it, but the truth is I really have missed his face, and I've missed my memories. They weren't all bad.

We sit on Chlo's bed and my friends hug me and listen as I waffle on.

'So are you gonna see him again?' asks Kas.

'Argh! I dunno. Maybe?' I say, flopping back on to Chlo's big pile of cushions and staring up at the ceiling. 'I feel like him coming back has filled my brain with a chocolate-and-sprout pudding. I wanna eat it and I don't wanna eat it at the same time.'

'I quite like sprouts,' says Kas, flopping down next to me.

Chlo delicately lies on the other side of me and we stare at the ceiling together, still covered with the glow-in-the-dark stars I gave her for her eighth birthday.

'What if I start to let him in and then he pisses off again? Which will be bad enough for me, but if he does that to

Noah?' I scrunch up my eyes, trying to squeeze out the heavy feeling left in them from crying earlier. Kas and Chlo both reach down and hold my hands.

I'm not overly keen on being served large dollops of sympathy though. It only makes me feel worse, so I shake them and the feelings off and leap up from the bed. 'Parents these days, hey? Screw it, I'm going for a wee and then let's talk about something else.'

They both sit up, smile and mumble something like, 'OK, if you're sure that's what you want.'

I walk to the toilet next to Chlo's bedroom, glad of the moment to take a breath, and then I stop in my tracks at the sight of Chloe's cat drinking out of the toilet bowl. He stops, his back paws on the seat while his front ones are splayed out in the bowl. He turns to me with a 'do you mind?' look.

'Chlo! Ryan Reynolds-Gosling is drinking from the toilet again!' I shout out.

They both rush through, giggling, as Ryan tries to escape with his dignity intact by reversing himself out of the bowl, only for his two back paws to slip off the seat and into the water. He leaps out in shock, then shakes his paws before straightening up and trotting, aloof, past us.

We all fall about laughing. It's just what I need.

'Aww, poor Ryan!' says Kas through her giggles.

'I know, right, but cats are totally only there to make us laugh,' says Chlo.

'That's totally cattist, Chlo – they should start a "MEOW TOO" movement!'

We all explode with more laughter. (Honestly, I don't think there's anything that's off limits for a joke, as long as it's well-meaning and funny.)

Ryan sits and licks toilet water from his paws, still managing to look more elegant than I could ever dream of being.

Back in Chlo's room, we sit on her floor and set up a game of Blue Scrabble, which is basically normal Scrabble, but every word has to be obviously rude or you have to justify it as being rude. Chloe begins with a solid start of 'buns', then Kas puts down a very strong 'fanny'. I'm just debating how best to argue for 'wonky' when Chlo starts banging on again about her 'hot hunk' Kyle from the summer and *his* amazing buns, how they were FaceTiming for forty-five minutes last night and how he's going to come over and stay at Christmas, which apparently her mum has OK'd. We 'oooh' and 'ahh' in all the right places in her story, though to be honest we're a bit tired of hearing about this bloke neither of us have ever seen.

'Still gunning for Watto too though, right?' asks Kas.

Chlo looks at Kas with a 'well, duh' frown. 'Oh, totally. You've gotta keep your options open, ladies! And I've got a new plan to let him know that I'm super bookish and stuff. I've started reading this full-on history book just when Watto's around. You know, that book by that history woman, Hilary Manuel –'

'Mantel,' says Kas.

'Yeah, the one who writes about Oliver Cromwell.'

'Thomas Cromwell,' says Kas.

'Same thing,' snaps Chlo with a splayed hand held up to Kas to stop her ruining the unveiling of the master plan. 'Then one of these days he's going to notice and ask what I'm reading, and I'll be like, "Oh, this old thing? Second time I've read it actually. It's *Wolf Hill*."'

'*Hall*,' says Kas.

Chlo's hand shoots up again. '*Whatever*. And he'll be like, "Are you enjoying it?" and then I've memorized this super-intelligent-sounding review I read on Amazon and I'm gonna pretend that's my opinion. You wanna hear it?' She clears her throat.

'No,' I say.

'Yeah, not really,' adds Kas.

'Well, fine, but it's a crazy-impressive plan, right? Gonna win him over and make him think I'm like a hot librarian or something . . . So, whad'ya think?'

'Well, that sounds . . . foolproof?' I say unconvincingly.

I look back down at my letters, hoping Chlo will be satisfied with my feedback, and notice I had an 'A' all along, which opens up a whole new range of indisputable word options.

'Yeah, totally,' says Kas, though unfortunately she doesn't leave it there. 'But, I mean, I know Watto likes history and books and stuff, but, well, have you tried talking to him about something else? Something you *do* actually know about?'

Chlo scoffs. 'What the *hell* am I going to talk to him about? I'm pretty sure nail varnish and how to do the perfect winged eyeliner aren't going to grab his attention.'

'Oh, come on, Chlo, you're so much more than that!' I say. Then I realize my mistake. I've lit Chloe's fuse and now we ought to be taking cover before the explosion.

'*More* than that? What, because that stuff's so silly and meaningless? Well, what if I'm not "more than that"? What if I'm happy not being more than that? I like doing this, Hay. I know it's not, well, it's not a very *feminist* thing to do with your life, but it's what I want to do; it's what I love. It's to me what comedy is to you, OK?'

'She didn't mean it like that, Chlo,' says Kas.

'I totally didn't!' I say. 'I just meant that you shouldn't try to be something you're not when you're brilliant and cool and interesting as you are! But it came out wrong. Because I'm an idiot.'

'Yeah,' says Chlo, thankfully smiling. 'You are.'

'And, by the way, of course beauty stuff is a "feminist" thing to do; why wouldn't it be?' I add, reminding myself as much as anything that this is how I feel.

'Fine, fine! We know!' says Kas with her hands in the air in surrender.

'Anyway, Chlo,' I say, 'the point is, just talk to him about anything you want: make-up and stuff or, like, what you watched on telly last week, or which teacher said the twattiest thing this week or *anything*.'

'Hmm, maybe,' she says. 'Urgh, he's just so cute with that little fringe and those dark eyes and everything, don't you think, Kas? I mean, you normally have the same taste as me in guys, right?'

'Erm, yeah . . . right,' says Kas shiftily.

I should ask her what's going on next time we're without Chlo. But then if she wanted to tell me she would, right?

We carry on with Blue Scrabble and giggle our way through the afternoon as we argue for the rudeness in our offerings of 'gibbon', 'sponge' and 'conkers'.

'So have you heard from Dylan since yesterday's scandalous hand-holding incident?' asks Kas.

I check my phone again. 'Still no.'

'Aw, don't worry though, Hay. I mean, he held your hand. That's a great sign he's proper into you, right?' says Kas.

'It was pretty awesome.'

'Dude, he *held your hand* after you've been going out for what, two months?' says Chlo. 'That's like ordering a burger, then staring at it for like an hour before finally nibbling at the lettuce.'

'Chlo, that analogy is eww in so many ways,' says Kas.

'Yeah, I did feel it's eww-ness as soon as I started it, to be honest,' says Chlo, laughing.

I'm a bit annoyed they're playing the whole thing down. I mean, he *did* kiss my hand too! But it feels silly to try to up the sexiness by adding in a peck on the back of a hand. I raise my eyebrows saucily. 'But what you have to understand is that it was some *guud* hand-holding, some of the best I've ever had. I dunno, you've got a point though, Chlo. At this rate, we'll be using matching Zimmer frames in an old people's home before he finally gets round to snogging me. Anyway, I can't even think about that at the moment. I just can't get over the fact that I actually met with my dad today.'

'So you any closer to a decision? You gonna see him again?' asks Kas.

I think about how heavy the conversation got at the end and the feeling that I just had to get out of there. But also how comforting it was to see his face.

'I really don't know.' I start pacing round the room, talking fast as my words try to catch up with my thoughts. 'It was kinda cool to see him again, but then it would be easier to go on pretending he doesn't exist. On the other hand, I might miss out on actually having a dad who seems to want to be my dad again, but then it might just screw with Noah, but then again it might be good for him, and how is Mum gonna deal with him being in our lives and . . . urgh!' I flop down on the bed again, one arm over my face. 'Help me, wise ones – how am I supposed to decide?'

'Oooh, I know!' squeals Chlo, leaping up. 'Let's do Quick-Fire!'

In case you don't know, Quick-Fire's that thing where you're asked super-fast questions and you have to say the first thing that comes into your mind to understand how you really feel about something. And, sure, you might think it's a ridiculous way to decide on something so major, but have you got a better idea?

'Yeah, OK, go for it,' I say, closing my eyes tight and clearing my mind.

'OK . . . marmalade or Marmite?' says Kas.

'Oh, easy. Marmite,' I answer quickly.

'Bath or shower?'

'Bath.'

'Netflix or YouTube?'

'YouTube.'

'Oooh, controversial. Toilet paper: scrunch or fold?'

'Scrunch.'

'Sunset or sunrise?'

'Sunset.'

'Fingers or toes?'

'Fingers. Stop giggling, Chlo!'

'Tina Fey or Amy Schumer?'

'ARGH, GOD, WHY MAKE ME CHOOSE? Amy Schumer.'

'Red or blue?'

'Blue.'

'Normal or weird?'

'Weird.'

'Cat or dog?'

'Cat.'

'Dad or no dad?'

'Dad.'

And there it is. You can't argue with Quick-Fire. It's scientific. The decision has been made.

But if I'm going to see him again I know that I've got to – oh crapballs.

I've got to tell Mum.

THIRTEEN

When I get home, my heart feels heavy as I walk through the front door. I know I need to talk to Mum about Dad, about seeing him and wanting to see him again. I can't lie to her; it'll totally do my head in. And she'll sniff out the truth eventually, as always. She's like Sherlock crossed with a Rottweiler in a nurse's tunic. The longer I keep it a secret, the more it'll upset her. And I don't want to upset her.

Though there is also the fact that I'm pissed off with her. After all, Dad told me that she'd made it difficult for him to see us when he left, which is kind of understandable considering what an arse he'd been to her, but that's not the version of the truth she'd given to us.

I walk into the hall and hear Noah's and Mum's laughter erupting out of the living room. Surprisingly though, no Ruben's ho-hoing, booming laugh over the top of it all, which I guess will soon be a daily occurrence.

That's a good thing, right? It will probably make Mum less likely to be a) mad that I saw Dad without telling her and b) upset about him being around again as she's all loved-up and making plans with Beardo Boy.

I walk in and see Mum lying on the rug with Noah suspended above her, held up by her arms and legs in a 'flying angel'. They both look over to me and smile as Mum's legs fold and Noah collapses on to a well-padded, bosomy landing and bursts out laughing again. And any bad feelings about Mum not telling me the full story go. It's like turning over a hot, stinky pillow to the comforting and refreshing cold side.

It's home; it's familiar. It's just Mum, Noah and me and everyone's happy.

And that's all she's ever done: worked her butt off to keep us happy. Dad ruined the happy and she was only protecting us by keeping him away.

'Haylah!' shouts Noah.

'How you doing, Hay?' asks Mum.

I smile as I walk over to them both. 'All good. How's the training for this little Olympic Flying Angel champion going?'

'Oh, very well. Noah, let's show her what you got.'

Noah rolls off Mum and stands at her feet with his little podgy arms in the air.

'Do the common-tree, Hay! Do the common-tree!' says Noah, handing me the TV remote control.

I slump down into the sofa next to them, hold the TV remote 'microphone' in front of my mouth and clear my throat as Noah's face lights up with excitement. I put on my best low, calm, nasal, posh-bloke TV sport commentator voice: 'And here we have the leading Flying Angel competitor for Great Britain, Noah Swinton, now on his final lift of the day. Currently in second place, with Switzerland's Enzo Schmid, the tournament favourite, taking the lead after the second lift, but it's all to play for. Swinton is limbering up and really showing us what a crowd-pleaser he is, his warm-up moves now almost as famous and beloved as his medal-winning lifts . . .'

Noah, beaming, starts stretching his arms out while bending over and doing a slow, deranged twerk as Mum's chest wobbles about as she giggles.

God, I love these two nutters so much.

'But now the time has come and –' I start whispering – 'the crowd has hushed to a silence; you really could hear a pin drop here, ladies and gentleman, as the tension in the room rises and all eyes are on Noah Swinton to see . . . just what he can bring . . . to this final lift . . . as he goes for gold . . .'

Noah reaches down and takes Mum's hands as she bends her knees to her chest and places her feet on his belly, looking like a huge balled-up hedgehog. Then she straightens her legs out and pushes him high above her on shaky legs while trying desperately not to laugh and drop him.

'AND THEY'RE UP! And that really is a perfect start, and if he can only hold that position for a few more seconds . . . Just a little wobble there, but that should be OK, and here comes the dismount. There's so much hanging on this, not least the hopes and dreams of the British audience here and at home as they hold their breath, waiting to see if it's enough to bring home the gold . . .'

Mum pushes Noah up a little, which lifts him into the air for a moment before he lands on his feet with a floundering thump. He raises his chubby arms triumphantly.

'AND HE'S DONE IT! A HUGE lift at the end, and landing with such style! And there's a triumphant roar from the audience here as they realize that Noah Swinton has brought home the GOLD FOR GREAT BRITAIN!'

'Again! Again!' shrieks Noah.

After three more Olympic golds, two with me as the lifter and Mum on commentary, we finally tire Noah out and he settles in with his iPad while me and Mum go to the kitchen, her to sort tea, me to fix myself a snack. I start thinking about Dad again. How the hell am I going to bring this up with her and escape alive?

'No Ruben today then?' I ask, nervously eating a fistful of 'Chocopops' cereal straight from the box.

'Haylah, I do wish you wouldn't do that. But no, he's got an early start at work tomorrow,' she replies while rooting around in the freezer. 'Fish fingers OK tonight?'

'Yep, fine.'

She straightens up and squints at the fish-finger box while holding it at arm's length.

'Why do you old people do that? Are you trying to be down with the kids? Cos you should know that when we do that we're taking a selfie and you really can't get a good pic from a packet of fish fingers.'

'I'm trying to read the cooking instructions, smart-ass.'

'Then I think you need reading glasses, dumb-ass,' I reply. And really I'm just stalling for time.

She smiles. 'Fine, you read it then,' she says, shoving the packet in my direction.

I wave it away. 'Just put it on for twenty minutes at two hundred degrees. Everything that goes in the oven takes twenty minutes at two hundred degrees.'

'Right,' she says, turning on the oven. 'Remind me never to let you cook Christmas dinner.'

'No problem. I guess Ruben will be here this Christmas – maybe he could cook the turkey?'

Mum pauses and gives me a questioning look. 'Yeah, I guess he will. Is – is that OK?'

'Yeah, it's cool,' I say. Though to be honest it does feel weird, especially after seeing Dad today. Sure, Ruben is comfortable to be around these days; it's just, well, he isn't my dad. But, if I want Mum to be cool with me seeing Dad again, the last thing I should do right now is be an arse about Ruben.

'Thanks, love,' she says with a smile, then in a split second she scans my face and her mum sensors pick up on something else.

I go to leave, hoping I can put off the whole dad discussion for another time. But it's no good – she takes one of my hands as I walk past her.

'You OK? Everything else OK?' she says, staring deep into my eyes.

'Yep. Of course,' I say, then I sigh.

Fine, yes, you're right. I know I can't keep it from her.

But, as I'm about to blurt it out, Noah comes running through the door with his own out-of-the-blue blurt.

'Do giraffes and hyenas ever get married?' he asks, his big brown eyes darting from me to Mum urgently.

This interruption is a sign, I tell myself. *A sign to shut the hell up about Dad*. And it is, right? It's totally a sign from the universe, and you can't argue with signs from the frickin' universe.

'Yeah, I'll let you field that one, Mum,' I say before fleeing to my bedroom.

As I climb the stairs, I hear Mum saying, 'Well, I don't think so, Noah, but who are we to decide which relationships are right and wrong? Love is love.'

Up in my room I take a deep breath and text Dad. I say that if he wants to we could meet up again. And after I've pressed send I'm nervous as hell about it. What if he doesn't reply? What if seeing me today was all he was really wanting and after finding me such a disappointment of a daughter he's done now?

I put on Dylan's playlist and lie back on my bed. Aretha Franklin smoothly yet furiously shouts at her man to give her some 'respect'.

I look at my phone. There's no response yet and still no message from bloody Dylan, even though he knew I was meeting my dad today. Maybe after the hand-holding thing he's too embarrassed to make contact. Or disgusted at himself? On the other (kissed) hand, thinking back to when I was nervous at the pub and he started flipping beer coasters, and at his house when the whole dead-mum thing came up and he squirmed his way through the conversation, maybe dealing with any kind of emotion is just beyond him. To be honest, it's beyond me right now too. After all the Dad stuff, there's no more room in my brain to mull over the Dylan stuff as well.

So instead I start to think about what Chlo was saying earlier – how wearing make-up isn't 'feminist'. And of course the point of feminism is that ALL women, *as they are*, be they super-feminine, blonde, flirty bombshells or shaven-headed, Dr. Martens-wearing, ballsy, bookish intellectuals, or anything and everything in between, are *equal* to men, deserving of equal rights, pay, respect, and are equally free to be themselves WHATEVER that may be. God, I love feminism.

So I sit and write before making another sarcastic rant video in my ultra-patronizing American accent again.

I give it the same kind of title as the rest of my videos. It'll look super controversial and hopefully get lots of views. 'Feminists Are Idiots (But They Can Still Look Pretty!)'

'Hey, everyone, it's your PFG back again! It's not easy being a teenage feminist, right? Why not? It should be the easiest thing in the world – all it is, is believing we have the same rights as guys! That's it! Literally nothing else about you has to change! There is no typical feminist! Yay! So why the title on this vid? I didn't write that. Our stylist in residence, Stacy Beeatch, did . . . Stacy, over to you . . .

'*Hi, it's me, Stacy Beeatch, and I'm back with my latest fashion tips for the unfortunate.*

'OK, *this one's aimed at all you strange little FEMINISTS, all you hairy-legged, blotchy-faced, angry girls, who for some silly reason want to be equal to men. Even though you hate them. I know, right? You girls are super cray-cray, but we love you anyway!*

'*Now I understand that you think that to be taken seriously you need to look more like men. Because really why would anyone be interested in what our little-girl brains have to say? So you don't wanna do anything that normal women do that makes them look pretty, like using make-up and washing your face. But you probably don't wanna live in a cave with small children running screaming from you either, so here are my top tips for feminists who still wanna look vaguely female. Isn't this fun . . .?*'

I go on to suggest that they don't need to be scared of handbags – just get one with diamond studs, which will look pretty and can also cause serious harm when used to bash men round the head; that they *can* wear bras – just make sure they're at least 50 per cent polyester as that'll give off a brighter flame when they burn them; that a good lip balm is essential otherwise their lips will dry out from all that ranting, but the best thing is they don't need to spend money on a waterproof mascara as true feminists never do anything so girlie as crying.

I press upload. It feels pretty good and takes me just the right distance away from reality. Then my dad texts me back, plunging me right back into it. I hold my phone at arm's length and wince as I read the text, as if I'm afraid it might jump out of the phone and mortally wound me. But actually it's OK. He hasn't rejected me again. Yet.

Thanks for agreeing to meet up. Can't wait to see you again. Cinema? Dad

I agree and now we're going to the cinema on Wednesday, like a normal dad and daughter might do. Which is nuts. But, yeah, why not let the guy pay for me to go to see a film? Doesn't change the fact that he's still a lying, cheating arse-wipe. I mean, we're hardly gonna end up being best buds.

FOURTEEN

So it turns out my dad is awesome and we're definitely gonna be best buds.

OK, OK, I know all the stuff about him being a big jerk in the past is still true, but over the next few weeks we start spending more and more time together – at the cinema, bowling, meals out and whatnot – and the thing is he's really funny and interested in my comedy. Turns out he's pretty wise when it comes to advising me on my new material, suggesting extra jokes or where to leave a pause for a bigger laugh. And it's nice having an adult to talk to – Mum's always busy with work or Ruben, Grammo's always out with her friend June or talking about their next dodgy adventure, and it seems weird talking about it with Ruben.

We also make each other laugh a lot and it feels like a break from other more weighty things, like Mum and her nagging about Dylan or homework, or the thought of her sharing a bed (urgh) with Ruben, or awkwardness with Dylan (who if anything has been even *more* physically distant since the hand-holding event).

The problem is, I still haven't told Mum I'm seeing him. And the longer it goes on, the harder it gets. I just don't know how to tell her. And I don't know how she'll react. I'm fairly sure it wouldn't be pretty.

I've lied to Dad, telling him she said it was fine for me to see him as long as he doesn't come to the house. He thinks it's cos Mum won't let him see Noah yet. He doesn't get that if he ever came to the house she'd probably aim a nuclear missile at his crotch. And she'd be justified in doing that, right? What he did was unforgivable. I know that. I know I'm being a traitor to myself, to Mum, to the sisterhood. But I can't help enjoying having a dad again.

Last night we drove to where I fell off the slide all those years ago. We walked up and down the beach, hurling stones into the sea, then got fish and chips and ate them on a bench. For some reason, fish and chips always taste better when you're sitting on a bench.

'There ya go, Hay. Get that down ya neck.'

I look at the fish-and-chip shop logo on the bag. '"The Cod Father". God, I love a good punning fish-and-chip shop name,' I say.

'Me too. Where I lived up north, we had Oh My Cod and The Plaice to Be.'

Somehow 'lived up north' stings. It's not like I can forget he went away or anything, but I prefer it when I can almost pretend there hasn't been a five-year pause in his parenting. Almost.

'Both classics,' I say. 'Though I'm not sure they're trying hard enough.' I hope he takes the bait (another fish pun!)

and this conversation heads down Humorous Avenue rather than towards the dodgy end of town that his mention of living up north is sending my brain to.

He thinks for a moment while chewing on a chip. Then thankfully he goes for it. 'OK, well, what about Cod the Father, Cod the Son and Cod the Holy Ghost? Too much?'

I snort. 'That's just trying too hard.'

'Well, OK, what would you go with?'

I think about it then say, 'Chip Happens.'

He laughs. I've started to love it when he laughs at a joke I made. It's like I'm finally getting his approval or something. Yeah, I know that sounds super lame. He adds, 'How about Chip Happens and Then You Pie?'

'Genius,' I say.

On the way back home, I finish off my chips in the car as he asks me why I want to become a comedian.

'I don't know. I think I always enjoyed making people laugh in primary school. I guess it was the classic defence mechanism against bullies and stuff . . .'

'Oh, Hay,' he says sadly.

'Nah, it's all good – it kinda worked. And, well, I guess it was probably after, well, after you left that I got a bit obsessed with it.'

I chew on a chip as I think about this. I'd never realized it before, but it's gotta be no coincidence. I dunno, maybe it was my way of coping. I grabbed hold of the funny and let it drag me away from the misery.

'I guess I should thank you,' I say, licking ketchup off my fingers. 'Most of the great comedians use comedy to cope with personal trauma. If you hadn't supplied the trauma, maybe I wouldn't be as great as I am.'

I was being sarcastic and expected maybe a small laugh, but instead he goes quiet before saying, 'I'm so sorry, Haylah.'

And I really think he is.

'I know. At least, I think I know,' I say.

'I'll take that,' he says. And for the next twenty minutes we travel in silence until we get back into town and I point out the sign that says WELCOME TO WOLKERTON, PLEASE LOWER YOUR and some genius has crossed out the word SPEED and added EXPECTATIONS. We both laugh and then he pauses before saying, 'Hay, how does your mum feel about you seeing me?'

I know I should tell him I haven't told her, but the thing is that, although in one way it feels like he never left and it's so easy being in his company again, I also feel I hardly know him at all. I don't know how he'll react. And I don't want to give him any reason to be pissed off with me cos, well, cos then he might leave again.

'Yeah. She's fine,' I say before stuffing another handful of chips in my mouth in an attempt to look like I'm just being breezy about the whole thing.

'And . . . "Ruben", is it? What's his take on it all?' Dad does his own attempt at trying to sound breezy when he says Ruben in a weirdly high-pitched tone, but I can tell that, like the chips we're eating, the word sticks in his mouth.

'Yeah, he's fine,' I say, probably too quickly. So I add, 'I'm not sure Ruben has "takes" on things. He's like Noah, really;

he just sort of plods along quite happily in his own little world, reacting in a very basic way to life as it crops up.' I suddenly feel bad though, because, unlike Dad back in the day, Ruben's been nothing but gentle and brilliant with Mum. With all of us, really. So I add, 'He's a good guy though.'

'Good. I'm glad your mum found someone to treat her right – she deserves that.' He sounds genuine. 'And maybe, well, maybe you could put in a good word for me about seeing Noah?'

'Don't push it,' I say. It's one thing to consider that Dad might just up and leave and hurt me again, but if he did that to Noah I'd so rip his balls off.

'No, fair enough. Sorry. I just . . . Sorry. How about you tell me a bit about him instead? Just what he's like, what he's into, that kind of thing.'

I consider this for a moment. He is his dad after all. So I talk to Dad about Noah. About how when he grows up he wants to be a scientist so he can spend his life making 'potions and explosions', how he also wants to change his name to 'Eugene Griffin' for no reason whatsoever, how the other day he drew circles round all his bruises to 'cordon them off as safety zones', how he wants to get a cloning machine so that for Christmas he can 'give everyone a me', and how this morning he announced that his new favourite song is 'Spice' by George Peppers, even though there's no such song or singer.

Dad listens and laughs, and before he drops me off, up the road from my house because I lie and tell him I need to get some stuff from the Tesco on the corner first, I glance over to him and see him wiping away tears. Which makes me feel awkward, but also super crappy: for him, for Noah, for all of us.

'God. I've missed out . . . on so much,' he says, his eyes fixed on the road ahead.

'Yeah,' I say. 'You have.'

When I get into the living room, Noah is sitting on the floor surrounded by a sea of Lego and building a 'dinosaur toilet', while Mum sits on the sofa with her feet up on Ruben's lap, having a heated discussion about Edam cheese.

'Oh, hi, Hay!' says Ruben.

'Everything OK, love? Have fun with the girls?' says Mum brightly.

Oh knobnuts. I smile sheepishly, the great weight of the guilt of seeing my dad crushing my treacherous brain.

'Yeah, great,' I say too quickly. I start backing out of the room before her mum sense starts tingling. 'Just gonna go and do homework, 'K?'

'You sure you're OK, babe?' Mum calls after me.

'YEP!' I yell back.

In my room, I shlump down on my bed and stare up at the ceiling. Spending the last few weeks getting to know Dad again has been hard but great, but lying to Mum about it has been a big sack of dung chunks. Though I'm convinced that if she looked into my eyes for long enough she'd figure it out. Cos that's what mums do, right? She's

167

like a big-boobed Yoda; she might look unthreatening, but the truth is she knows all.

I know, I know, I just need to tell her.

I will.

Tomorrow.

After school.

Promise.

And I'm sure she'll be fine about it.

Except that she probably won't be fine about it.

Just make sure they put this on my gravestone: *I told you she wouldn't be fine about it.*

FIFTEEN

OK, so I didn't tell Mum today either. Sorry. It's just too hard. So I'm still avoiding her, which continues to be super awkward.

Since seeing Dad, my relationship with Mum isn't the only one that's gone a bit wonky. There's also the Dylan situation.

Instead of dwelling on it, I write and upload some new videos, including 'Facebookers Are Idiots' and 'Teachers Are Idiots'. They're not *too* rude to these people, just the right side of rude, and, I think, pretty funny. AND they start to get me more and more subscribers – just enough to encourage me to keep going.

Anyhoo, back to the Dylan thing. It's been a month now since I went round to his house and he told me about his mum and we held hands and everything looked good. Then back at school it went cold again. We still hung out with the group together at lunchtime, and sometimes he'd tell me he'd added a few more songs to my playlist and we'd talk about those, and he vaguely asked how it was going with my dad, but we haven't really seen each other outside school because I've been so busy with Dad and everything . . . and because I came up with excuses to say no. It was just too much on top of everything else to keep worrying about why he doesn't seem to *like me* like me all that much. Now though I kinda feel bad about it as, at times, he's started to look a bit like a massive, sad, rejected puppy at school, standing at the edge of the group, hanging his head low, shuffling his feet and weeing in the corner. OK, I made that last one up.

At other times, he's still as loud-mouthed as ever though, so it may be that he hasn't even noticed anything. The whole 'we had a relationship and now we kinda seem to have split up' thing may have passed him by entirely.

Then today things sort of changed.

At lunchtime, we're hanging around on the steps at the back of the science block. Ginger Dan, Belge and Watto are doing keepy-uppies, using their backpacks for footballs, cos they're just that sophisticated. Near me and Chlo, Kas is sitting on the corner of the bottom step being proper geeky, reading some GCSE revision-tips book called something like *The No-Pressure Guide to Getting 100% in Your GCSEs So You WIN! WIN! WIN! at Life and Don't End Up a Massive Loser!!* Chlo is showing me before-and-after pics of makeovers, as if I'm interested. I tell her that it seems to me the only reason the poor sods look better in the 'after' pics is because they're smiling. Maybe because the makeover is finally over.

'Nonsense,' she says with a dismissive wave of her hand. 'Look, what do *you* think, Dylan?'

Dylan, who's been sitting on the top step and drumming on his thighs the entire time, leans down and laughs. 'Yeah, I'm with Hay.'

Yeah, but are *you?* I think.

Then Chlo stands up, links her arm through Watto's, grabs his face and they full-on snog as we all uncomfortably look away. Dylan sits down next to me as I try desperately not to catch his eye, the snogging below us kind of highlighting yet again the fact that we don't, and haven't, and, I guess, won't.

Oh yeah, so, about two weeks ago, Chloe and Watto started going out. Chlo told me she went along with Kas to one of her many after-school revision sessions in the library, as Kas had told her Watto was usually there. They sat next to him and when Chlo got her Hilary Mantel book out of her bag Kas desperately wanted her to avoid the fast-approaching humiliation, so she suggested that Chlo go and get herself a glass of water so her voice would be lovely and smooth when she recited her *Wolf Hall* review. Chloe bought it and disappeared, and when she did Kas whispered to Watto that Chloe liked him and he should ask her out. So he did. And she said yes. And now they snog. A lot.

Chlo makes it all look so simple. Like when you see the fit girls showing off and doing cartwheels and flips on the school field and you think, *Yeah, I could do that, looks easy; it's just a confidence thing, right?!* Then you try it and end up with your face in the dirt, your arse in the air and your dignity splattered across Instagram. Or so I imagine. I mean, obviously that didn't happen to *me*.

Anyway, that's how simple relationships are when you're Chloe.

Nothing so simple as that for me.

I accidentally catch Dylan's eye and he awkwardly raises his eyebrows at me before offering me an awkward, teeth-sucking grin. He clears his throat. 'So, you gonna do the next open-mic? Isn't it on Friday?'

Oh nuts, what with everything else going on I'd completely forgotten about it.

'God, yeah, I guess it is. Yeah, maybe. I'll see if the girls are going.'

'OK, but, you know, if they're not, I could always go with you?'

And I can't take it any more, this running hot then cold. After all, I don't need a boyfriend to 'complete' me or whatever; I'm perfectly complete on my own, thank you very much. But I like the guy and, if he's in, I'm in and, if he's out, I'm out. JUST MAKE YOURSELF CLEAR, DOOFUS!

My cheeks burn red as I lower my voice and say, 'Well, yeah, but . . . look, this is driving me mad, Dylan. Are we a thing any more or what?'

He squirms and takes a deep breath.

My heart hammers as I wait for what feels like an eternity for a reply.

'Well . . . erm . . . do you want us to be a thing? You're the one who's been . . . off lately.'

'Off'? I haven't been 'off'. I've had bloody big life stuff to deal with! And he *knows* about Dad coming back. What am I supposed to do: prioritize my we-once-held-hands boyfriend over a huge life thing like that?

'Well, my dad came back into my life, Dylan. You get that, right?'

'Yeah, sure, I'm sorry, I know. That's why I've, I dunno, been trying to give you space or whatever, but I was worried maybe I'd backed off too much and that was it.'

And now his coldness over the last few weeks at least makes more sense. Which is cute, but the problem is he was already so far backed off he's now just reversed out of view altogether.

'So . . .? Are we a thing still?' I ask.

'Well, I want us to be a thing . . . Do you? I definitely want us to be a thing.'

And his hand, which has been resting on his thigh, slides down to the cold concrete between us and gently holds mine. And it feels chuffin' amazing.

'Well, OK then,' I say, looking away from him, trying to disguise the big grin spreading across my face.

'Don't . . . turn away,' he says. 'I like it when you smile.'

Did you hear that? That's like a proper gorgeous romantic thing he said right there!!

So obviously I respond like this: 'Oh, shut up, dumbass. I have a terrible smile,' I say, giggling a bit.

'So . . . can I come round some time? Tomorrow maybe? I still haven't seen the last episode of *Flight of the Conchords* so . . .'

'Yeah,' I say, looking up into his eyes for the first time. 'That would be fab.'

'Fab'? Why the hell did I say 'fab'?! I'm the only kid in the world who sounds like she's trying to be down with the kids.

He smiles, which makes me smile back. Then Ginger Dan breaks the magic by turning to face us all and burping insanely loudly before taking a bow.

Dylan immediately lets go of my hand. Brilliant. So as usual it's one step forward and two steps back with us, as he's still embarrassed to show me any affection in front of his mates.

'I'm crazy bored,' says Belge.

'Me too. Let's do something,' says Kas.

'Let's do a fight run!' shouts Ginger Dan.

'What's a fight run?' I ask.

'Come on, we'll show you,' says Dylan, and he jumps up and GRABS MY HAND.

HE GRABS MY HAND! IN FRONT OF EVERYONE!

And, as my heart jolts into overdrive, he drags me down the steps and round the corner as the others follow on behind. It all happens in a split second, but long enough for me to see Chloe as we bolt past her, looking down at our joined hands, then up at me with a cheeky grin and raised eyebrows. We run round to the main quad where various groups, from geeks to cool kids, are milling around.

'FIGHT!' shouts Dylan as we run through the groups.

'Fight! There's a fight!' shout Belge, Watto and Ginger Dan as we continue to run aimlessly round the quad.

Soon an air of excitement builds as rumours of who it might be grow out of nowhere. Any student or even teacher seen having any kind of argument this morning is soon named as a possible contestant in this apparent 'fight'.

'Fight! Fight! Fight!' we all now chant as the seven of us run out of the quad, Dylan still leading the way and holding my hand while I try to stifle my giggles.

Soon the whole quad follows on behind us, many of them now joining in with the chanting. 'Fight! Fight! Fight!' We run past the all-weather pitch as the kids playing football pick up on the excitement and start after us.

'What do we do now?' I puff as my boobs start to hurt with all the bouncy running.

'Run!' And we pick up the pace some more, as now the entire school seems to be racing behind us, chanting along. My heart races, partly with the adrenaline of being chased by an angry mob, partly with the hot electricity travelling up my arm from where Dylan's big hand is holding on to me.

We run down the narrow gap between the art block and the gym, then turn the corner and Dylan, with his non-hand-holding hand, pushes open the door to the maths corridor. The seven of us duck inside and hide behind the stairs, laughing uncontrollably as we watch the whole school hurtle past the doors, still chanting 'fight' and desperately looking for this imaginary battle.

'That. Was awesome,' says Chlo breathlessly as we emerge from behind the stairs to watch the crowds pass, each group looking ever more confused as the information about what they're looking for, vague as it was to start with, becomes ever more diluted.

Dylan gently lets go of my hand and walks towards the door. He turns to us all. 'Check this out,' he says.

And we all stare on in excitement, though my hand now feels a little lonely without its partner.

Dylan opens the door as people rush past it, some still chanting.

'What's going on?' he asks a group of Year Sevens.

'Haven't you heard?' says a tiny girl with pigtails. 'Apparently, Big Joyce from Year Nine is about to kick the crap out of Fran from Year Ten because she said her hair looked like a pineapple.'

We're all holding back giggles as a red-faced boy from Year Nine shakes his head passionately and cuts in. 'What? That's not what I heard! I heard Mrs Patel got the caretaker in a headlock because he refused to put the chairs away after her crap assembly.'

'Well, go on then – you'd better not miss it!' says Dylan, waving them on. He shuts the door as we all burst out laughing.

Then Dylan turns to me, looks me in the eye and smiles. My heart does a little skip.

For the rest of the afternoon, I'm walking on air. Until I get home with Noah and remember I promised myself (*really* promised this time – don't look at me like that) that I'd tell Mum about Dad tonight.

I pause with my key in the door. It could wait another day surely?

'Hay?' says Noah, tugging on my school shirt. 'You doing a farty-pop?'

'Shh, Noah, I'm thinking,' I hiss.

'Your think face is the same as your farty-pop face,' he says.

But I'm not listening. *I mean, maybe she never has to know?*

Then I imagine my wedding day, when I can finally hide it from her no longer as Dad walks me down the aisle. And the headline in the papers the next day reads: MOTHER OF THE BRIDE EXPLODES WITH HEARTBREAK AT SHOCK DISCOVERY OF DAUGHTER'S SELFISH SECRET.

I need to get this over with. I just can't take the guilt any more.

I hold my breath as I turn the key.

SIXTEEN

After the usual bosomy Mum-cuddles on the sofa and
Noah showing off his pictures from school (crap as always,
but Mum seems to like them), I get Noah settled in front
of some insane cartoon on TV and then follow Mum into
the kitchen.

I sit at the kitchen table as she makes herself a cup
of tea.

'You not getting a snack, babe?' she asks, piling the
sugar into her cup.

'Nope. No, no, no, no, no.' For some reason, I keep
saying 'no' as if it will cover up the previous 'no' sounding
so nervous and weird. It doesn't.

Mum immediately picks up on this, stops mid-stir and
aims a frowny, concerned expression my way.

There's no avoiding it any more. I've just gotta dive
right in.

'Mum, I've got something to tell you.'

'Oh *God*,' she says. She sits opposite me at the table,
reaches out, holds my hand and whispers, 'Are you . . .
you know?'

'WHAT?!' I yell, yanking my hand away from her. 'No! Crazy lady! Me and Dylan haven't even snogged and I'm pretty sure holding hands doesn't impregnate you!'

'OK, OK!' She smiles. 'Sorry, love, was listening to a *Woman's Hour* special earlier on teen pregnancies. So what is it?'

I look down at the table then back up at her, swallow hard and just say it: 'I've been seeing Dad.'

The smile drops off her face. She sits back in her chair, takes a shaky breath and says, 'What? Where? Did he say anything to you? That bastard, he should have told me if he was in town.'

I take a deep breath. 'No, Mum, you don't understand. I've been seeing Dad willingly. For a few weeks now.'

And now I'm kind of wishing I was pregnant. I have a feeling she would have coped with that way better. Her mouth falls open and her nostrils flare. I bite my lip then continue. I've got this far, I may as well let it all spill out. A dark frown is fixed on her face as she listens, her breathing ragged. I tell her about him showing up at the open-mic night, how I went mental at him then decided to give him a chance, how apologetic he was, that he's moved down here, that he's split up with Tits McGee, that he took me to the beach and bought me chips.

'CHIPS?' she yells.

Really, that's her main concern here? I recoil from her in my chair. 'Erm, yeah, chips.'

'Well, that makes up for everything then, doesn't it?' she sarcastically spits. 'I mean, what's years of neglect and heartache compared to a bag of chips?! Were they good chips, Hay?'

'Yeah,' I say stupidly, before quickly adding, 'but not the best. Not as good as the ones you make.'

She looks down at her clasped hands resting on the table and shakes her head. 'Why didn't you tell me?'

'I'm sorry, Mum. I'm sorry.' And I really am. I can feel the burn of tears behind my eyes and in my throat. 'I knew you wouldn't like it. I didn't know how to tell you.'

'Did he tell you to keep it a secret?'

'What? No, nothing like that. He, well, he thinks that you know.'

She takes another deep breath, blinks hard as if rebooting her brain, forces a half-smile and reaches out to stroke my arm. I can tell she's gone into practical-nurse-mum mode. 'Well, I do now. It's not your fault, Hay. I know you think you want to see him, but he's just manipulating you. Where's my phone? I'll tell him where to stick his chips, and you don't have to see him ever again, OK?'

She avoids eye contact with me and takes a gulp from her tea. I wipe away a tear and stare at her. Part of me wants to agree, to make her happy again, to take away the hurt. But another part, a bigger part, knows I absolutely want to continue seeing him.

'No, Mum. I know what he's done. I know what he did. So does he. But I want to . . .' She slams the drained mug down on the table, but I try to stay strong. 'He hasn't manipulated me. Come on, you know I'm not easily manipulated. I *want* to see him again.'

'He'll hurt you, Hay,' she says in her most sinister, quiet, angry voice, 'and I can't let him do that to you. Not again. You *cannot* see that man. You understand?'

And now I'm angry at her. She can't stop me seeing him. It's not my fault they split up; it's not my fault she stopped him seeing us in the first place. I dramatically get up, the chair flying out from under me and hitting the wall behind as I stand on slightly shaky legs.

'That "man" is my dad, Mum. And I *am* going to keep seeing him.'

I turn and leave, stomping down the hall. Of course I knew she'd react badly, but I thought she'd be upset, not go into complete controlling crazy-woman mode.

She throws her own chair back and marches after me, yelling at my back, 'Do NOT leave when I am talking to you. We are NOT done here, young lady!'

Oh God, and now she's 'young ladied' me, which will probably trigger a local red warning from the Met Office – take action and expect widespread damage to property and infrastructure. I need to get out of here.

I can't believe she's being so unreasonable without any kind of concern for how this all makes me feel. I grab my keys off the hook and throw open the front door. I turn to her and in my most sarcastic voice say, 'Wow, *thanks* for being *so* understanding, Mum. I don't know *why* I was worried about telling you this!'

She stands at the bottom of the stairs with her hands on her hips, her red frowny face looking every bit like the angry-face emoji. 'Don't you *dare* walk out that door, Haylah.'

'WATCH ME!' I yell as I walk out and slam the door behind me.

As I storm down the street to God knows where, tears start pushing their way through, making my eyesight all blurry. People start to stare at me when I walk past. I decide to go to Grammo's, as it's the nearest house belonging to someone who might be sympathetic to me.

When I get there, she immediately sees I'm upset and brings me in for a much-needed big Grammo hug. Which forces the tears out more.

'What is it, sweetie?' she asks into my hair.

'Had . . . an . . . argument . . . with . . . Mum,' I manage to get out.

She tells me everything will be OK, which, even though I know she has zero idea of the details of the situation or whether it will, in fact, all be OK, I find strangely comforting anyway. She tells me to come on in, not for tea and crumpets like other grans might, or indeed like Grammo would have done before Uncle Terry died and she started doing what she liked. Instead, she offers me a G & T and the leftovers from the takeaway pizza she and June had last night. I do love the fact that at seventy you can still go through a rebellious phase.

I turn down the gin, but start munching on a triangle of cold margherita as we sit next to each other on the sofa. The house still looks the same as it ever did though, and its comforting surroundings immediately make me feel a bit better, sort of safe and warm. It reminds me of family Christmases here when I was little. I can almost smell the dumplings steaming in the kitchen. By which I mean the adults getting drunk.

Grammo has one hand clasped round a giant gin glass and the other hand, weighed down heavily by cheap, sparkly jewellery, on my knee. 'What is it then, darling girl?'

So as she sips I tell her. About Dad, about Mum's reaction. All of it.

'Well, you should have told her sooner, love, but, well, there's no use crying over steamed milk.'

'Spilled.'

'What have you spilled?'

'Nothing, it doesn't matter,' I say, and somewhere in the back of my brain I make a mental note to write that one down later. 'But *you* get that he's my dad and that she's being totally unreasonable not letting me see him, right?'

Grammo takes a thoughtful pause and sips her gin. 'She just needs time, Hay. You have to remember how much of a git he was to her. You can't blame your mum for being protective of you.'

I take another bite of pizza. 'Yeah. I know,' I say. 'And I do get how hard it is for her.'

Though I'm still thinking she could try a little bit to get how hard it's been for me without a dad for so long. But I don't press it any more with Grammo. I change the subject and we talk about her next plans with June.

'Oooh, you should come with us – we're going to a burlesque night. Bring Chloe and Kas and that strapping young boyfriend of yours!'

'Thanks,' I chuckle. 'I think you have to be eighteen to go to one of those, plus I'm not sure it would be Dylan's thing. In fact, I'm not really sure what his thing is, but probably not that.'

'Well, you're his thing though, aren't you, sweetie?' she says with a squeeze of my knee and a slightly evil glint in her eye.

'Erm, I suppose so.' I think back to the hand-holding at school in front of everyone, which had felt pretty damned good and like we were moving forward. But, still, it's not exactly going at lightning speed.

At least Grammo has calmed me down and made me feel better about the whole Dad thing. I need to remember that he was a git to Mum, and how angry I was when he showed up out of the blue.

I creep home and, other than letting her know I'm back, which gets a grunt from the kitchen, I avoid Mum and she avoids me. Grammo's right, she just needs time, but I'm also still mad at her for freaking out at me like that and making me feel terrible about seeing *one of my parents* – something that most kids do every day.

So I make another video: 'Mums Are Idiots'. (I know she'll never see it, Mum's online life being very much separate from the wilds of YouTube.) But people who don't know me do seem to like my ranty takes on things, as my subscribers are still creeping up. Plus, these vids get the frustration out, which is way better than bottling it up, right?

'Mums are like bras – either they're making things uncomfortable and offering very little support, or way too much support to the point of being pushy and always trying to mould you into something you're not . . .'

I go on ranting about the contradictions between mums when they're in advice mode compared to when they're in mothering mode.

'So Mum'll advise me, "Ask questions in life, hun, and always make sure you get answers." Then, whenever I ask her why, she says, "Because I said so!"

'One of her favourite "wise" pieces of advice is, "Never settle for anything less than what you want." But when I say, "Mum, can I have beer at my party?" she says, "No frickin' way – you'll have orange squash and you'll be grateful for it."

'Then there's, "Even if others are cruel to you, never be cruel back to them." Yet, when I told her that her arse did look fat in that dress, she threw a baguette at my face.'

Maybe that was a bit much, I think when I'm done. Then I see the latest comments on the last video I uploaded.

PFG, ur the BEESSSSSTTTT! 😘

Ouch! Loving the brutal honesty – keep up the rants! 😆

Soooooo funny! More pls, PFG! 🙏

So I press upload. You've gotta give the fans what they want and, really, what harm can it do? I need to stop feeling guilty and follow my instincts, and they definitely say this is funny stuff, this is what you were built for – you're getting yourself out there and making people laugh. Go with it, girl!

SEVENTEEN

For the next few days, me and Dylan feel way more like a couple at school, and the hand-holding, even though it's just hand-holding, is pretty hot.

At home, things are way frostier. I make excuses not to see Dad as I don't want to fuel the Mum-fire, and me and Mum avoid each other as much as possible. She's at work a lot anyway, and when Ruben's here they sit on the sofa, disgustingly close to each other, and Ruben tells me what Mum's told him to say, like what's left over in the fridge for tea, when Mum's next at work and when I need to put Noah to bed. I nod in reply and he offers me a sheepish grin.

Then one evening as I get in from school I hear the strangely comforting sound of Grammo and Mum passive-aggressively arguing with each other about the bolognese sauce Mum's making in the kitchen.

'I didn't know you could put peas in a bolognese, darling,' says Grammo.

'Yes, well, there are probably lots of things you don't know when you think about it, Mum. Anyway, it's a very good way to get more vegetables into Noah without him noticing.'

I pause in the hall and smile.

'Lovely. Does the boy really need *more* food smuggled into him though? I mean, he's hardly wasting away.'

'He's not *that* big, Mum.' Then there's the large clanking sound of a wooden spoon being enthusiastically whacked down on the counter.

'No, he's not big at all, dear. Why would you say such a thing? He's perfect! Why are you getting upset?' says Grammo in her sickliest of sweet voices.

'Why do you always think I'm getting upset, Mum?' says Mum through clenched teeth. This is priceless! 'Why don't you have a glass of wine? That always relaxes you, doesn't it?' Ouch.

'I'm perfectly relaxed, darling. I'm sorry if you think I'm not . . .'

'Drink the wine, Mum,' snaps Mum.

As Mum's glugging half a bottle of wine into two huge glasses, I go in and give Grammo a hug, fully expecting the silent treatment from Mum, but instead she asks me how my day's been.

Could this be the breakthrough moment?

'Oh, er, yeah, not bad,' I say. She nods in reply then turns back to her sauce-stirring. 'Just gonna go to my room and get some homework done.'

'Righto,' says Mum to the sauce, and as I turn to leave I see Grammo elbow her in the ribs and whisper something to her.

I get into my room and lie back on the bed. It seemed Mum was softening for a moment, but then maybe not. I check my phone for messages. There's just one from Dad asking if everything's OK and if I wanna go bowling with him this week. I want to, but I still feel I'm somehow 'cheating' on Mum if I do. I'm about to message back some excuse when Mum knocks (and she never normally knocks).

'Erm, come in,' I say, wondering if I should take cover.

She comes in and wanders around a bit, tidying a few things up as she goes. I stare uneasily at her as she finally sits on the end of my bed and takes a deep breath.

'I'm sorry, Hay,' she says, then she reaches out and strokes my foot.

I hate it so much when we fight. It feels like I've been holding my breath for days and now I have full access to oxygen again.

I put my phone aside. 'I'm sorry too, Mum. I should have told you. And I haven't seen him since you said not to.'

She half smiles and nods. 'But you still want to, right?' she asks with a sigh, because she already knows the answer.

'Yeah. But I don't wanna do it behind your back.'

She looks down at the floor, takes her hand away from my foot and shifts her weight around on the bed. Then she starts nodding slowly. I bite my lip as I wait for her answer.

'You don't have to, love. It's OK.' She looks back at me, leans forward and forces a smile. 'If you want to see him, you can see him.'

Relief spreads through me, but I can literally see how hard this is for her, and how she's going against everything inside her to do the right thing for me and to make me happy.

My face lights up. 'Mum, thank you. I know this is . . .' But I can't get the words out, so instead I just say, 'I love you.'

She climbs next to me on the bed and I lift my head as she puts her arm under my neck. We both stare at the ceiling together.

'Love you too, Hay,' she says. 'Though you're a pain in the arse sometimes.'

'Right back atcha,' I say, and we both laugh.

After a few moments, she calmly but strongly sets out a few ground rules, telling me she doesn't want Dad at the house and she doesn't want Noah to know, which I totally get. The last time Dad phoned the house, Noah answered and ended up crying and confused, and of course I don't want that either. Mum continues listing her terms and conditions, including wanting to know exactly where we are when I'm out with Dad and when I'm coming home and all that stuff.

It all seems fair enough, and I can't exactly expect her to be jolly about it, so I agree to her terms. Then she draws me in for one of her Mum-hugs, making me realize how much I've missed them recently.

I gulp hard and pluck up the courage to ask her if it's true that Dad had actually wanted to see us more than she'd let on.

She sighs as we both sit up with our backs against the wall. And I'm thinking she's going to brush my question away, but she doesn't. She tells me she's sorry if she made it hard for him to see us at first, but it was all such a mess and she had to find the best way for us all to move on without him.

'Hay, we were fighting all the time. I think, in retrospect, I had postnatal depression after Noah was born, but it wasn't picked up on and . . . well, I probably wasn't the easiest person to live with at that time. Then he had the . . . affair, and I was just heartbroken. I needed him completely out of my life. I dunno, I probably did the wrong thing.'

It's weird that I so want to hear this, to understand what happened, but at the same time I so don't want to hear it. The thought of Mum, the one solid, strong, reliable thing in my life, going through all that is hard to bear.

I swallow down the lump in my throat. 'Thank you for telling me, Mum,' I almost whisper.

She strokes my hair as I rest my head on her shoulder. Then after a few moments her voice goes all wistful as she says, 'You think when you become an adult you'll have things sorted, make wise choices, be less hot-headed. Then you learn that that's absolute BS.'

'It is?'

'Totally. Adults still make stupid decisions; we're just better at pretending they're wise. We're basically just big kids with jobs.' Her tone has lightened and I'm glad of the break from the heavy atmosphere.

'Not even proper adult jobs in Ruben's case,' I joke.

'Shut it!' she scoffs, stopping the hair-stroking for a moment to playfully hit me on the side of my head.

'Ow!' I laugh.

'The only real things that adults know that kids don't are how to bleed a radiator and that Kinder eggs are actually rubbish,' she says as she climbs off the bed. 'Right, better go and stop the bolognese from overcooking and Grammo from overdrinking.'

'Thanks, Mum,' I say.

She stops with her hand on the door handle and turns back to me. 'I'm not completely OK with it, Hay, but it's your decision.'

'OK,' I say, and I realize that's probably the best I can ever hope for.

She points at me. 'Just make sure he knows that if he hurts you I'll rip his balls off.'

'Oh, he knows,' I say.

She nods with a resigned smile and I can see again how hard this is on her.

'One more thing, Mum. You're wrong . . . about Kinder eggs . . . They're awesome.'

She proper smiles again as she opens the door to leave. 'Kinder eggs are like life, hun – the surprises are disappointing and there's never enough chocolate.'

'Ooh, that's good. Can I write it down?'

She laughs as she closes the door behind her. 'I'd be disappointed if you didn't, babe.'

*

So things aren't perfect with Mum, but she's letting me see Dad and at least I don't have that bastard guilt slapping me round the brain the whole time. The next day I wake up (after hitting snooze about twelve times) and feel like a weight has lifted, and the day just continues getting better.

It starts with Noah telling a super-cute joke at breakfast. 'What do you call a flying skunk?'

'I dunno, Noah. What *do* you call a flying skunk?'

'A STINK-copter!'

He chews on his 'Chocopops' for a few moments as me, Ruben and Mum stare at him blankly. Then, just as we're about to file it under 'Noah being weird', he holds his spoon in the air to silence everyone and announces, 'SMELLY-COPTER! I meant smelly-copter.'

We all laugh, which he wrongly assumes is us laughing at the joke, not at him.

'Very good, Noah,' I say. 'Cos it rhymes, right?'

'Yep,' he says, his mouth full of cereal, 'with aeroplane.'

On the way to school, now with Mum's full approval and no guilt, I text Dad and arrange to meet after school for bowling. Yeah – get me – I'm a two-parent kid again!

Me, Kas and Chlo come up with a new game in registration called Fart Music, which involves blowing raspberries of your favourite songs and the other two trying to guess what it is. Then Dylan spends the ENTIRE lunch break holding my hand and making me laugh, which is just delicious, and we make plans to walk home together tonight and go to the open-mic night again on Friday.

I mean, could this day get any better?

I sit in maths next to Chlo and after the work is set I do the bare minimum early on so that I can daydream through the rest of the lesson about Dylan and the cute dimples he gets in his cheeks when he smiles at a joke I've just made. Chlo hasn't missed the slightly glazed look in my eye and the smile that keeps playing around on my lips, and occasionally she elbows me and whispers, 'Look . . . why don't you just grab the boy and snog him? It's obvious he really wants to. He's probably super inexperienced and shy.'

'Hmm, maybe,' I say, and I rest my chin on my hands and look out of the window, thinking it all through. *Why hasn't he kissed me yet?*

'Hmmm, my boyfriend, Dylan, is sooo lurvely . . .' Chlo purrs into my ear.

'Oh, shut up!' I respond with a smile, and she giggles and carries on copying my work.

'Yeah, could you just move your infatuated elbows over though, as I can't see your first answers?'

'Yeah, sorry,' I say, dreamily shifting over a bit.

I think about Dylan and maybe, *eek*, possibly kissing him later. I totally want to snog his face off.

Chloe's right: there's no rule that says the boy has to make the first move. If he's shy, maybe I have to step up and be the non-shy one. It's what a good feminist would do, right?

And then. And *bloody* then. Vicki happens. And the good day goes supersonic tits up.

When most of the class, including the teacher, have given up caring about the work we're supposed to be doing and the general noise and shifting about has increased, Chief Megabitch Vicki strides over from the back of the classroom and then crouches down next to Chlo.

'Hey, snot-hair.'

'Piss off, Vicki,' says Chlo as she pretends to carry on with her maths work.

'Really? That's the best insult you can come up with? "Snot hair"?' I say.

We're all terrified of Vicki, but I'm feeling rather confident and ballsy after my Dylan excitement.

'Well, her hair *was* the colour of snot,' she sneers. 'So I think that's pretty accurate, yeah. I'd like to hear *you* come up with better, fat girl.'

Oh, when, when, when are people going to realize that *the* most boring insult ever hurled at anyone is calling them 'fat'? I am well aware of my size, thank you very much. You may as well point out that I have brown hair or size-six feet and expect me to be shocked and hurt at that revelation.

'Oooh, "fat girl" – wow, I take it back, you *are* the queen of inventive put-downs. OK, how about, "Your hair's SNOT looking too bad today," or, "What did you use, Greenier-Nutrisse?" or, "Hope that new hair colour doesn't make you KERMIT suicide," or –'

'HAY!' shouts Chlo, cutting me off before I grab a mic and start performing an entire set based on green-hair jokes.

'Sorry,' I say, realizing I'm not actually helping.

'They're actually pretty good. Thank you,' says Vicki, smirking.

Well, that backfired. Vicki regroups and aims her bitch gun directly at me.

'So how's it going with Dylan, *Pig*?' she says with a pouty, evil grin.

'It's "Haylah" to you,' spits Chlo.

'*Whatever*,' Vicki continues, not taking her scowling eyes off me. 'Anyway, he's such a good kisser, right? I'm sure he told you me and him hooked up last Christmas at the disco. Man, he was full on, really passionate, you know?'

What? Seriously WHAT? The blood drains from my face and sinks down to my toes.

Chlo glances at me with a concerned look, then scowls at Vicki. 'That's BS, Vicki, and you know it.'

'Totally BS-free actually. Ask anyone.' Vicki notices my mortified look of horror and shock, like I've just accidentally clicked on a 'Fifteen photos that will make you vom' link. 'Oh, what is it? Have you guys not kissed yet?' She places a perfectly manicured evil hand on my arm and does an impression of a concerned and caring friend. 'I didn't want to say this, but it's probably better that you hear it from someone. I think he's just with you for a joke, Haylah. Think about it. Why else would a popular guy be with you? Aww, I'm sorry. Anyway, give him my love, won't you?'

My mouth dries up so I can't even respond.

Vicki stands up and turns to Chloe. 'Oh, and FYI – me and Jason from Year Seven did NOT have a fight a couple of weeks ago because he "stole some of my knickers" – so, next time you and your little group of saddos start some stupid fake-fight chant, get your FACTS STRAIGHT!' Then she saunters off to the back of the room.

I look down at the table and scrunch my eyes closed for a moment, trying to fight the hot sting of tears. There's no way I can give Vicki the satisfaction of that.

Chlo puts her arm round me and whispers, 'Hay, she's just talking crap, OK? She thinks we started a rumour about her and she's lashing out like a . . . stupid . . . lashing-out . . . gibbon . . . Look, you know I'm not very good at the put-downs.'

'But how did she know,' I say in a shaky whisper, 'that we haven't kissed yet? She must have done if she knew she could wind me up like that.'

Chlo swallows. 'Actually, I do know . . .'

I shoot her a questioning look and she offers me a guilty grimace back.

'Don't get mad, but me and Kas were talking in the toilets the other day and, well, it *may* have come up and when we were done we came out and saw Vicki standing at the sinks, smiling her evil smile at us.'

Well, at least Dylan hasn't been telling people, but wow. This is just *great*.

'It "came up"?' I whisper-shout. 'How the heck did it "come up"? "Hey, Kas, pass me some bog roll, and, ooh, that reminds me – Dylan still hasn't snogged Hay!"'

Chloe twiddles with the hair behind her ear. 'It wasn't exactly like that, but, yeah. I'm sorry! I feel awful!'

'It's fine. Doesn't matter.'

Except that it TOTALLY MATTERS. And why are they talking about me and Dylan anyway?! I mean, sure, me and Chloe talk about Kas when she's not there, and me and Kas talk about Chloe when she's not there, but them talking about me is not allowed!!

I don't have the energy to be bothered about that right now, though, and I need Chlo onside.

I lower my voice so it's barely audible as I open up to Chlo. 'I thought he hadn't really snogged anyone. I thought that was the reason he wasn't doing anything with me. Now it seems pretty clear – he just doesn't fancy me.'

'Oh, Hay,' says Chlo, stroking my arm. 'I'm sure that's not it.'

And Vicki's 'fat girl' comment, however predictably dull, comes back to haunt me. Is it just the case, that however confident and fabulous I feel, I'll never quite be what the world wants?

'It is, Chlo. You know it; I know it. Yeah, he might like me, but he can't work his stupid boy brain past the fact that I'm fat, and boys aren't supposed to want to snog fat girls. That's what it comes down to.'

'You're not fat, Hay.'

'I don't care if I am! But other people do, and you know as well as I do that I'm definitely no Vicki to look at. Maybe she's right: he's just with me for a joke. After all, that's all I'm good for.'

I somehow drag myself through the rest of my lessons and at the end of the school day Dylan's waiting for me at the top gates. With Kas (who was obviously beside herself with remorse about the whole toilet/Vicki thing when I filled her in) and Chlo on either side of me as backup, I charge past him. I don't even want to look at him right now.

'Hay? HAY! Wait up!' he yells as he follows us.

'You need to talk to him, Hay,' says Chlo as we storm up the road.

Kas chimes in. 'She's right. He doesn't know what Vicki said to you today. Maybe give him a chance to explain?'

And I guess they're right. So I stop, my cheeks red from the storming and the anger and humiliation inside me. 'You guys go on. I'll catch up.'

'If you're sure,' says Chlo, and they walk off as Dylan jogs alongside me.

'I thought we were walking together?' he says, a little out of breath.

'That was before your ex-lover "Vicki" spoke to me earlier,' I spit, still looking straight ahead and starting up my fast, angry walking again, which makes my boobs bounce around and probably makes me look more comical than fierce. *Stupid boobs.*

'W-wait, ex-what?' stammers Dylan.

Oh, like he doesn't know!

'You remember *snogging* her at some party?'

'Er, yeah, so? That was way before, y'know, us.'

I stop walking. He stops too. And I look at him with my evillest frowny face. He looks back at me with a vacant expression that screams 'CLUELESS'.

'You really don't get it? You spend one night with that brazen hussy –' to be honest, I'm not *exactly* sure what a 'brazen hussy' is, but Mum always used the phrase to describe Dad's secretary so I'm going with it – 'and you're all Snoggy McSnoggisson. We spend months apparently as a 'thing', but clearly even that's not long enough cos you still think I'm too disgusting to come anywhere near. Do you have any idea how crappy that makes me feel?'

'Oh.' He looks down to his shoes for answers, but clearly doesn't find any. 'I don't know what to say . . . erm . . . sorry?'

'And she says you're just going out with me for a joke, is that right?'

He looks lost, confused and almost scared, like a toddler who's been asked where the nearest train station is by a stranger. And, I mean, REALLY, can you believe this? It's not exactly a hard question!

'What? No, I dunno, no,' he says.

Unbelievable. I think he does truly mean no. I don't think he's been going out with me for a joke, but, still, if your girlfriend asks you if you're going out with her for a joke, surely you respond with a massive, 'No, *of course* not, babe. How could you even think that?'

'Really? That's all you got? Goodbye, Dylan. This "thing", which was actually a complete non-"thing", is now officially over.' I start walking again.

'Wait!' he says, and just for a split second I hope he says or does something to persuade me otherwise, like this could be that moment in the romcom when it's all solved in one massively romantic moment. *Oh, come on, Dylan, you can do this.*

I turn to him. 'What?'

'Erm . . . nothing.'

He really can't do this. Or doesn't want to. Either way, I'm out. I don't need a guy to make me feel bad about myself. I can do that quite well on my own, thank you very much.

'Brilliant,' I say, turning on my heel and marching away.

And, more than with him, I'm angry at myself. Why did I think, for even one tiny moment, that he was with me for anything other than, OK, maybe not a joke but a laugh, or maybe out of pity or boredom or some other deranged reason only understood by boys? Why else hasn't he come close to kissing me? I'm no Vicki; I'm never going to be – I don't want to be! But being me seems to mean that, sure, I can make the boys laugh, but I don't make them fancy me. That's just never going to be the case.

Give up now, Pig. You're destined to be alone forever.

Chlo and Kas wait for me further up the pavement.

'It's over!' I dramatically announce as I hurtle past the two of them.

'Wait up, Hay!' they yell, trotting along after me.

'It's fine, really! I've gotta go,' I pant as I try to put as much distance as possible between me and them, between me and the beautiful ones who'll never really feel that kind of rejection. Sure, they'll have break-ups, but it'll be because they 'want different things' from their boyfriends or they've got 'nothing in common'. It'll never be a straight-up rejection because they're too unattractive. So how could they possibly understand?

I take a different route home in case they try to catch up. I'm not angry with them or anything, but I don't want to talk to anyone about how I feel right now. I just wanna have a pity party for one. Is that too much to ask?

Apparently, it is. A few roads later, with my phone buzzing in my pocket with what I'm sure will be messages from them that I can't be bothered to look at right now, I suddenly hear a voice from behind me.

'Hey, Hay!'

Oh my God, it's Leo. Great. Thank you, universe, for piling another dollop of crap on this day.

Yet another boy who strung me along for no reason only to reject me cos I didn't fit the bill of his thin, beautiful 'type'. Which is, of course, everyone's 'type'.

I spin round, and he's on his own, coming to the end of a jog, apparently to catch up with me. 'WHAT?' I snap. Though, God, it's difficult to be pissed with a guy who looks as downright gorgeous as he does.

'Whoa! Calm yourself, dude. I only wanted to see if you were all right. I saw you charging up the road, looking like someone had just run over your kitten. You all right?'

I sigh, his concern for me softening my mood. 'Nothing. It's . . . well, if you must know, I just dumped my boyfriend.' I'm guessing he won't have a lot to say to that, so I turn and start walking again, but he runs up and walks alongside me.

'Bummer. Why?'

'Oh, shut up. Like you're interested in my little love life. Jog on, Mr Popular.'

'Argh, come on, Hay. Don't be like that. We're friends, right? Tell Unkie Leo all about it.'

I laugh. 'Unkie Leo?'

'Yep. Come on, why'd you dump him? And, if you're the dumper not the dumpee, why are you so upset about it?'

And because I'm an idiot for his charms I tell him. 'Argh! Fine. I think he was just going out with me for a joke or, I dunno, I'm just unfanciable.'

Why did I say that?! Could I not have said something that at least makes me sound *cool, even if I'm not?!*

Leo stops walking and grabs my arm, spinning me round to face him.

'Haylah, if that dirtbag doesn't realize what an amazing babe he's got in you, then he doesn't deserve you.'

My head spins. I'd almost forgotten how charming this boy can be. But he's still a git and I can't have him thinking he can just sweep into my life whenever he wants and I'll be like, 'Oh, Leo, you're my hero!'

'Well, that's rich coming from you. You might remember that not so long ago I wasn't good enough or fanciable enough for you either,' I say, though I can't help my face from offering him a slightly flirty smile when I say it.

'That was *never* the issue, girl, and you know it. Look, I gotta go, but you did the right thing in chucking him. You're a goddess. Remember that.' And he flashes me that gorgeous smile, lets go of my arm and starts backing away. 'Remember that!' he says again with a wink, before turning and leaving.

'I will,' I say a little too breathlessly. And I can't help but smile.

Oh, Leo, you're my hero! Shut up, brain.

Then he's gone and the brief lift in my mood disappears with him.

EIGHTEEN

I get home and Ruben is there, so I don't tell Mum about Dylan. Plus, although the official line is that she's fine with me seeing Dad, she's definitely pissy about me seeing him tonight. Up in my room I get changed before I meet him down the road. I try desperately to keep my mind off the Dylan thing, but it keeps wandering back into it without my say-so.

Stupid mind.

It keeps torturing me with images of Dylan kissing Vicki. Beautiful she-beast Vicki.

But is it misery I feel about our break-up or relief? Maybe it'll be nice to not have to worry about Dylan any more. The whole is-he-or-isn't-he-into-me thing.

Sod it. Sod 'em all. I'm better off without any of this boy crap.

Me and Dad go bowling, and it's great to do something and think about something totally un-Dylan related. We joke, we laugh, we talk about TV shows and comedians and things of no consequence whatsoever, which is exactly what I needed. Then he asks how my day's been.

For a moment, I think of saying, 'Yeah, fine,' but then I think, *He's my dad. I can tell him stuff.* That's what daughters do with their dads, right? So I tell him about splitting with Dylan.

He clears his throat and his eyes roam round the big warehouse ceiling, as if the right thing for a 'dad' to say in this moment will be written on it somewhere.

'It's OK, Dad,' I say, laughing, 'you haven't had a lot of practice at this. You don't have to say anything.' But secretly I'm a bit disappointed.

Then he puts down his bowling ball and sits on the plastic seat next to me. 'I know I don't have to, but I want to. Haylah, you are an incredible girl, am I right?'

I smile. 'Well, yeah, obviously I'm awesome,' I say, somewhat unconvinced.

'I'm serious. Getting to know you again over the last few weeks has been phenomenal. I mean, I knew I was missing out on a daughter, but I guess I didn't realize I was also missing out on getting to know one of the most interesting, quick-witted, driven, exciting and cool people I've ever known.'

'Aw, shut up, Dad, you're gonna make me blush.' Though I so don't want him to shut up. His words are lighting up my insides.

'I will not,' he says. 'Look, teenage boys are messed-up hormonal lumps of confusion. They don't know what they're doing. And I hate that they're gonna hurt you. But, believe me, there will be a ton of them after you as you grow up, and I'll probably hate every one of them by the way, but there will be, because you light up any frickin' room you're in, girl.'

And it's just about the nicest thing anyone's ever said to me. And it's definitely not something I thought I would ever hear from my dad, who up until recently I thought was a complete arse-wipe. A huge smile takes over my face and I don't really know how to respond. I think he senses the awkwardness, and he says, 'Anyway, enough of that soppy crap, I'm up,' before jumping to his feet and bowling a strike.

'Thanks, Dad,' I say as he sits back down.

He nods with a smile. 'C'mon then, show me what you got.'

'OK, but brace yourself, cos this is gonna be awesome,' I say.

My own technique is a little different to his. I can't be bothered with the holes so I carry the heaviest ball I can find to the edge of the lane, thump it down on the floor and roll it towards the pins with my foot, saying something like, 'Go on, son, knock 'em all out!'

By the time the ball reaches the pins, three people have taken their turns on the lanes either side of us. It's not pretty, but it's surprisingly effective. And throughout the game I don't get any strikes, but it makes Dad laugh. Every time. And, when it comes down to it, any idiot can get a strike. It takes a special kind of idiot to get a laugh.

When we're done, it's only 7 p.m. and I have a day off tomorrow, so I message Chlo and Kas and get Dad to drop me at Kas's house.

I'm feeling bad about storming away from Kas and Chlo earlier. It's not their fault they're the beautiful ones and that their lives are easier than mine. And, yes, I know deep down that's kind of not true, but I'm still stinging from the Vicki thing.

'Are you sure you're all right, Hay?' asks Kas when I get into her room and shlump down on her bed.

'Yeah, I really am actually,' I say, hugging a cushion.

Chlo, sitting on the edge of the bed and painting her nails a disgusting entrails-pink colour, shoots me a questioning look.

'No, really, I am,' I say, picking at the cushion. 'It's weird, but I feel almost relieved. I don't need to worry about Dylan and me any more cos there is no Dylan and me. Sorted.'

I figure if I keep up this train of thought eventually I'll convince myself. Fake it till you make it, right?

'Hmm. Well, if you wanna talk about it some more?' offers Kas, who's sitting cross-legged on the floor, doing some biology homework that I didn't even know we had.

I really don't wanna talk about it some more. Thinking about it only makes me feel crappy about myself, and after the Leo thing last year I swore I wouldn't let a boy make me feel that way again. As Mum's always telling me, 'No boy's opinion of you has any actual bearing on your true worth.' I know that, I really do. But sometimes it's difficult to *feel* it too.

'No, really. It's done. And, hey, things are good. I know it's Thursday, but in case you need reminding we are on

208

holiday for a week now, thanks to the beautiful gift that is the PD day tomorrow. Sod it, I might even do the open-mic tomorrow evening. Who needs boys, right? You guys wanna come?'

'Oooh, I can't, sorry, Hay,' says Kas. 'I've got a . . . study-date thing with Lola.'

'Oh, have you now?' says Chlo, blowing her nails dry. 'New bestie, is she?'

'What? No! Come on, dudes,' says Kas.

'So she doesn't just look at you and think of you crapping yourself then?' I ask.

'Hay!' Kas explodes, before pointing a highlighter pen at me. 'You're not supposed to EVER talk about that EVER again!'

'Sorry,' I say, laughing. 'How about you, Chlo? Wanna come with me?'

'I can't, I'm sorry.'

I'm disappointed, but after the Dylan break-up I'm probably not exactly in the right mood to stand up and make people laugh anyway. Maybe I'll do another ranty YouTube vid instead.

Chlo goes on to explain why she can't come. 'Watto's coming round,' she says. 'Although I've gotta time it right as Kyle's FaceTiming me tomorrow night too. God, it's hard work juggling all these hunks.'

'My heart bleeds for you,' I say.

I roll my eyes and glance at Kas for support, but she's not listening. She has that weird, pained, distant look on her face again. Almost a smile but not really, more like she's smiling on the inside, but something is stopping it from coming out. As if she's smile-constipated.

I turn on my side, spooning several of the cushions on Kas's bed as I try to figure it out. Then my brain cogs start whirring and I've got it! *Oh my God, she's got a secret crush! She fancies Watto!*

Kas and Watto make far more sense than Chlo and Watto anyway, since they're both into books and school stuff. Poor Kas. She may be beautiful, but no one's ever going to be able to get a bloke away from Chloe.

'No, that's cool that you're both ditching me,' I say. 'I guess I should probably do some studying of my own at some point this year. Gotta make sure we all get through to the sixth form next year, right, dudes? Not that they're fussy at our school. I mean, I think they'd accept Ryan Reynolds-Gosling into the sixth form if he promised to work hard.'

'Hmm,' says Chlo, speedily applying her second coat of varnish.

Kas also focuses a little too intently on her science homework.

The air around us seems to have changed.

It's the first awkward silence I think I've ever experienced with these two.

'What?' I say. Then the penny drops and I sit up. 'Hang on. What *are* you guys doing next September? I mean, we're all still staying on for A levels like we planned, right?'

Both of them remain silent for a moment, staring down at their nail and biology-based activities.

'Right?' I ask again.

'Erm . . .' says Kas.

'Well . . .' clarifies Chlo.

'Oh,' I say. And suddenly the entire picture of my future, however fuzzy it might be, has completely changed.

Kas gets up, sits next to me on the bed and puts her hand on my arm. 'I'm sorry, Hay. We were going to talk to you about it,' she says, making it clear that they've talked to each *other* about this and not me. She goes on. 'But, what with everything that's been going on, no time seemed like the right time, y'know?'

And, yeah, OK, that does seem fair enough. But, still, the three of us make decisions together, don't we?

'I know it's a shock, hun,' adds Chlo, looking over her fanned-out nails at me. 'It's just . . . well, you know me. I'll totally suck at doing A levels. So I think I'm gonna apply to go on the beauty therapy course my sister's on.'

'And with me it's my mum and dad, y'know? They think I'll be better off if I leave and go to one of the sixth-form colleges, get into a better university, that kind of thing.'

'And what do *you* think, Kas?' I ask, sounding more peed off than I intended to, but, I mean, why hadn't they spoken to me about this before? What were they going to do: wait until next September when I would show up for school and wonder where they were and why I'm walking around on my own like Billy bloody no-mates? On the other hand, why hadn't I worked out that sixth form probably isn't Chlo's thing? And, now I think of it, of course Kas's super-ambitious parents would want her going somewhere better. I've been wrapped up in my other relationships so much I've let these ones slide – and these two are everything to me. But that's why this hurts so much.

'I, well, I agree with them,' Kas says, looking at her feet.

'Right, well, that's settled then,' I say.

'Oh, come on, Hay. Don't be like that,' says Chlo. 'It's months off anyway.'

'And maybe you could apply to one of the sixth-form colleges with me?' says Kas hopefully.

I roll my eyes; she totally knows that's impossible.

'They're miles away and Mum wouldn't be able to afford the bus fare, you know that,' I snap a little too harshly.

They're both looking at me with wide-eyed, concerned expressions. 'It's cool,' I say.

'You sure?' says Kas doubtfully.

'Yeah, of course,' I lie. Then I try to imagine what life would be like if I didn't see these guys every day and it feels like my heart's breaking a little, so I pathetically add, 'We'll still be friends, right?'

'*Best* friends,' says Kas, hugging me.

'Always,' says Chlo, reaching out to stroke our hair with her palms, her fingers curled away to protect her ham-coloured nails.

After a moment, I get up, telling them I should get home as Mum is now super paranoid about me since the whole Dad-coming-back-on-the-scene thing. But the truth is I want to get out of here. Give my brain some space.

I realize I've been stupid to presume things would stay the same with Kas and Chlo. But we've always talked about how great it will be when we're top of the school in the sixth form, wearing what we want and strutting about like we own the place. Now I realize that we haven't actually spoken about this for months and I've been so consumed by Dad and Dylan and my determination to succeed as a comedian that I've not seen the bleeding obvious changes in them too – Kas being ever more obsessed with her school-work and Chlo being ever more obsessed with her beauty stuff. Of course these changes were going to affect their decisions about their futures.

It's fair enough. And at least they've told me now. Like ending it with Dylan, sometimes it's just better to rip the plaster right off. Doesn't stop it stinging like a bitch though.

Chlo decides to leave too, so we all say goodbye and go our separate ways.

NINETEEN

At home, I tell Mum about me and Dylan, but I play it down and say it's fine. She gives me a hug, but isn't hugely sympathetic. She's trying to hide her pissiness from me, but it's clear she's not happy I've seen Dad. Which makes me feel guilty and crappy.

When I tell her I can't do the open-mic night tomorrow as the girls can't come, she just tells me I can have a 'lovely' evening with Ruben at home as she's out at some 'girls' night out' with her nursey friends.

Great, I think, *could this day get any worse?*

As I leave to go to my room, I say, 'Girls? A girls' night out? You sure you're invited? You haven't been a girl for decades, Mum, you do know that?'

'Oh, shut ya face,' she says.

I pace round my room. And I'm not so much upset now as angry. At Mum for making me feel guilty for not doing anything bad at all. At Kas and Chlo for merrily twitting off next year and leaving me in that crappy school alone. And at Dylan. Cos, however much I tell myself it's OK, it's not OK.

I know we had an actual thing there. I'm pretty sure he liked me. So why didn't he defend me when I told him I'd heard he was only with me for a joke? I go back to it. Maybe I'm just not girlfriend material, and maybe I don't frickin' wanna be.

I'm fed up with thinking maybe I'm not girlfriendy enough for Dylan, or Leo for that matter, because I'm not as much of a 'girl' as I should be. And so I make my escape into the funny, and film another ranty comedy video: 'Girls Are Idiots (And There's Nothing Wrong With That)'. Cos the people in the real world might be as difficult as hell, but the dudes in virtual YouTube-ville bloody love me. This one's less funny and more just a straight-up feminist rant though, so I guess it might not go down too well.

At this point, I don't care.

'Hey, dudes, it's your friendly PFG back again, this time with a proper feminist rantathon, so, if you don't like that kind of thing, well, you have been warned.

'Mo Mum's going on a girls' night out. Not a women's night out, no, a girls' night out. This is something she does now, that and a weekly fitness class called, I dunno, "ladies who lunge" or something. Cos apparently us females don't mind being called "ladies" and we don't mind being called "girls"; both terms are patronizing, but we're used to that. It's familiar to be patronized – comforting, like a kidnapper patting you on the head to say, "Well done for not screaming."

'But for some reason we don't want to be called "women" quite so much. The term seems a bit serious. It conjures up images of angry protesters, cardigans and jam-making.

'Now I'm a girl, and I'm proud of being a girl. But, dammit, I can't wait to become a woman. And when I'm a woman I want to be called a woman. Cos for boys that's the case, isn't it? We appreciate boys, and we appreciate men, and transitioning from one to the other is seen as an important step. Males go from one cool period of their life to another. "You're no longer a boy, you're a man now, and so your journey towards world domination begins."

'Now compare that to: "You're no longer a girl, you're a woman now, and so your downhill, withering, crumbling journey towards irrelevance begins." Cos that's a little bit how society still sees "women", so it's understandable why women want to cling on to girlhood as long as is humanly possible. Hence that bloody "Here Come the Girls" song, which normally accompanies some group of link-armed middle-aged women strutting along, desperately pretending they're still teenagers. You don't need to pretend you're teenagers! You're probably all massively accomplished lawyers and doctors and artists and whatever, just really cool, exciting women – embrace that instead! Or be massively flawed, overweight, stinky, selfish, stupid women and embrace *that* – after all, that describes eighty per cent of men, and the world still embraces them.

'Boys want to become men. They don't want to be called a boy when they're forty-six. But society still thinks that calling a woman a girl is paying her a compliment! Because for females it's apparently a "good" thing to remain young, innocent and fresh. Which, by the way, bears no resemblance to the actual girls I know who all have potty mouths and could fart for Britain.

'I'm not kidding. Us girls are not the weak, innocent, delicate flowers the word "girls" conjures up – little girls still wanna roll in the mud as much as little boys do, and teenage girls, well, we're frickin' idiots! Recently, one of my best friends dyed her hair green to try to impress a boy, and the other one is on a crazy diet that gave her the squits so bad she shat herself and I accidentally walked round school with my skirt shoved into these hideous pants – ' I hold my pants up to the camera – 'which as you can see – and indeed the whole school could clearly see – say "SUNDAY".

'My arse might not know what day of the week it is, but this I do know: girls are idiots, just like boys. And there's nothing wrong with that! The point is, the stuff we attach to all these terms – "boys", "girls", "women", "men" – it's all pressured crap and we need to let people just be people. And valuing youth and beauty in women over and above intelligence, ability, kindness, strength and personality is just dumb as frick.

'Personally, I don't want to be a girl for any longer than necessary – I want to be a woman! A big-titted, farty, inappropriate, funny, fabulous woman. Bring it on.'

And, yeah, I probably shouldn't have said all that about Chloe and Kas and I'm not even sure I believe everything I said about being called a 'girl', but, well, it's fun to rant and no one I know's watching this stuff anyway.

TWENTY

In the morning, I roll out of bed late. I mean, that's what PD days are for, right? Doesn't it stand for Pillow Day?

As I walk into the kitchen, Mum, Noah and Ruben, who clearly slept over again (and yes, I know I'm OK with him moving in, but somehow there's something way more 'eugh' about him just 'sleeping over'), are eating a late breakfast.

I get myself some toast and join them at the table. Ruben pours a second helping of 'Cheery-Oos' into Noah's bowl while reading out the 'fun fact' on the back of the box.

'Ooh, interesting fact here, Noah: what's the closest living relative of the T-rex?'

'Is it his Auntie Susan?' I answer with a mouth full of toast and 'Nutello'.

'Nope, it's a chicken,' Ruben answers.

I roll my eyes at Ruben's lack of humour.

'It's always a chicken! Why is every joke about chickens?' exclaims Noah.

'No, Noah, the thing about the T-rex isn't a joke,' says Ruben.

'No, not a very *good* one,' says Noah.

I laugh and stretch out my palm to Noah, who obliges me with a high five although he and Ruben have no idea why.

As Ruben and Mum ramble on to each other about the latest Netflix show they're bingeing, all I can see are the toast crumbs dancing around in his beard, which is looking stragglier than ever. Dad's clean-shaven face is so much more handsome. I mean, I'd kind of got used to Ruben's beard recently, like you get used to the brown mould round the edge of the bath, until you see someone else's bright, clean bath edges and you realize yours is actually super gross. He offers to clean up the kitchen while Mum 'takes the weight off her feet'. (I mean, seriously, is he calling her fat or what?)

'Thanks, Rubidoobs,' says Mum.

'"Rubidoobs"?' I say with a wince. But, come on, has there ever been a more vomit-inducing pet name?

Mum shoots me a look.

'Dawny,' says Ruben, 'you really can't get anything more in this dishwasher, you know. It's like –' then he puts on a deep, grand voice in an impression of the dishwasher – 'I'm so full, I couldn't eat another thing . . . Oh, go on then, just one more . . .'

Mum laughs as he closes up the dishwasher and I stand there, watching him with my hands on my hips. Then he notices the rinse-aid light flashing and continues with the dishwasher's voice as he tops it up. 'No, no, I can't possibly be expected to function in these circumstances. I do have *needs* you know and, if they're not met I shall simply go on strike. I mean, what am I to you? A slave? Look at this stuff, you dirty animals – I just washed all this yesterday. Is it too much to ask that you keep just one cup clean for twenty-four hours?!'

Ruben's all right. I know that. But now I've got Dad back again I can't help but compare the two . . . And Dad's so much funnier and *cleaner* than this bearded twit. Mum's still laughing as I roll my eyes. I grab some toast and disappear back up to my room.

I get busy making another video called 'Mum's Boyfriend Is an Idiot', to take my mind off things.

'So my mum has a boyfriend. And, ugh, that sentence in itself is just plain wrong. Mums should have book clubs, unused gym memberships, hysterectomies, that kind of thing, not boyfriends, right? But there it is: she's got a "boyfriend".

'And that's what she calls him, her "boyfriend". Not "partner" because she thinks that'll, God forbid, make her sound like a lesbian or, worse, a lawyer. Nope, he's her "boyfriend". Though how something with a beard so wild it comes with its own handler could be called a "boy" I'm not sure. I'm not kidding: his beard is so overgrown the neighbourhood have petitioned the council to come and mow it.

'So, yeah, when your mum has a boyfriend, you suddenly realize how they feel when you get a boyfriend. You become the parent, all paranoid and asking stupid questions, like: how long's he staying? How much have both of you had to drink tonight? You know I can hear everything that goes on upstairs, right? Does he even know how old you are? You do realize Dad's not going to like him?

'Ugh. I do get that my mum needs to have her own life. That's cool, just so long as it does not interfere with her meeting every one of my wants, needs and desires. That's fair enough, right? And then, of course, the boyfriend starts to move in and, I dunno, I guess it's the little things that annoy you, like his actual existence in the world . . .'

When I'm done, I press upload.

But now that distraction is over I start thinking about Dylan. So I check my messages. There's nothing from him, but then I guess there never will be again. Clearly, he doesn't care that we've broken up.

I lie back on my bed, listening to music – a thing that I do now since Dylan introduced me to the world of cool female artists who sing about real stuff. The problem is, my old way of coping with things by watching comedy was far more uplifting. Now when I'm sad I just listen to sad music, which only makes me sadder.

Maybe I massively overreacted. I'd SO wanted to kiss him yesterday. Truth is, deep in my insides, I still do. *Stupid insides.*

But he snogged Vicki – VICKI! Perfectly thin, preened, luscious-haired Vicki. How can I ever compete with that? And, surely he's thinking the same thing, I'm out of his normal league. Maybe that's why he never went to kiss me, because I would never live up to all the other gorgeous proper girlie girls he's snogged before?

At the end of his playlist, Spotify chooses similar songs I might like by other cool female artists. 'At Seventeen' by a singer called Janis Ian starts playing. It's the most depressing song I've ever heard, which is perfect for my mood right now. It's all about how you learn the truth as a teenager that life was built for the perfect and beautiful, not people like me.

I add the song to Dylan's playlist and wonder if he'll notice. It might make him understand where I'm coming from. Then again, he's probably too busy texting Vicki pictures of his lips right now and asking for a snog rematch and laughing with her about my utter patheticness.

I check my phone again. There are a few encouraging thumbs ups and good comments on my new vids. And Kas and Chlo have both sent me several messages saying something along the lines of 'sorry we didn't tell you we're leaving the school next year – we'll still be BFFs', etc. And I've replied back with messages along the lines of 'yeah, it's all cool'. And it is, I guess, and it's months away and everything.

Then at the top of my emails is – OH MY GOD – a message from Van, the impossibly cool London-comedy-club woman. I sit up in bed and hold my breath as I open it.

Hi, Haylah, it's Van here. Soooooo sorry it's taken me an age to get back to you – all crazy busy as always. But I have GOOD NEWS! We're putting on a comedy night in a few weeks' time at The Hawker Club in London, and a seven-minute spot has opened up. I know the owner well and it's a nice, friendly, clean place, and they're cool with you coming along as long as you're with an adult. So, if you've got any new stuff I thought maybe this would be a good chance to give a proper gig a go? It'll be £50, not much, but something, right? Let me know what you think ASAP!

Van x

OH MY GODDY GOD!!!!!! I have a proper comedy gig!!!!!!!

My heart pounding with excitement, I immediately email back with a massive YES and, worried that she might change her mind, I send her a link to my YouTube channel to show her I've definitely got some new stuff.

Then I text Kas and Chlo and Dad with the news before running downstairs to tell Mum and Ruben, who are now binge-watching *Game of Thrones* in the living room. They panic trying to find the remote and pause what looks to be medieval porn as I rush in.

'Haylah! Give us some warning before you explode into the room!' says Mum, red-faced.

I ignore her and stand right in front of them. Then I grandly announce, 'I have a gig – in London – a proper paying gig!'

Mum leaps up and gives me a massive hug. 'Oh, Haylah, that's fanTAStic – you clever girl!!'

'Whoa, dude, that is phenomenal!' says Ruben. 'Here, have some Pringles to celebrate.'

He passes me the tube of crisps as Mum releases me and I tell them the details. Mum sits back down on the sofa, grinning at me with one hand on her chest. 'That's MY girl!' she says proudly. 'How much does it pay?'

I laugh. 'Mum!'

'What? I'm not saying that's what's important – just interested, that's all!'

'Fifty pounds. For seven minutes.'

'Damn, that's a good hourly rate,' says Ruben. 'Well, cheers to you, girl. We're super proud. You deserve it.'

They both raise their coffee mugs to me and I clink them with the Pringles tube before tipping it up and 'drinking' the Pringles from it, making Ruben almost spit his coffee out with laughter.

I like that he's easy to make laugh. He's not that bad really.

As he smiles up at me, I actually feel guilty about the video I made earlier. I'll delete it later. Right now though I just wanna enjoy this feeling. I've got a gig. An actual paying comedy gig! Nothing's gonna bring me down from this high, for I, Haylah Swinton, AM A COMEDY GODDESS!!

TWENTY-ONE

Knowing there is work to be done, I make a plan. I'm going to do the open-mic tonight, cos I need to practise my new stuff, even though I've got no one to go with. Maybe Dad can take me? That would be awesome. I'll text him later. Before that, I'll watch about two hours of stand-up videos, taking notes on the best jokes and why they work. Then I'll have lunch and a nap so I'm in tiptop condition for tonight, spend a few hours on my set, and pick my outfit for this and the proper gig to treat it like a dress rehearsal.

The plan goes well until my planned short nap actually renders me unconscious for half the day. I'm just starting to come to when Noah bursts into my room and starts rolling around on the floor.

'Noah,' I mumble, squinting at him over the edge of the duvet, 'what are you doing?'

'I want to do a forwardy roll.'

'Why do you want to do a forward roll?'

'Because Humphrey in my class can do one and he said I was too fat to do one.'

Well, that immediately wakes my brain up with an overwhelming urge to slap Humphrey round the face. Then I remember that assaulting five-year-old children is unfortunately frowned upon.

'You're not fat, Noah. You tell that Humphrey to f– to leave you alone.'

'Oh, it's OK,' he says brightly. 'I bit him so he won't say it again.'

'Right, well, that's probably not the best way to deal with the situation, but well done for sticking up for yourself.'

And part of me is a little bit pleased.

He carries on with his task, looking like a small old person falling down then getting up, then falling down again on a never-ending loop.

'And why do you need to do this in *here*, Noah?'

'Because you have all this padding everywhere so it doesn't hurt my noggin.'

I look round my room and see that the floordrobe is currently so expansive you can barely see the carpet any more, which is actually a good thing because the carpet is super disgusting.

'Yeah, fair enough,' I say. 'Oooh, Noah, I have some good news!'

'Have slugs gone extinct?'

'What? No. I have a comedy gig, in London, a proper one!'

'Oh,' he says, getting up and falling over again. 'Is that why Mum and Ruben are cross with you?'

I freeze. 'What? No they're not. Wait, are they? Why?'

'I dunno, something about YouTube.'

Oh . . . my . . . giddy . . . goddy . . . God . . .

My heart starts hammering away inside my chest. My thoughts tumble over each other in quick succession. Somehow Mum and Ruben must have seen my YouTube channel and, oh frickin' crapballs, the stuff I ranted about Ruben. Maybe it's OK. Maybe they've seen that I've got a channel ... Maybe they haven't seen the video about Ruben yet. Or the one about Mum's girls' night out. Or, argh, the one about bad mums. Maybe there's still time to delete them. There's still hope.

Noah babbles on while I desperately search for my phone, which has somehow got lost in the lining of the duvet.

Eventually, I locate it and fish it out.

I stare at it, open-mouthed, my thumb frantically pawing at it. And for a moment I think about hiding the phone and myself back in the duvet lining in the hope that no one ever finds me. Because things are NOT good.

A quick glance at the crapstorm of messages I've received since I last looked at my phone this morning destroys all hope, not only for retaining my relationship with Mum and Ruben, but pretty much every other relationship too. *Everyone* has messaged me. Several times.

In a shaky voice, I tell Noah to go downstairs and tell Mum and Ruben I'm still asleep.

'Why?'

'Because otherwise I'll put a slug the size of Jabba the Hutt in your bed tonight.'

He runs out of my room, slamming the door behind him. And, yeah, OK, it was a cheap shot using his fear of slugs against him, but desperate situations call for desperate measures. *Who exactly has seen my channel and what the hell was I thinking putting so much ranty, borderline-offensive stuff out there?!*

I clutch my phone to my chest. I can't bring myself to look at the messages on there in any detail. I feel sick as I think about the huge potential for a massive nuclear fallout that I've created. Stuff about Dylan, stuff about my friends, stuff about Ruben, Mum and, urgh, Dad.

For a moment, a faintly hysterical voice in my head says, *It'll be OK. Just go and delete your channel now. No harm done. It'll be fine.* But deep down I know it's way too late. Like when you've flushed after doing a big poo and using way too much toilet paper, and you can see the waters rising, and you desperately hope and pray that they subside, but you know in your heart of hearts that there's no chance this situation will end in any other way than you standing in a sea of your own turd water, wearing nothing but socks and shame.

My hands shake as I force myself to rummage through my phone, discovering exactly what's happened, like doing an autopsy on a really grisly dead body.

So it turns out the good news is that Van replied several hours ago to say she 'love, love, LOVED' the stuff on my YouTube channel and that the gig's definitely on, and that – the very, very, VERY BAD news – she hoped I 'didn't mind' if she shared the channel on social media.

So she did. A lot. I wince as I read through the posts. And, yes, there's a tiny bit of me that's excited that she's bigging me up, but there's a colossal bit of me that just wants to leave the country, maybe the universe, right now.

Move over, old farts, there's a new young comedian in town – Haylah Swinton, the PFG (Pretty Funny Girl). Come and see her live on 12 November @TheHawkerClub, and check out her HILARIOUS videos *here*.

The PFG – Pretty Funny Girl – Haylah Swinton on bad dads: 'Having a dad is like weekday afternoon telly. It's all just pathetic dramas and *Pointless*.' Watch the whole hilarious rant *here*.

The PFG – Pretty Funny Girl – Haylah Swinton on Mum's new boyfriend: 'His beard is so overgrown the neighbourhood have petitioned the council to come and mow it.' Such a natural comic talent, watch her *here*.

The PFG – Pretty Funny Girl – Haylah Swinton's beauty tips: 'Repeat after me: I do not need full use of my internal organs. I DO need to look thinner.' This young feminist comedian is SOOOO funny. Watch her *here*. Then come and see her live on 12 November @TheHawkerClub.

As a result of Van's tweets, in the last few hours, my channel's gone, well, not exactly viral, but definitely mildly and horribly contagious. What with running lots of comedy nights and being a successful comedian herself, Van has a shedload of followers on social media, including a lot of comedians, many of whom have reposted her links. Which – argh! – would be SO exciting if it wasn't for all the crap I've said on there about people I know!

Then it seems a few people from school who follow her (friends of Leo's who met her at the comedy competition in London) saw that it was me and reposted them too, which led to lots more people at school seeing them and probably resulted in someone in the mums' network seeing the links. And I can only guess that one of them alerted my mum to it. And that's why she and Ruben are now wanting to kill me. And, of course, they're not the only ones.

Chlo sends a message. Then Kas.

C: Dude, can't believe you told the world I dyed my hair green to impress a boy! And Kas is going TO KILL YOU.
K: YOU TOLD PEOPLE I *SHAT* MYSELF?!

My heart sinks further as I read Dylan's message.

So did you *really* have to tell *everyone* I was such a crap boyfriend? And I thought you liked the key ring!

Oh God, oh God, oh God.
Nothing from Dad yet so I message him a casual 'Hey, how you doing?' sort of thing, but get nothing back.

And then, waiting for me downstairs, is Ruben. And, argh, Mum, who is going to go apocalyptic on my arse and for good reason.

I look up my channel on YouTube and see that the views keep going up. Which should be a brilliant thing, but it's not. It feels awful.

Then I also see the new comments. Some nice ones. Some not so nice. I sink down on to the bed as I read.

I agree with Stacy Beeatch – fat girls should hide themselves away. So should you, PFG, you unfunny ✢✢✢✢✢✢✢.

Get this Unattractive Unfunny Girl off my screen NOW. MY EYES, MY EYES!

Why you so mean to people? Maybe take a look at yourself, girl.

And on and on.

Of course I know about how crappy people can be to each other on the internet. It feels very different when it's directed squarely at me. But I didn't mean those things I said about my friends and family, not really. I just got swept up in the rants.

Blunt anger and viciousness sells; it's what people want. Look at Trump. Oh God, I'm the Trump of comedy. I don't want to be *that*! I don't want to be known for slagging people off and going for the easy laugh at the expense of others. I delete the videos where I talk about Kas, Mum, Dad, Chlo, Dylan and Ruben.

But it's out there now; it's too late. The metaphorical toilet has indeed overflowed and I am now standing in a rising stink-tide of my own poo juice. And I deserve it.

TWENTY-TWO

Still too scared to face the music downstairs, I have a shower and get dressed, wondering what the hell I'm going to do about it all. Then another message pings in. Holding it at arm's length and wincing, I look at my phone, bracing myself for further hideousness.

It's Dylan again, simply saying, **You OK?**

I sigh and sit on the edge of my bed as I stare at the message. I've dumped this guy and publicly called him a bad boyfriend, but he's worrying about me and asking if I'm OK. Frankly, it's way more than I deserve.

Eventually, after composing about seventy-two different versions, I reply.

H: I'm OK, thanks. I didn't mean any of that stuff and I do genuinely like my key ring. I was just 'trying' to be funny and not really thinking it through. Sending you a big fat sack of sorry.

I wait, staring at my phone for a reply. Eventually, the three dots of anticipation start dancing on my phone as he types.

D: Sack of sorry accepted. And it's true I *was* a bit of a crap boyfriend. It's cool. And it *was* funny.

I can't quite believe it.

H: Thanks. Still sorry though. I'm such a knob.
D: You are. But luckily I like knobs.
H: Er . . .?
D: Wait, that came out wrong.
H: Now, come on, you KNOW I make it a policy never to write 'LOL', but I gotta tell you I'm dangerously close to typing that right now.
D: Hehe. Are you still doing the open-mic tonight?

God, the open-mic. I'm not exactly feeling in the right mood to get up and make people laugh. But it might help to remind me I can still be funny without upsetting or attacking anyone. And I could really do with the practice for this London gig. Ugh, if Mum even lets me do that now. And Dad still hasn't got back to me.

H: No, I don't think I have anyone to go with and I don't think I should.
D: Balls, it'll all be fine. U should totally do it. I'll come with you. If you want.

And at this point I almost cry.

H: Really?
D: Really. If you can get a lift there, my dad'll take you home.
H: OK, that would be cool.
D: See u tonight. I'll be there at 7.

I put my phone down and breathe a sigh of relief. Flopping back on my bed, I stare up at my Comedy Wall of Hilarity and Greatness. 'The show must go on, right, guys?'

And, if Dylan can forgive me, maybe Kas, Chlo, Mum, Ruben and Dad can too?

But I can't bring myself to try to sort all that out yet. It's like when you've exceeded your pain threshold plucking your first eyebrow. It may leave things unbalanced, but there's no way you can immediately put yourself through a second ordeal. I'm not ready to have the big angry conversation with Mum and see Ruben looking all pathetic and hurt, and I'm not exactly sure how the hell to apologize to Kas and Chlo. And then there's Dad. We've only just started rebuilding our relationship. What if I've killed it before it's begun? On the other hand, I let him back into my life after some truly crapola behaviour on his part so surely the man could cut me some slack?

I need to get away from it all, from everyone, from the horrible guilt-butterflies swirling round my insides. I go to my desk and write a note to Mum simply saying, *Sorry, Mum. Feel awful about it all. Gone to Grammo's.* Then I creep downstairs, where I can hear the murmuring of the TV from the living room. I leave the note on the bottom step and tiptoe down the hall and out of the door to escape to Grammo's house.

I tell Grammo about it all and she does what grandmas are supposed to do: tells me everything will be all right, gives me hugs, bakes me cookies and then we binge-watch *Queer Eye*. Thankfully, there are very few situations that can't be improved with hugs, baked goods and Jonathan telling us that, in his world, 'Everything that's romantic is topless.'

Then I fight back my laughter as Grammo says, 'I do like a well-groomed man. I tell you what, if that Karamo's married, his wife is one lucky lady,' revealing that she hasn't quite got the point of the show.

Before the fourth episode starts playing, she turns the TV off. 'You know you've got to talk to your mum, right?'

Argh, life's so much easier with your head well and truly shoved in the sand.

'Yeah, I know. I'm just not ready, not yet.'

'Look, your video about Ruben: I get why you're not wild about him, Hay. He's not your dad. Plus, well, he's a bit of a drip.'

I laugh, which then makes me feel worse. Even if he's a drip, I've never heard him say or do anything that wasn't super kind.

'That's the thing, I'm fine with him. He's cool. I don't know why I said that stuff really. I don't know why I said any of it. It's just all been so crazy lately and I guess I wanted to get it all out, to faceless people whose judgement didn't matter. I didn't think it would hurt anyone, but I guess I wasn't really thinking about anyone but me.'

'Well, yeah,' says Grammo, which was a slightly blunter response than I was expecting but nothing less than I deserve. She puts down her cookie and turns to me on the sofa. 'Haylah, love, I know it's tough that things are changing, that you and your friends are going to be doing different things next year, and Ruben's moving in and you've got your first boyfriend so no doubt your hormones are hammering away at your brain, making you say some silly things.'

'Can we leave my hammering hormones out of this?'

She laughs. 'Sorry, dear. But the fact is things change. Sometimes for the worse and sometimes for the better, but you can't really stop it. That's just life: it's a never-ending rollercoaster with ups and downs –'

'And a questionable safety record,' I add.

'Correct,' she says, 'and your dad is an OK guy, and a pretty good dad when he's around. But to be honest he was a terrible husband and your mum's better off with drippy Ruben.'

'Harsh,' I say. Though I know it's true.

'Harsh but fair,' says Grammo.

'I know. Argh, I'll talk to her later. I'll just give her a chance to calm down a bit first.'

'Probably a good idea. I spoke to her on the phone when I was baking . . .'

I'm not sure I wanna know what Mum said. 'You did?'

'Just to tell her you're all right. Anyway, she said she was relieved to hear you're OK, but, well, the conversation came with a loud soundtrack of a lot of crockery being flung round the kitchen.'

Oh God, angry-mum kitchen sounds are the worst sounds in the world.

'Yikes. I'd better give it a few more hours.'

She phones Mum while I cower in the corner in case Mum jumps right through the phone to strangle me. Grammo asks if I can stay for tea and whether it's OK if she takes me to the open-mic where my friends are going to meet me, which, yes, isn't exactly the truth as it's only Dylan meeting me there, but, hey, he's a friend so it's not *technically* a lie.

After a lot of persuasion from Grammo, involving her telling Mum that I'm feeling crazy guilty and stressed about the whole thing, and that maybe it's a good idea if me and her have a bit of a break from each other for the evening, Mum says OK. Grammo's such a boss.

Later we pull up outside the pub and Grammo says she's not keen on just dropping me off, but she has a salsa group to get to with June. 'But I could cancel it and come in, dear, if that's what you want?'

And I know Grammo's cool, but can you imagine turning up for a comedy gig, and what could possibly be a romantic reunion with your ex (please, God), with your grandma holding your hand?

'No, it's fine!' I garble. 'They've just texted me. They're in there now – look.'

I point vaguely to the pub, relying on Grammo's bad eyesight, hoping she doesn't actually see that the only people I can actually spot are two middle-aged men in Barbour jackets.

'Oh, OK, love.' She squints through the window. God, she really shouldn't be driving with her eyesight as bad as it is, but it's worked in my favour tonight so I don't mention it.

'Someone wants to pull in behind you though, Grammo, so I'll just jump out quick. Thanks for today – you're a star. Love you. Enjoy your salsa-ing.'

I kiss her goodbye and walk into the pub.

Immediately, I realize this was a bad idea. Dylan isn't here. But Leo is.

TWENTY-THREE

Argh, I hadn't even considered Leo being here. Yet there he is with a group of mates. Luckily he's not with that girlfriend of his though, as I think the sight of them all over each other would have finished me.

Why do I feel like this though? I haven't seen him that much lately. And I (maybe) have Dylan now. But every time I see Leo he makes me feel special, like I'm someone. Not something to be ashamed of. But isn't he like that with everyone? Didn't I learn *anything* last year?

Even with everything else going on, as with every other time, seeing him reignites all my old warm, electric, stupid crush feelings. I mean, yes, he did turn out to be a selfish git, but he was super nice to me last time I saw him and when he turns on that charm it's hard to remember the bad stuff.

And he chose to kiss me. Just once, but still.

I really don't want him to see me though. It'll be insanely embarrassing that I'm here with no friends. So I hang around the toilets, like a weirdo, then skulk at the back of the pub, pretending to be engrossed in my phone for what feels like an eternity.

If only Dylan would turn up. I mean, I don't know if we're even together any more, but at least if Dylan was here and Leo did look over he'd see me with a boy that wasn't him.

I look at my watch. Dylan is already twenty minutes late. *Brilliant.*

Keeping my head down, I walk round to the other side of the bar as far away from Leo as possible. I order a Diet Coke from Kingston, hoping he doesn't turn round and tell his son, 'Look who's here – that fat loser girl who used to follow you around!'

Instead, he asks, 'You putting your name down for a set tonight then?'

And I know that's why I came here, but now, on my own, after the day I've had, I can't even begin to think about getting up on stage and trying to make people laugh.

I smirk awkwardly at him and mumble, 'No, probably not tonight,' as I pay him and take my drink.

I sit at a table in a dark corner and stare down at my phone, even though I still have no messages (still nothing from Dad) and nothing to look at. But I'm sitting alone in a public place, so if I choose to stare around the room instead of at my phone I'll just look like a complete nutter. Plus, I don't want to risk catching Leo's eye.

The pub fills up and the first act goes on. They're right over the other side of the pub, but I can just about see, and unfortunately hear, them. It's some wet female duo, one lightly tickling a guitar while the other warbles on, refusing to enunciate her consonants.

Dylan is now almost an hour late. I send him a text asking when he'll be here, but get nothing back. I realize with a sinking feeling that he's not coming. He must have decided that I'm not worth the effort. After all, I did describe him on my video, which has now been seen by thousands, as smelling weird and barely moving unless he's eating. Or maybe this is all part of the 'joke' that was going out with me in the first place – a way to get me back or humiliate me further.

Another ten minutes roll past and I know I need to get out of here. What was I thinking? I'm not going to do a set anyway, and what I really should be doing is sorting out stuff with Mum, Ruben, Dad, Kas and Chlo, not sitting here like a fat lemon.

I decide to get some air. I'll ring Grammo from outside. It's way too noisy to make a call from in here anyway, and if I text her I'll be lucky to get a reply by next Thursday, and I really don't fancy being here that long.

I muddle my way through the crowd as they cheer on the current act, a large woman singing opera to a muffled backing track.

I push my way out into the dimming night air and sit on a bench next to the door.

I look at my phone. Still nothing from Dylan. Still nothing from Dad.

I phone Grammo to ask her to pick me up, but there's no answer. She's probably in full salsa-dance swing with June.

Out of desperation, I text Mum, obviously not telling her that my friends aren't here, but instead saying that I'm feeling a bit depressed about everything and just wanna come home. Which is pretty much the truth anyway. She sends a short, sharp text back telling me that, In case you forgot, I'm at a girls' night out, but fine – I'll be there in twenty minutes. Which only piles a dollop more stinky guilt on to the toilet-load I'm already feeling.

'You going without saying hey?' says a voice so smooth you could skim it across water.

I look up and see Leo walking down the pub steps towards me. My stupid heart does a backflip through my ribs.

'Oh, hey, Leo, didn't, erm, didn't see you in there.'

He smiles *that* smile. 'Yeah, you did.' He sits next to me on the bench, his thigh almost touching mine.

Stop it.

'You doing a set tonight?' I ask as casually as possible.

'Yep, I'm up later. Got some cool new stuff I wanna try out; you should stick around for it. Are you doing something?'

'No, Jeez, no. I don't know why I'm here, really. I was going to meet someone, but, well, he hasn't showed so . . .'

Why did I say 'he'?! Oh, please don't ask questions and just go now, Leo. This is bad enough as it is.

'He? Ah, so is this the guy you dumped or, what was it, the "smelly iguana" that buys you "bitch" key rings?'

Oh crapballs, so he saw the videos too. Yep. Of course he did.

'Hmm.' I force a half-laugh. 'Yep, that's him. So you saw my videos then?'

He leans back on the bench with his arms behind his head. 'Yeah, I think everyone did.'

'Oh God,' I say, unable to keep up the pretence of being cool and fine about everything any more and flopping forward with my head in my hands.

'What? It's great stuff – and you've got a gig with Van in London. Man, I'd kill for that!'

'Yeah, but I've managed to piss everyone off in the process. I mean, it's not worth all that, is it?'

Leo shrugs. 'I dunno – they'll get over it. You were being funny and you were being honest. You've gotta be true to your truth. They'll understand.'

'I was being a knob.'

'Yeah, well, it turns out your truth is being a knob – there's no shame in that.'

We both laugh. And, although he doesn't seem to get the weight of what I'm feeling, I like that he's making the effort to try to make me feel better.

I lean back next to him, but carry on looking straight ahead. He turns to me and I can faintly feel his breath on my ear as he says, 'So has no-romance boy stood you up then?'

A small tingle of excitement runs up my spine. *Stop it.*

'Yeah, but I don't blame him.'

'I do,' he says. 'Hay, like I said, you're funny, you're cool, you're gorgeous – anyone would be mad to stand you up.'

And I know he's just being flirty because he's Leo, but, man, it feels good.

'Oh, come off it,' I fake-protest.

I turn to him to shoot him a sarcastic smirk, but his calm, serious expression only centimetres from my face wipes the smirk away and for a moment we just stare at each other. Then time slows as he moves towards me . . . What is happening . . .? But before my brain has a chance to stop my mouth from being an idiot . . . we kiss.

Only it's not like last time. There are no explosions going off in my head, no sparks of electricity. Instead, I'm desperate to feel something other than the crap I've been feeling all day. And OK, yes, it also feels amazing to be wanted, to feel like I'm not just the joke, the embarrassment, that I'm the leading lady rather than the comedy sidekick. But this is insane. I've barely seen this guy recently and all he has to do is say a few nice things and *boom* we're sucking face? Really, am I that desperate?

After just a couple of seconds, I totally know I don't want this and I pull away.

'Sorry,' I say. 'Not what I'm after, mate.'

He shrugs again, though with a slightly confused expression. I doubt he's used to being turned down. 'Suit yourself,' says Leo. 'I hope you do find what you're after.'

Then both of us whip our heads round to look over the other side of the road, where someone just shouted, 'Haylah?'

And, of course, it's Dylan.

Argh, crapnuts!! Thanks again, universe. Except this was my doing. It's not the universe's fault I'm a total idiot.

Dylan frowns at us, his mouth hanging open in disbelief, and then starts marching away.

I leap up from the bench. 'Dylan, wait!' I yell, but he ignores me. Which is fair enough.

'Whoops,' says Leo with a laugh – an *actual* laugh, the git.

I shoot him a look. 'Sorry,' he says, and I think it's genuine. 'Look, can I help – go and tell him it was all me or something?'

'No,' I say shakily. 'Forget it – this is my bad.'

'All right,' he says, looking relieved. 'See you around, Hay, and good luck!'

Then he gets up and actually winks at me before wandering back up the pub steps. Smug git. What the hell was I thinking?!

I cross the road and run after Dylan, hoping he'll listen and that I'll say the right thing, whatever the hell that is. When I reach him, I grab his arm to turn him round to me.

'What?' he snaps. He frowns down at me, jutting his jaw out. I expected him to be mad at me, but, to make things worse, his eyes actually look more sad than angry.

'Wait,' I bluster. 'I'm sorry – that was nothing. It was just Leo; he's nothing. You were late and –'

'I was *late*? Really? That's what you're going with? Cos if you must know I dropped my bloody phone in the toilet and then Dad was stuck at work with that stupid band and I've been feeling terrible all evening about leaving you here on your own, but now I can see you're not on your own, are you? So I'll go.'

Ouch. I felt bad and now I feel terrible.

He goes to turn from me, but I keep a hard hold of his shirt sleeve so he can't. 'Please, just hear me out.'

He yanks his arm out of my grip and for a moment I think he's going to storm away, but thankfully he folds his arms with a stern 'I'm listening' look.

I go on. 'Dylan, I'm really sorry. I dunno what I was thinking. It's been such a weird, crappy day. It really was nothing though. And,' I add stupidly, 'we were on a break?' Yeah, cos that line always works so well.

He huffs angrily through his nose, and I brace myself.

'You broke up with me because I snogged Vicki ten months before we were together, but it's OK for you to suck face *just* after we break up?!'

Yeah, OK, I deserved that.

'I didn't break up with you for *that*. I broke up with you cos when I told you Vicki said you were only dating me for a joke you didn't even defend me. In fact, I think your exact inspired words were "dunno".'

His cheeks go a little red – with what? Anger? Frustration? Embarrassment? It's hard to tell. But his tone definitely sounds pissy now. 'I didn't know what to say! Clearly, I'm not with you for a *joke*. I mean, it would be the longest build-up to a punchline in history, right?'

And I can't help but love that he's just used the science of comedy to make a point. But I need more explanation than that and he knows it.

His voice softens. 'I'm sorry. I know I get it all wrong, Hay.' He runs his fingers through his hair. 'We're not all as good at this stuff as *some* guys are.' He nods towards the now-empty bench on the other side of the road. 'I've never been someone's "boyfriend" before; I don't know what I'm doing. But I thought that was part of what made you so cool – that you didn't mind about that stuff, wouldn't want all that meaningless other crap, flowers and grand romantic gestures and, I don't know, pink bloody bows.'

'I don't want pink bows. But I do want someone who makes me feel wanted, someone who isn't embarrassed to be with me.'

'I'm not embarrassed to be with you, Hay. I'm just not good at showing it.'

'Yeah, well, if I'm gonna be with someone, I want to know that they wanna be with me.'

He looks down and shuffles his feet on the pavement, going redder in the face, like he's building up to something. And I can't tell if it's a good something or a bad something. Then he looks directly at me with a serious and forceful look I've never seen on him before.

'Hay, I *really* like you,' he says quietly, 'like really, massively, can't-stop-thinking-about-you, wanna-be-with-you-all-the-time *like* you . . .'

My mouth drops open. And my heart does a little jump. Hearing him say this reminds me of just how much I also massively like him.

After a long pause, he continues, still looking down at his feet. 'And I . . . really wanna kiss you, but . . .'

'But what?' I ask in a shaky voice, my insides doing somersaults of excitement.

He sighs and looks back down. 'But I'm scared about getting it wrong, OK? I keep thinking about that bloody tea-drinking cartoon thing they showed us in sex ed. You know, the big analogy where, if you don't *know* if someone wants tea, you shouldn't just pour tea down their throat. I didn't know what you wanted and I didn't know how to ask you without sounding like a total spanner, so I . . . stupidly ended up doing nothing instead of maybe doing something wrong, and now –'

'Shut up, I want tea!' I bluster like a big tea-drinking slag. 'I want you to make me some tea. But not, you know, actual tea. I'm saying I want you to kiss me. In case I wasn't being clear.'

He looks at me and I think there are tears in his eyes, which immediately makes my eyes fill as I already know what he's about to say.

'Too late, Hay.'

'No it's not – don't say that,' I plead pathetically.

'It is. You know it is. You were literally just snogging another guy. And not just any old guy. I've seen the way you look at Leo whenever he's around. I don't wanna be with someone who makes me feel like crap, either, Hay. We're done.'

And I'm speechless.

It never crossed my mind that Dylan had noticed that I go all crazy whenever Leo's name is mentioned, or how I acted that night in the pub when they were both there. Seeing me snogging Leo just now must have made him feel as bad as I did when I caught Leo snogging Keesha last year. I was so wrapped up in whether or not Dylan was being a 'good boyfriend' it hadn't occurred to me that my girlfriending abilities weren't all that either. I've completely blown it. There's nothing else I can say or do to make it right.

We stand there in silence for a moment.

'Have you got a lift home?' he asks gently.

'Yeah,' I say, staring down, too ashamed to look him in the eye. 'My mum's coming.'

'Then I'll wait with you till she's here.'

Dammit, he's such a nice guy. Which of course makes me feel worse.

And he walks a few steps away and leans against the shop door behind us and drums softly on his thighs while I keep staring straight ahead.

Then, desperate just to say something, I pathetically offer, 'Sorry about your phone.'

'Doesn't matter,' he mutters from behind me. 'SIM was fine and I've shoved it in my dad's old smashed-screen one.'

'Erm . . . Ruben knows a guy in town who can fix them real cheap.'

Oh, do shut up, mouth.

'It's not worth it,' he says flatly. 'Some things just aren't fixable.'

Ouch.

I continue to stare up the road and put all my efforts into not crying.

I can't believe I've done this. I can't believe I kissed stupid bloody Leo and I can't believe I've only just realized how much I want to be with Dylan AFTER we've broken up. WHY AM I SUCH A LOSER??

I see our car in the distance and brace myself because now, to top it all off, I'm going to have to deal with a rage-filled Mum.

She pulls up next to us.

'Bye, Hay,' mumbles Dylan as he turns and walks away.

But I can't answer him because my throat's got a lump in it the size of a pine cone and my nose has filled with snot and my head's pounding behind my scrunched eyes.

Even though Mum can tell I'm upset, she's obviously decided she's not in the mood to comfort me – which I guess is fair enough. She says very little in the car, just short, sharp sentences about practical stuff like, 'I've gotta get back to the girls', yes, GIRLS' night out . . . There's lasagne in the fridge . . . I'll be back late.'

She drops me at home and I run in, ignore an alarmed and confused Ruben as I charge past him into the kitchen to fill my arms with anything and everything snackable, then disappear to my room, possibly for the rest of my life.

TWENTY-FOUR

The next morning I cry a lot and sleep a lot and generally wallow, like a soggy bit of scummy bread disintegrating in a soup of misery and guilt.

I avoid Mum and Ruben. There's nothing I can say to them that'll make it better.

From the safety of my bed, I text Kas and Chlo and Dad with apologies, but hear nothing back.

I think about Dylan. With all my thoughts about what crap us teenage girls face, I guess it's easy to forget that teenage boys get it pretty tough too. Whilst teenage girls have ridiculous expectations placed on us that we're supposed to live up to, boys have pressures weighing on them too. They can't all be as confident and cocky as Leo and I don't want them to be. It's presumed they're all 'after one thing', when they're not. The fact is that on paper Dylan might be the classic loud-mouthed, loutish boy, but when I'm with him I've never felt anything other than respected, appreciated and safe. And, ugh, the reason he didn't kiss me wasn't because he didn't fancy me, but because he saw me as something more than a thing to be fancied and grabbed at.

I text Dad again. I still reckon if anyone owes me a bucket of forgiveness it's him. And he's pretty good with advice, which I could really do with right now. But I get nothing back.

Mum said if I got close to him again he'd only leave and hurt me. I guess she was right. He's spent some time with me, realized I'm not worth the effort and now he's left me. Again.

I bury my head under my duvet, taking my phone with me, which is pumping out Lizzo, but even her relentless positivity isn't shaking me out of my brain funk.

Mum shouts angrily up the stairs that she and Ruben are going out for a few hours and they're leaving me in charge of Noah. I loudly grunt a reply and when the door slams shut I emerge from my wallowing and head downstairs. Me and Noah eat Pringles and watch *Harry Potter*. While it's on, Noah sits on the rug and builds a Lego model of an 'aubergine-fuelled spaceship hotel' while I lie back on the sofa, slipping in and out of sad naps filled with disturbing dreams.

Halfway through the film, Noah climbs up to sit on me and I look up as his little round freckled face stares down at me intently. 'Why you grumpy?' he asks with a frown.

'Noah, am I funny? I mean, do you think I should carry on with this whole comedy thing?'

'Erm, yep,' he says.

Quite why I continue to put so much faith in the career advice of a dude who thinks the days of the week are

Oneday, Twosday, September, Sleepy, Happy and Steve is beyond me.

'Yep. You funny, Haylah. You make people laugh and that makes them happy.'

'At least it should do,' I mumble to myself.

'I like questions. Ask me more.'

'Hmm . . . OK, am I pretty?' I say, doing my best over-the-top pouty selfie look.

He giggles, then leans in and examines me, using a teaspoon to push and prod my facial features around before concluding, 'You have bogeys. But the bogeys are very pretty.'

'Thanks.'

'You're welcome,' he says, still unable to detect sarcasm.

When Mum and Ruben return I disappear, back upstairs and force myself to watch my PFG videos one more time, to see if they were worth losing my friends and family over. And, of course, they weren't. They had some funny lines in them, sure, but getting a laugh is not worth it if it's at the expense of others. Or yourself. It makes the laughs cheap and easy. I read the comments again and start to side with the trolls.

But they've got me wrong too. I'm not a fat, angry, self-hating girl lashing out at the world because it's easier than trying to fit in – that *isn't* me. Not the real me. I like me. OK, not right now, not today, but generally speaking, if I saw me in a room, I'd wanna be friends with me.

That's the Haylah I need to put out into the world. The lovable, honest and confident one, with maybe just a touch of sass and sarcasm, sure, but not the bitter and twisted angry thing I'm seeing in these videos.

I realize now why I got into comedy when Dad left. It was a way for me to escape the crap, to escape from myself, to avoid the realities. But maybe it can be something else. Maybe it can be about delving further into me, not away, about being vulnerable and genuine and proud of who I am, instead of angrily running away from it. So I grab a fresh notebook and start writing new stuff. Genuine stuff. Stuff from the heart. Stuff girls need to hear.

I keep the sarcasm, but I ditch the bitchiness. I keep the wit, but aim it in the right direction. I write about the value of friends, about what the world would be like without mums, about how hard it must be to date a single mum with kids, about valuing your own beauty and ignoring the haters, about the good guys who are out there and the bad rap they get because of the bad guys. And, of course, I make sure it's funny AF.

Here are a few of my favourite bits:

I gotta give my mum's boyfriend some respect cos dating a single mum is a tough job. Can you imagine the job interview? 'Yeah, so there's no training and, as for health and safety, well, we don't have those things. The other guys in the office will either constantly annoy you or hate you. You will never be the boss, or even the boss's favourite. And there'll be lots of screaming, and not just from you. But, hey, if you like chaos, Cheestrings and exhaustion – the job's yours!

The difference between *friends* and *best* friends is that, if you fell down a hole, a friend would smile and sympathize, whereas a best friend would laugh so hard at you they'd fall down there too. Then you'd both PMSL so hard you'd float your way out on a sea of wee. Best friendships — they're not pretty, but they save your life.

Us girls waste a lot of time working out why we don't fit in. But, like the last size-eighteen outfit I bought, sometimes you gotta realize that if you don't fit in, it's the label that's wrong, not you. Or, in this case, the fact that you thought the number referred to size, not months old. Though I still think I'd look damned fine in a Peppa Pig playsuit.

I've been told I dress like a boy and I've been told that I dress like a lesbian. But not only are neither an insult, they both can't be true, right? Cos I haven't met many lesbian boys. And in a lot of ways the most girlie thing you can be is a lesbian. A *girl* who likes *girls* so much she wants to be with other *girls*. That sounds pretty frickin' girlie to me.

When I'm done, I send the link to my new vids to Van with a message saying I'm not going to be doing the ranty comedy any more, so if she wants to cancel my spot at the gig I'm totally OK with that. And I am. Truth is, getting gigs and subscribers is great, but not if I'm paying for it with my soul.

I message links out to Dylan, Kas, Chlo, Mum, Ruben and Dad.

I'm sorry x

No one replies. And somehow the most hurtful non-reply is Dad. I mean, haven't I forgiven him a lot to let him back into my life? Does he not owe me one? Or actually, like, a thousand? He seemed so genuine. He seemed to really like me, to really want to be in my life again, but maybe he just liked the idea of having a daughter again, and the reality is too much. So he's left me again. Making me the idiot that believed him. And making Mum, urgh, right all along. I'm about to chuck my phone across the room in anger and frustration when Mum replies.

When you're ready, come downstairs. I want to talk to you.

For a moment, I wonder how quickly Amazon could deliver a bombproof jacket and a hard hat. But I know I've gotta face this sooner or later. It's as unavoidable as a fart in a tent. And, the worst thing is, it's my own fart.

TWENTY-FIVE

After Noah's gone to bed, I pluck up the courage to go downstairs. I brace myself for a Mum-attack. But when I walk into the living room she gives me a soft smile and pats the sofa seat next to her. Relieved, I go over, Radio 2 wafting in from the kitchen where Ruben is keeping himself busy, loading his friend, the dishwasher.

I sit next to her and she pulls me in for a big hug. I hug her back. And the tears start to flow.

'I'm sorry, Mum. I've really stuffed up,' I whimper into her cleavage.

I expect her to agree and say, 'Yeah, you really have,' but instead she makes a few sniffling sounds of her own and says, 'Well, it runs in the family cos so have I.'

I sniff and pull back from her, our hands falling into each other's. 'What you talking about, woman?' I say. 'You haven't done anything wrong.'

She nods sadly. 'I have, Hay. I've been a selfish prick. Yes, your videos were a bit, well . . . they were pretty rude.'

'I know,' I say, my guilty eyes looking down at my lap.

She lets go of one of my hands and cups my chin, gently raising my face until my eyes look into hers – 'But, like I said before, us adults should know better, yet we don't. I've been pissed off that you're seeing your dad and that's not fair of me.'

Instead of getting angry (I've done enough of that), I listen and try to get it from Mum's point of view. She does all the hard work, working doubly hard so we can eat, watching dismal children's TV with Noah and pretending to enjoy it, nursing us through the night when we're sick, watching all our school plays, putting up with all our moaning and constant snack demands, and then Dad waltzes back in and Mum's gotta just suck it. And, let's face it, it's easy to be a good parent if you're just taking the kid to the beach or bowling, but it's the never-ending snot-wiping, parents'-evening-attending, school-shoe-buying and soft-play-centre-enduring that's the real test of parenting.

'That's OK, Mum,' I say. 'I get it.'

She smiles, then heaves a big sigh and I know whatever she's about to say is hard for her to get out. 'He wasn't a bad dad though, Hay, and he did, *does*, love you, and it's selfish of me to make you feel bad about that.'

I swallow hard. 'Thanks, Mum. But, I dunno, maybe you were right. He's not been replying to my messages and maybe he's left me again, Mum.' I dip my head into her chest again and sob like a pathetic baby.

'Oh, Hay, I'm so sorry,' she says, stroking my hair. 'He wouldn't do that, baby. He wouldn't frickin' dare. Look . . .'

But she can't find the words for some reason, and then she stops stroking my hair and the air in the room changes somehow. I pull my head away from her. Her face is scrunched up, all guilty and sad, like Noah's when you catch him stealing a biscuit from the cupboard.

I sniff back the tears. 'What is it, Mum?' I say suspiciously.

'Hay, I'm sorry, but the truth is I told him to back off, to leave you be for a while so I could sort all this stuff out with you. I'm sorry, but you need to know it's nothing you've done, Hay, honestly.'

And, although I'm relieved he hasn't stopped contacting me because of something I've done, for a moment I'm totally pissed that she did this and didn't tell me – didn't tell me! I frown at her, my eyes still red from the tears.

She holds my hand again. 'Look, I saw those videos and how angry you were at me, Ruben and your dad, and I wanted him to give you some space to figure it all out. But I was wrong. It was a stupid thing to do. I know he's not the only one to blame for how you feel.'

And my pissiness goes. I know she's not perfect, believe me. But I also know how crappy Dad made her feel when he left, and that this is crazy hard for her. I also know that she wouldn't do anything to hurt me on purpose.

'No, Mum, I know he was a git to you.'

'Yeah, but that was a long time ago, and I need to get over it. For you. For Noah.'

'Noah?' I say, wondering where she's going with this.

'Yeah.' She leans over, picks up her glass of wine from the coffee table and takes a huge gulp, before saying, 'I've invited Dad round for lunch tomorrow.'

'Holy crapballs, really?' I say, grinning from ear to ear and not quite believing what I'm hearing. Could it possibly be the case that this is the start of our broken family actually finding a way to work like a regular broken family? 'You sure?'

'Yeah. I think so. In fact, I know so, especially now I see the smile it just put on your face. Your dad's moved back here, so I have to assume he's not going anywhere. I need to suck it up and let him see you guys. If that's what you want.'

I can't believe she's doing this for us. Dad's a good dad. I'm pretty sure of it. A really truly terrible husband, but a good dad. And I'm sure he could be a good one to Noah too.

'I do. Thank you.' I hug her again.

'Oh, and I love the new videos, Hay. So much more you,' she says into my hair, making me grin some more.

Then Ruben pokes his hairy head out of the kitchen door. 'Room for a wild beard and its handler?' he asks.

'Of course,' I say, extracting myself from Mum's boob canyon and giving him a sorrowful look that I hope doesn't look sarcastic. He really didn't deserve the video I made about him and I know he's also a good dad to Noah (and the more the merrier, right?). He sits down on the other side of Mum as she puts on Saturday-night trashy TV.

'Sorry, Ruben,' I say, hanging my head in shame.

'Nah, it's cool,' he says. 'I thought that video was bloody hilarious. And I've been thinking of shaving the rug off anyway,' he adds, stroking his face.

'No,' I say. 'Don't. I like it,' I lie. But I feel like I need to throw the dude a bone.

The next morning, I come downstairs and stop at the door to the living room as I overhear Mum talking to Noah about Dad.

'So he's coming over later. For lunch?' Noah asks. 'My real dad?'

'Yeah,' Mum says quietly. 'Is that OK?'

'Yeah, course. Will he remember me?'

I close my eyes and swallow hard.

'Of course he will,' says Mum, and I can tell she's holding back tears too. 'Who could forget you, Noah?'

I can hear in her voice how much she's having to fight back her natural inclination to protect us against any possible hurt or sadness. So I walk in and, without saying anything, give her a hug, and just hope that that shows her how much I get it.

At lunchtime, Dad knocks on the door and I run down and answer. It's so weird seeing him walk into this house again after so many years.

'I'm sorry I didn't reply to your messages, Hay,' he says when he gets into the hall. 'Your mum, she *rightly . . .*'

'It's OK,' I say. 'You're here now. And I'm sorry about the videos.'

'No need, girl. In fact, I got you this to help you out with your next ones.'

He hands me a box, and when he does I notice his hands are shaking. I guess this isn't easy for any of us.

It's a GoPro camera!

'Wow, Dad, thank you!'

Mum appears in the doorway behind me, her arms crossed. 'John,' she says sternly.

'Hi, Dawn,' says Dad with an awkward smile. 'You're looking good. It's good to, y'know, see y–'

'Oh, shut up,' she says.

And I wince, wondering if this is actually the worst idea since Trump last had an idea.

Thankfully, she gives him a half-smile afterwards to let him know she's not actually about to attack him.

'Right.' He nods. 'Thanks for . . . I know it's not easy. Thank you.'

'Yeah, well, I'm not doing this for you,' she says in a calm but firm voice.

'I know,' he says.

The three of us stand for a moment in a silence so awkward it's the atmospheric equivalent of an autocorrected text where you meant to say 'I'm getting Pringles tonight' but it changes 'Pringles' to 'pregnant'.

'Well, this is fun, isn't it?' I say, trying to cut through the wall of tension. 'And you guys thought this would be awkward!'

Thankfully, it works and they both laugh. A little.

As we walk through to the living room, Ruben appears and shakes Dad's hand before disappearing into the kitchen, whistling through his beard as he goes like some demented overgrown eighth dwarf.

'Noah,' says Mum, 'this is . . . this is . . .'

Noah looks up from where he's sitting in his nest of Lego. He gives a slight frown and looks back down at his model. 'I know who it is,' he says.

Mum puts her hand over her mouth and looks up to the ceiling, fighting back tears.

Next to me, Dad lets out a shaky breath. I walk over to Noah and sit with him.

'Dude,' I say softly as Mum and Dad (SO weird to put those two names together) look on, 'it's OK. He just wants to say hi, that's all. Is that OK?'

Noah thinks about it for a moment, then lowers his voice to a whisper, which of course the whole room can still hear. 'I want him to stay for more than a "hi" cos me and Ruben bought him special yoghurts for puddling.'

And I can almost hear the cogs turning in his little brain; he wants Dad to stay, but he's scared he's gonna leave.

'He's not going to go anywhere, dude. He's totally up for those banana yoghurts with the weird chocolate flakes, isn't that right?' I look over at Dad.

'Yep, oh absolutely, my favourite,' he says, smiling, though his voice is shaky.

Mum is still holding her breath next to him.

Noah keeps looking down at his Lego, but says to Dad, 'Do you wanna make something from my Lego?'

Dad swallows back the tears and looks questioningly at Mum.

'It's OK,' she says softly.

'Yeah, I really do,' Dad says, and he walks towards us. I get up so he can take my place next to Noah.

I walk over and squeeze Mum's hand and she nods and gives me a sad smile back.

There's another knock on the door and I seize the opportunity to leave the heavy atmosphere in the room and answer it.

It's Grammo. I guess Mum thought the more people here to diffuse the situation the better. She hugs me and asks how things here are going in a voice she thinks is quiet and subtle, but is actually louder than a foghorn.

When I tell her it's about as comfortable as pooping in a holly bush, she says, 'Well, that's to be expected at first, but you can't break an omelette without baking eggs.'

She sashays into the living room and greets Mum with an especially big hug.

'Mo, lovely to see you,' says Dad, getting up to greet her. 'You're looking fabulous as always.'

'John,' she replies, 'you're looking old. Like someone who used to be good-looking, but didn't keep up the payments.'

Dad laughs through his nose before sitting back down with Noah.

'Hi, Grammo! This is "Dad".' Noah says the word 'Dad' like you would say, 'This is Rob,' or, 'This is Brian.'

'That's right, Noah,' says Grammo. 'A title so often given out before it's earned, but we'll see.'

She winks at Noah, who grins cluelessly back, then glares at Dad with a half-smile and raised eyebrows.

Dad nods in return. He knows he's on probation. One step out of line and he's out.

We have lunch together, keeping the conversation light and centring it mostly on Noah, as he's the only one blissfully unaware of the thorny environment everyone else is trying desperately to tiptoe through.

While shovelling forkfuls of shepherd's pie in our faces, we play Noah's favourite games: Facial Stereotypes, Guess What I Can Smell and Word Tennis, which was generally going well until the words 'man' then 'husband' came up. Mum said 'cheat', which was painfully awkward, then Grammo said 'wrong', and next up was Dad who said 'forgive?' Mum only just restrained herself from throwing a saucepan at his head. But slowly the atmosphere moves from horrendously awkward to manageable politeness and even at times to reasonably enjoyable. And in those moments I get a glimpse into how the future might be, when this becomes our new normal, of how a group of people who have been thrown together, torn apart, hurt each other, yet still find themselves tied to each other with strings of love can find a way to be a family.

After lunch, the adults drink coffee in the living room. When I go through, Dad is explaining to Noah that he's gotta go now, but hopes to see him again soon, and Noah seems OK with that. Dad lifts himself out of the Lego nest. 'I'd best be off then. Thanks for lunch and, well, for everything, Dawn.'

'No problem,' says Mum with a half-smile.

'Wait, before you go,' I say, then swallow hard as everyone looks quizzically at me. 'I wanted to say . . . Erm . . . I know this is super weird for everyone, but thanks for making it kinda work for me and Noah. And, everyone, I'm sorry, for the videos and everything.'

'Don't worry about it, Hay,' says Ruben. 'Seriously, me and John were just laughing about it. It *was* funny. I mean, a bit harsh maybe, but funny. It's cool.'

'A bit harsh!' says Mum. 'Rubes, you are allowed to get pissed off with her, y'know.'

'Oh, come on, Dawn,' says Dad. 'She's just a kid; she didn't mean it.'

He immediately knows he's said the wrong thing.

I can see Mum's seething. 'I do know she's just a kid, John. I don't need to be reminded of that.'

'Yeah, of course, I know. Sorry, Dawn,' he says.

For a moment, the tension in the room is so thick it could be spread on toast. And I know this isn't easy for any of them. I think about Dylan losing his mum and realize that having three, well, two and a half parents who care enough about me to put themselves through this awkwardness, actually makes me one pretty lucky girl.

'Well, this is fun!' I say stupidly, trying desperately to break the tension.

'As I said, I'd better be going,' says Dad.

'Yeah, me too,' says Ruben. 'Gotta get up early tomorrow – the council's coming round to mow my beard off.'

There's a brief silence and then we all laugh.

'Again, sorry,' I say to Ruben with a sheepish grin. And his beard, which really isn't all that bad, smiles back at me.

Dad says sorry to Mum again as he leaves, and then me and her cuddle up on the sofa and watch *QI* together, while Noah sits on the floor twitting about on the iPad.

When it finishes and Ruben's out in the kitchen, tidying up, Mum says to me, 'It will get easier, you know, with me and your dad.'

'I know, Mum. There's no rush though. I just like that you're trying.'

'You're the trying one,' she says, then an evil grin spreads over her face and she grabs my sides, and before I know it I'm begging for mercy as she tickle-bombs me like a pro. Noah immediately piles on to help her out in an unfair pincer attack.

All the while the Dylan thing is throbbing away at the back of my brain. And I don't know exactly how it's possible to be really sad about something yet laugh hysterically at something else at the same time, but it is. Just one of the weird wonders of the human brain, I guess.

TWENTY-SIX

A few gloomy days roll by and I'm grateful it's half-term because I really don't know how to face Kas and Chlo again. I send them more apology messages. But I don't hear anything back.

I do hear from Van though – and she LOVES the new videos! Says she thinks it's all 'just as funny, but with way more integrity and exactly what the comedy world needs right now – young female comics who are positive and unapologetic about themselves'. She posts it online and it starts getting even more hits than before! The comments are mostly great on the YouTube videos and although the troll-y stuff is still there I don't care so much now, because I have complete confidence in what I'm saying. I know it's good, I know it's truthful and, if people don't like that, if people don't like *me*, I don't care. I like me. And they can shove it. I just wish I could share all this excitement with Kas and Chlo. And Dylan.

Then, when I'm up in my room on Thursday afternoon, I hear Mum shouting at Noah to get the door, but there's no response from Noah. I suddenly realize that I forgot to 'unpause' him after the game we were playing twenty minutes ago, when I was pretending to control him with the TV remote. Turns out since then he's been standing stock-still in the middle of the living room. You have to respect that level of dedication to the imagination.

'Haylah, can you PLEASE unpause your brother?' Mum shouts up the stairs as she goes to get the door.

I go to the top of the stairs, shouting back down, 'Noah, I've pressed play – you can move again!' And then I see Kas and Chlo at the bottom of the staircase.

'Can we come up?' says Chlo.

'Er, yeah, hi, yeah,' I say, nervous and excited all at the same time. Oh God, I've missed them so much. What if they haven't forgiven me yet?

They walk into my room, which is untidier than ever and genuinely looks like there's been a break-in.

'I like what you've done with the place,' says Kas as she sits on my bed.

'Yeah, sorry, it is a bit, er . . .'

'Disgusting?' offers Chlo, using her thumb and forefinger to remove one of my bras from the bed at arm's length like it's radioactive, as she sits down next to Kas.

'Well, yeah,' I say, my anxiety levels rising as I sit a safe distance away from them on my desk chair.

'We've been talking, Hay,' says Chlo, 'and what you did, telling everyone online about our . . .'

I hang my head in shame.

'It stinks,' she finishes.

'It really does,' says Kas, 'but we know you've been going through it lately, with your dad and everything, and, well, we feel bad about not telling you about us going off after school next year and, well –'

'We forgive you,' says Chlo. 'And we miss you. Ya big plum.'

I look up at them and smile.

'And we love the new videos,' says Kas.

I get up and run over to the bed and jump on them, bowling them over with a huge hug.

'Urgh! Careful, Hay. I'm too pretty to die young!' says Chlo, laughing.

'Thank you, guys. I don't know what I'd do without you,' I say into their hair.

I realize as I say it that next year I really am going to have to learn how to do without them. But that's months away. And we'll make it work somehow.

We're back together now; that's the important thing.

I tell them all about Dylan and Leo. They 'oooh' and 'aah' in all the right places, and apologize for not being there for me over the last few days. When I'm done I feel fantastic that I have them back to share this stuff with, but I'm even more depressed about the Dylan thing. Truth is, I miss him. So much.

'Argh, it all sucks and it's all my fault.' Desperate to snap myself out of this brain fart, I leap up from the bed and lie on the floordrobe, making floorscum angels in my clothes with my legs and arms. They laugh. 'Right, someone change the subject, please,' I say, now sitting cross-legged in the valley between Stinky Mountain and Pants Peak.

Chloe tells us in graphic detail about all the time she's been spending with Watto.

I cringe and look to Kas for signs of jealousy, but she seems to be OK with it now. Perhaps she's had to get used to the idea of them being together. Poor Kas.

'Ugh, I don't know if it's gonna last though. Watto's a bit dull, and also a bit of a prick. The other day he told me I wear too much make-up.'

'He did what?' I say.

'Yeah, you would have been proud of me though, Hay. I said to him, "That's interesting that *you* think that; what's that got to do with me?"'

'Oh my God, Chlo, I've never been prouder,' I say, my hands over my heart.

'I always thought Watto was a moron,' says Kas.

Huh, I think.

'So you think you guys will be over and done with before Kyle comes to stay at Christmas?' I say.

'Yeah, defo, but, well . . .' Chlo squirms in a very un-Chlo way.

'What is it?' asks Kas.

'Nothing!' Chlo protests.

'Oh, come on, Chlo. I've aired all my dirty laundry in front of you,' I say, wafting some knickers around in the air.

'Eww! Argh, OK, but don't get mad at me,' she says.

'Why would we get mad?' asks Kas.

'Because I lied, OK? There *was* a guy called Kyle on holiday – he was eighteen and totally gorgeous – but, well, we didn't have a thing. Truth is, I fancied him, but he didn't fancy me back. Instead, his little brat of a brother who was, like, *twelve* did; he kept following me round the pool and everything. It was tragic. The closest I actually got to a thing with Kyle was when he handed me back one of my bikini tops that he had found in his brother's bed. God, it was disturbing.'

A laugh explodes through my nose and Kas fights back her own giggles.

'It's not funny; it was mortifying!' Chlo says, before a smile starts playing about on her lips. 'Yeah, OK, so I guess it was a *bit* funny. I'm sorry I lied though.'

'Why did you? It's *us*, Chlo. We're all tragic here!' I say.

'I don't know. You've got your comedy thing, Hay, and you're a bloody genius, Kas. I guess I was just worried you'd outgrow me or something. So I tried to make myself sound more interesting, I guess. Look, I know it was stupid.'

'Aww, Chlo,' says Kas with a sympathetic hand on Chlo's knee.

'It was stupid,' I say.

'Hay!' exclaims Kas.

'But *only because* you don't need boys to make you interesting, Chlo! And we're never going to "outgrow" you. We're in this together – we're stuck with each other, whether we like it or not!' I say.

Chlo beams. 'You're right. No more secrets, OK, guys?' she says.

I get up and plonk myself on the bed with them, thinking we'll probably laugh it all off now with a rude game of 'Would You Rather?' before watching *Pitch Perfect* for the hundredth time. But Kas shuffles away from us, leaning up against the wall, then weirdly clears her throat. We both look at her as she swallows hard and looks down at the pillow she's turning over in her hands.

'What?' I say, concerned that in this new spirit of 'no secrets' she's going to announce that she's in love with Watto.

'Yeah, what is it, Kas?'

Kas pulls my pillow up to her face and shouts into it, 'Urrrggghhh! Why is this so hard?'

Me and Chloe shoot a look at each other before Kas emerges from the pillow, that familiar look on her face again. A light smirk at the edge of her lips, a flush to her cheeks, like she has a wonderful secret, and I'm no longer sure that it's Watto, cos she wouldn't look so happy about that . . .

'Kas,' I say, 'are you all loved-up with someone?'

'Whoa! Really? That's so cool! Who with?!' explodes Chlo with an excited hand clap.

Kas looks down at the pillow. 'Well –' she clears her throat again – 'you know Lola . . .'

'Yeah . . .?' say me and Chloe, waiting.

Kas looks up at us with a shy smirk and I realize, of course, that Lola *is* the story.

'Oh!' I say with a smile as my heart swells for Kas. She must have been going through so much lately – and she's being so brave right now. Although she really shouldn't have to be. I crawl over to her and grab her for a big hug. 'Kas, that's awesome – why didn't you tell us, ya big prick?'

She laughs and hugs me back. 'I dunno, because I'm a big prick, I guess? But thanks, Hay.'

'I don't get it,' says Chlo as me and Kas break apart, but I keep holding her hand.

'Seriously, Chlo?' I say.

'What? What am I missing?' she says, throwing her arms up in the air.

'Well,' says Kas, '*me* and *Lola* are, y'know . . .'

We both stare at Chlo and you can almost hear the cogs turning in her brain, eventually ending with a triumphant *ping* as the penny drops. She gasps and throws a hand to her mouth. 'Oh my *God*, that's epic!' she squeals, climbing over me and grabbing Kas for her own hug. 'And, dude, Lola's *really* pretty – you are punching well above your weight.'

We all laugh, and as we release her from our hug-bundle Kas's eyes are filled with tears. We both hold her hands.

'Thanks, guys, for being cool about this,' she mumbles, still smiling.

'Are you kidding me? Thanks for telling us, dude,' I say.

'Totes what she said. That is so cool that you chose to tell us,' agrees Chlo.

Kas sighs. 'God, I'm so relieved. The thing is, it's all so weird because I feel deliriously happy all the time and yet I kind of feel as if I have to tell people like it's a bad thing, something I should be sorry about. But the thing is I'm not.'

I can't begin to imagine what Kas is going through, but I feel so proud of her right now. And I also hate the fact that I'd just presumed she was into boys, like an idiot, and that telling us she has a girlfriend was so difficult for her. I hate that this has to be something she worries about at all, that anyone has to think that there's a bit of themselves that they have to keep boxed up and not admit to because we live in a screwed-up world that says, 'Until you tell us otherwise, we're gonna go right ahead and presume you're a bunch of stuff we've decided is "normal".'

'It's not a *bad* thing. It's the opposite. It's a frickin' awesome thing – it's lurve!' I say.

'Yay!' squeals Chlo.

Kas beams.

'Does anyone else know?' I ask.

'No, not yet. And I kind of want to keep it that way. For now.'

'Of course, whatever you want,' I say.

'However you wanna play this, we're in your hands, OK?' says Chlo. Then her face lights up like she's just been switched on. 'And, oh my GOD, this is so great – now we have a reason to go on the pride march!! You're my way into the fabulous gay community – thank you!'

I roll my eyes at Kas.

Kas grimaces. 'I don't think it's all feather boas and leather thongs from here on in.'

'Oh, let me have my fun!' purrs Chlo.

Kas smiles. 'I just fell in love with Lola, that's all.'

Chlo claps her hands together. 'That's amazing, that's like *pan*sexual. I wonder if everyone will be pansexual in the future? God, you're so ahead of the game, Kas.'

'Oooh, which one's pansexual again?' I ask.

Kas giggles and Chlo fans out her fingers, glowing at being the one in the know. 'You muppet. Pansexual is fancying someone cos of what's on the inside, not what's on the outside. It's personality that matters, not ya bits. It's really cool,' says Chlo.

'Except,' says Kas, 'that you're basically the opposite of pan, Chlo; you *only* fancy boys *regardless* of their personalities.'

'Oh, very strong,' I say, high-fiving Kas.

'Oi!' says Chloe, throwing cushions at our heads. 'OK, so at the moment I'm one hundred per cent boy crazy, but who knows what might happen in the future? With ANY of us. We're fifteen, free and fabulous, darlings – it's all to play for!'

'Hell, yeah,' I agree, and we chuck cushions at each other, fall about in hysterics and spend the next hour hearing all the details about Lola and Kas's relationship. It just feels so great to all be this close again, and you can almost see the huge weight coming off Kas's shoulders as she's finally able to share her happiness with us.

I wince at my earlier stupidity at thinking they were the beautiful ones and so didn't have their own issues and insecurities. I'd been so wrapped up in my own Dylan-and-Dad-based dramas I hadn't even noticed that Chlo was making up the stuff about Kyle or that Kas was prepping to come out to us, for goodness' sake. Lying back on the bed together, I say, 'It's pretty rough, isn't it, being a girl?'

'Yep,' says Kas with a sigh.

'Damned *straight*,' says Chlo, before adding, 'No offence, Kas.'

Kas flops another cushion on to Chlo's head.

I reach over and grab my phone to check my messages as usual, to see if something's come in from Dylan. Which, of course, it hasn't.

'Dude, just call him,' says Chlo, watching me.

'Nah, he doesn't wanna hear from me,' I say, sighing.

'Didn't he say something about big romantic gestures when you broke up?' asks Kas.

'Yeah, he just said he didn't think we needed all that stuff,' I say.

'Yeah, but he also said that *you* didn't do any of that "stuff" either. I dunno, maybe he wants you to? He said all those nice things to you, so maybe you need to make it super clear, after the Leo thing, how much you like him too?' says Chlo, playfully wiggling her eyebrows up and down at me.

'And it shouldn't all be down to boys, you know,' adds Kas. 'If you want him, don't wait for him to come get you. Let him know!'

They've got a point. He let me know how he felt about me and I've never really let him know how strongly I feel about him. Why should the boys get to make all the big romantic gestures? I am super desperate to get him back. And so me, Kas and Chlo hatch a plan.

TWENTY-SEVEN

The next evening Chlo manages to persuade her sister, Freya, and Freya's boyfriend, Jake, to help us out. If they don't, Chloe threatens, she'll tell her mum that Freya and Jake *did it* in her bed the last time she was on a spa day.

Me, Chlo and Kas squish into the back of Jake's bad joke of a car and we drive to Dylan's house.

Only as soon as I'm jammed in the middle of the back seat it all becomes real and my stomach fills with a thousand vomiting butterflies.

'You OK, Pig? I mean, *Hay*, dammit!' says Chlo with a hand on my knee.

I realize again that when Chlo and Kas call me 'Pig' I feel comforted. It's what the people I love called me for so long, and though everything is changing, and I know I can't stop that, there are some things I want to stay the same.

'Guys, I've been thinking. If you two wanna keep calling me Pig, I'm cool with that.'

They both stare at me as if I've set them some sort of trap. 'I'm serious,' I say.

'But you're never serious,' says Kas suspiciously.

'OK, fair enough, but on this occasion I am. Truth is, I miss it. When you guys call me Hay, it just sounds like my mum or something and it makes me nervous.'

'Oh, thank God for that,' Chlo says with a sigh. 'I mean, what with all the school stuff they're cramming into our brains this year, trying to remember to call you something different was doing my head in.'

'I know what Chlo means,' says Kas. 'I mean, the thing is, I look at you and think Pig – no, wait, that came out wrong. I don't mean you look like a pig, I just – Chlo, help!'

'You're not *a* pig, but you are, most definitely, Pig.'

I laugh. 'I get it. And I totally agree.'

'Yay! Pig's back!' says Kas, leaning across me and fist-bumping Chlo.

'Anyway, back to today. I don't think I can do this,' I say, nervous as hell.

'Oh, come on, Pig, what's the worst that could happen?' says Kas.

'Er, crippling humiliation, fatal injury, arrest, Dylan hating me forever more?'

'Yeah, but *apart* from that,' says Chlo, examining her nails.

'Of course you can do this,' says Kas, 'and, even if it doesn't work, you'll have given it your best shot, right?'

Oh. Holy. Bum cracks.

'So you think it won't work?'

'I didn't say that!'

'I'll say it then,' says Jake from the driving seat. 'There's no *way* this is going to work. He's gonna think you're an absolute plank.'

Brilliant. Thanks, Jake.

'Oh, don't be such an old grouch, Jake,' says Freya, who turns round to face me. 'I think it's lovely what you're doing, Hay. You know you're gonna fail, but you're doing it anyway, and that shows *real* courage.'

'Oh God,' I say into my hands.

Chlo and Kas both put their arms round me.

'You can so do this,' says Chlo, though out of the corner of my eye I can see that she just pulled an 'eek' emoji face. But I've come this far, and I may as well see it through. Whatever happens.

We drive down Dylan's street.

'Blimey, this area is posh, Pig. You sure Dylan lives here?' says Chlo.

'Yeah, I know, doesn't quite compute, does it? You can only tell when you're in the rough end of the street because the kids on the corner are drinking Sainsbury's Sauvignon Blanc not Waitrose's.'

'Is that right?' says Freya.

'I think it was a joke,' says Jake.

'That's his house,' I say, gulping, and the reality hits me again. 'But, look, I think we should turn round – this was a bad idea.'

'Agreed,' says Jake, indicating to do a U-turn.

'NO!' screech Kas, Chlo and Freya.

'All right, all right!' he says.

Me and Jake both sigh as we roll up Dylan's huge front drive.

'Right,' says Chlo excitedly, 'we'll stay in the car; we don't want to ruin your moment. You get ready, and tell me when to send him the text.'

Jake passes me his speakers, which I plug into my phone with shaky hands, and I get out of the car, my heart pounding, and climb on to the bonnet and then up on to the roof. Well, I did tell you this was a bloody stupid idea.

'Oi! Watch the paintwork!' says Jake out of the window.

'Shhhh!' the others whisper-shout at him.

The car creaks as I stand shakily on the roof and tell Chlo, 'Send it now before I frickin' fall off this thing!'

'She'd better not; she'll dent the cocking bonnet,' I hear Jake grumble.

Oh God, oh goddy giddy crap monkey frickin' nutballs, what the hell *am I doing? There's a reason why girls aren't supposed to do this stuff, because it takes the kind of special stupidity only* boys *are capable of.*

'Sent!' says Chlo out of the window.

There's no going back now. I press play on my phone and I stare up at Dylan's bedroom. He must have read Chlo's text telling him to look outside because after a few seconds he opens the window and pokes his confused face out of it.

Just seeing him again makes me happy. Oh, please let this work . . .

He looks down, his mouth falling open as he takes in the alarming sight below him: me standing on top of a knackered old car, a red rose in my teeth, holding two small but fiercely powerful speakers above my head, which are playing Flight of the Conchords's 'I'm Not Crying' at FULL volume, and on my white T-shirt there's a large message written in black Sharpie across my chest, which reads PLEASE TAKE ME BACK, DYLAN!

And for some reason it only really strikes me now that, if he brutally rejects me after all this, I *really* am the loser of the century, and it's quite possible I may never again have the self-respect to show my face in public.

His mouth shuts after a while as I give him the most pleading look I can muster as I sway along to the music.

For a heart-stopping moment, I think he's just going to shut the window, possibly call the police and definitely book himself some intensive counselling to get over this embarrassing ordeal, but instead a huge grin spreads across his face, which then turns into a full-on laugh. YES!!!!!!

'YOU'RE CRAZY!!' he shouts.

'I KNOW!' I try to shout back, but because of the flower in my mouth it actually comes out as, 'UH-UUHHH.'

He laughs. 'WAIT THERE!' he yells as if I'm gonna get back in the car and drive off to do this all again outside the next guy's house.

The girls in the car below me squeal with delight, which is great, although a little assistance getting down from here would be slightly more helpful right now. I sit and then manage to slide myself down the front of the car, which makes the girls laugh hysterically and Jake almost throw up at the sight of my buttocks flattened across his windscreen slowly descending with a drawn-out, high-pitched screech.

'Argh, COME ON!' Jake says in disgust.

Above the sound of the butt-screeching, the song from the speakers in my hands is still playing at full volume.

'Do you bloody mind?' shouts the next-door neighbour from their own aircraft-hangar-sized property.

''Orry!' I shout through the rose, trying to get the phone out of my pocket to turn down the music.

Dylan emerges from the front door. And, yeah, he looks happy about me making such an idiot of myself, but my heart races as I wonder what the hell he's going to say or do.

'Leave it,' he says, walking towards me and smiling. 'It's our song.'

I spit out the rose so the grin can fully spread over my face.

'I know,' I say as he stands right in front of me, the song bellowing out. I could have chosen a super-romantic song, but this is better, more us. It's funny, and stupid, and sweet. And, though we've heard it hundreds of times, we both still laugh.

'SHUT THAT RUBBISH OFF!' shouts the disembodied voice again from next door.

'Argh, shut up yourself!' shouts Dylan back, then he looks at me. 'What are you doing here, Hay?'

'What do you think I'm doing here, doofus?' I say nervously, then I gulp hard before I repeat the line he said to me last week back at him. 'I really like you, like really, massively, can't-stop-thinking-about-you, wanna-be-with-you-all-the-time *like* you.'

He smiles, takes a deep breath and says, 'Woman, that's a terrible line.'

I laugh. Though my heart is still hammering away like it's chosen this moment to do some frantic DIY in my insides. 'You're right. I'm actually just here because I was in the neighbourhood and I remembered that I may have left my high heels here.'

'You don't wear high heels.'

'Oh, that's right. I'll be off then.' And I turn to fake-leave, but he smiles and grabs both my hands in his.

'Just stop joking. For a moment.'

'I can't,' I say.

'Why?'

And for a second my stupid brain thinks about spewing out another joke, but I know this moment needs something real. So I take a deep breath.

'Because . . . my craziness for you manifests itself as constant rambling jokes, and I'm worried that the only reason you like me is because I'm funny so if I stop being funny you'll go and then –'

And then he interrupts me by leaning down and kissing me. ACTUALLY KISSING ME.

I'm kissing Dylan! *I'm kissing Dylan!!!*

It starts off soft and slow, then steps up a notch to proper running-hands-through-hair kissing, as everyone in the car behind me, plus Dylan's dad, who has just emerged through the front door, erupts into applause and whoops and cheers.

Fireworks burst in my head! This is actually happening!

I'm being kissed by someone I wanna kiss, by someone who wants to kiss me and doesn't care who knows it! And it feels motherflipping amazing!

When we stop, he smiles, pulls back and says, 'You are funny. Not to mention fun and clever and exciting to be around, but, well –' he looks awkwardly down at his feet then up at me again – 'I also think you're . . . hot . . . you know?'

'Yeah, ahem,' I say, flustered yet unable to keep the smile from my face, 'well, I get that now. That's, well, that's good to know. Really helpful information.'

He laughs, then glances around at my T-shirt, the rose and speakers on the ground, the people in the car with their faces pressed up against the windows (apart from Jake who's staring at his phone and shaking his head).

'You're also a complete doughnut,' he says, laughing.

I laugh too. 'I know I am, but what are you?'

'Oh God, I think I might have sucked all the decent comedy comebacks out of you,' he says.

'Maybe,' I say. 'Let's test that theory.' And I grab him and snog him again.

Everyone who was cheering is now laughing and shouting.

'Enough already!'

'Argh, get a room!'

'Have some self-control!'

'My eyes, my eyes!'

Late that night, Dylan sends me a message.

> I've always liked that Janis Ian song you added to our
> list. But, frickin' hell, it's depressing. And it's *not* you.
> I've added one too. See what you think.

I've never heard the song before. It's this cool, kitsch sixties thing called 'It's Getting Better' by this big awesome singer called Mama Cass. The further into the song I get, the more the smile on my face grows. It's all about how not all relationships are this big insta-love rockets, bells and poetry yuck-fest. Sometimes the best relationships slowly grow 'stronger, warm and wilder', becoming this incredible happy, comfortable thing that just keeps getting better every day. I listen to it over and over as I fall asleep.

TWENTY-EIGHT

A couple of weeks later and I'm on my way to Van's gig. My first proper comedy gig.

On the other side of the train window, trees chase lamp posts as we hurtle our way into London. My eyes refocus on the window itself where someone's drawn a willy in the window dirt. And I wonder what makes someone sit here and think, *You know what this window needs? A rudimentary knob drawing, and, dammit, I'm just the artist for the job.*

Next to the willy I see the reflection of Chlo, Kas and Lola squashed up on the double seat opposite, Lola looking at Kas with big admiring eyes, as Kas does some huge, weird braid thing to Chlo's hair, which makes her look like someone stuck a Cornish pasty to the side of her head.

Over on the opposite side of the train, Dad is sitting with Ruben, Noah and Mum at a table, playing Uno together. Mum sternly smiles at Dad as he tells Noah to watch out for Mum as she's known for her cheating. Out of Dad's sight, I can see Ruben holding Mum's hand tightly under the table to stop her from throwing a punch at him.

Behind them are Grammo and her friend June, who are still arguing about Grammo getting the window seat. 'I'm just saying, you *know*, I get one of my heads if I can't see out properly.'

Then I glance down and see my own hand resting on the seat between me and Dylan, and Dylan's hand clasped round it. And, yeah, it still feels awkward and weird. But good-weird. I just never thought that Dylan – DYLAN – would end up making me feel like this. But then aren't we all full of hidden surprises and depths that we only reveal to the right people at the right time?

And no one, not even your closest family and friends, nobody knows all the bits of you. You show a different side of yourself to everyone, but, like a dice, from any angle there are always sides that are hidden from view.

To Lola, Kas is this gorgeous and mysterious new girlfriend; to Chlo and me, she's our old brainiac pillock best friend.

To me and Noah, Dad is our dad, and, yes, he went away but now he's back and seems to want to make it up to us, but to Mum he's the ex who stamped all over her heart with his big man shoes.

To Mum, I'm her little crazy girl who always preferred playing in the mud to dressing up as a princess; to Kas and Chlo, I'm the one who always takes a joke too far, but they love me anyway.

And to Dylan, well, I don't know exactly what I am to Dylan yet, but I know that, unlike with Leo, he makes me feel happy and special. It's kinda fun working out exactly what I am to him as I go.

We're all a hundred different things to a hundred different people, and that's OK. That's why it's OK if some people don't like or get you, because others will see you from another angle and totally love what they see. And sometimes, like with me and Dylan, your angle will change and suddenly the person you've been looking at forever is still that same person, but now you see the sunnier side, and there's no going back to the way you saw them before.

And I'm tired of hiding my bits. It's time to proudly wave my bits in the face of the world.

And, argh, I'm about to get onstage and show another side of me to a whole new room of strangers. But these guys around me have now all seen my worse sides and are still here, so there's nothing that a bunch of strangers can throw at me that can be that bad, right? Unless they throw a grenade, I guess, but I strongly doubt my set will be *that* terrible.

I look down at my set notes for the hundredth time today. I let go of Dylan's hand for a moment as I scribble down a few changes. After all, change is a good thing, or at least it can be.

I know that things are going to change; it's just the way the world goes round. Ruben's moving in, Dad's come back and at the end of the school year me and my girls will go our separate ways. I just need to roll with it and see what happens – see! ROLL WITH IT! Dammit, I KNEW the dice analogy was a good one.

So what's my point? I dunno, maybe just that we should all be a bit less terrified about showing the world that we're pretty terrified of it, then maybe we can all laugh in its face together instead of running and hiding.

And hopefully I can help a little with that. After all, what is a comedian if not a crude drawing of a willy on a train window, just trying to make the world a little bit sillier, a little bit funnier, a little bit brighter against a constantly evolving backdrop?

I put my pen away, satisfied with the changes I've made. I hold on to Dylan's hand again and read through my set one last time as we hurtle ever onwards.

'Don't worry, Hay – you got this,' he whispers.

I let go of his hand and sit up straight. Boobs out, shoulders back.

Cos more than any other person's opinion of me, what matters is my own opinion of me, and right now I'm pretty convinced that, with all these guys around me, I'm pretty awesome.

'Yeah,' I say with a smile. 'I know.'

ACKNOWLEDGEMENTS

In my acknowledgements for *Pretty Funny* I said that it turns out that writing a novel is fun but it's also bloody hard. What I found with *Pretty Rude* is that writing a second novel is so much easier . . . in no way whatsoever.

So again I have to thank everyone, friends and family, who put up with me when I was writing this and whingeing on at them about plot structure, whether or not a joke was funny enough to include and why the hell they hadn't brought me Jaffa cakes in my time of need.

Specifically I need to thank my agent Laetitia who, if she's ever felt understandably frustrated with my numptiness, has always hidden it incredibly well and has remained relentlessly encouraging and beautifully supportive.

I also must send solid gold thanks to the wonderful team at Penguin Random House: Emily, Steph, Anne, Sophia, Michelle, Rosamund and particularly the lovely Naomi and Emma, without whom Haylah would never have existed anywhere other than in my brain. Thank you for your incredible belief in the book and patience with me

(I promise I *will* learn how to punctuate dialogue properly one of these days, honest).

Then there's all the gorgeous folks at Peachtree who have brought Haylah to the US audience, particularly Jonah and Elyse.

I'm forever grateful to THE Sharon Rooney who, and I still can't get over this, agreed to read the audio version of *Pretty Funny*. Watching her read was an incredible and humbling experience, as she truly *acted* my words and made what I'd written a whole load funnier. She was also a joy to hang out with and I'll never forget her particularly hilarious tale involving a wardrobe malfunction and Danny DeVito. Not my story to tell though, you'll have to ask her yourself.

Still my endless gratitude goes to my parents for their unconditional love and encouragement, and apologies to every delivery person, tradesperson and passer-by my parents' house who have had to put up with my dad waffling on about his daughter's career and doing an unrequested show-and-tell of my books. My mum, my hero, remains my first reader of everything I write and without her enthusiasm, assistance and support I truly believe I would never had written a word. Love you guys.

I also have to thank (because otherwise I'll never hear the end of it) my best friend, rock and podcasting partner ('Don't Laugh But' – check it out!), the hilarious stand-up comedian Kirsty Hudson. I just don't know where I'd be without you, you wonderful, crazy woman.

And then there's my two gorgeous, hilarious boys who never fail to make me belly laugh every single day. Toby, who remains my biggest fan and has read *Pretty Funny* more times than my editors, and Benjy, now eight, who, when I asked him the other day if he knew that one of the characters in *Pretty Funny* was based on him, replied in his most brilliantly sarcastic voice, 'Er *yeah*, Mummy, I remember that I couldn't say anything to you for a year without you writing it down.' And I'm forever indebted to my daughter Clemmie who, had she still been with us, would now be the same age as Haylah. I've said it before but dammit I'll say it again, you continue to inspire everything I do. Proud of you, girl.

Lastly I want to thank from the bottom of my heart and the heart of my bottom every reader of *Pretty Funny* and *Pretty Rude*. Especially the teenage girls. Keep bravely wobbling your funny bits in the face of life, girls. You got this.

Find out how it all started in . . .

PRETTY FUNNY

Does anyone ever really
want to 'fall' in love?
Knowing me I'll just trip
over it and graze
my knee on the gravel
of humiliation.

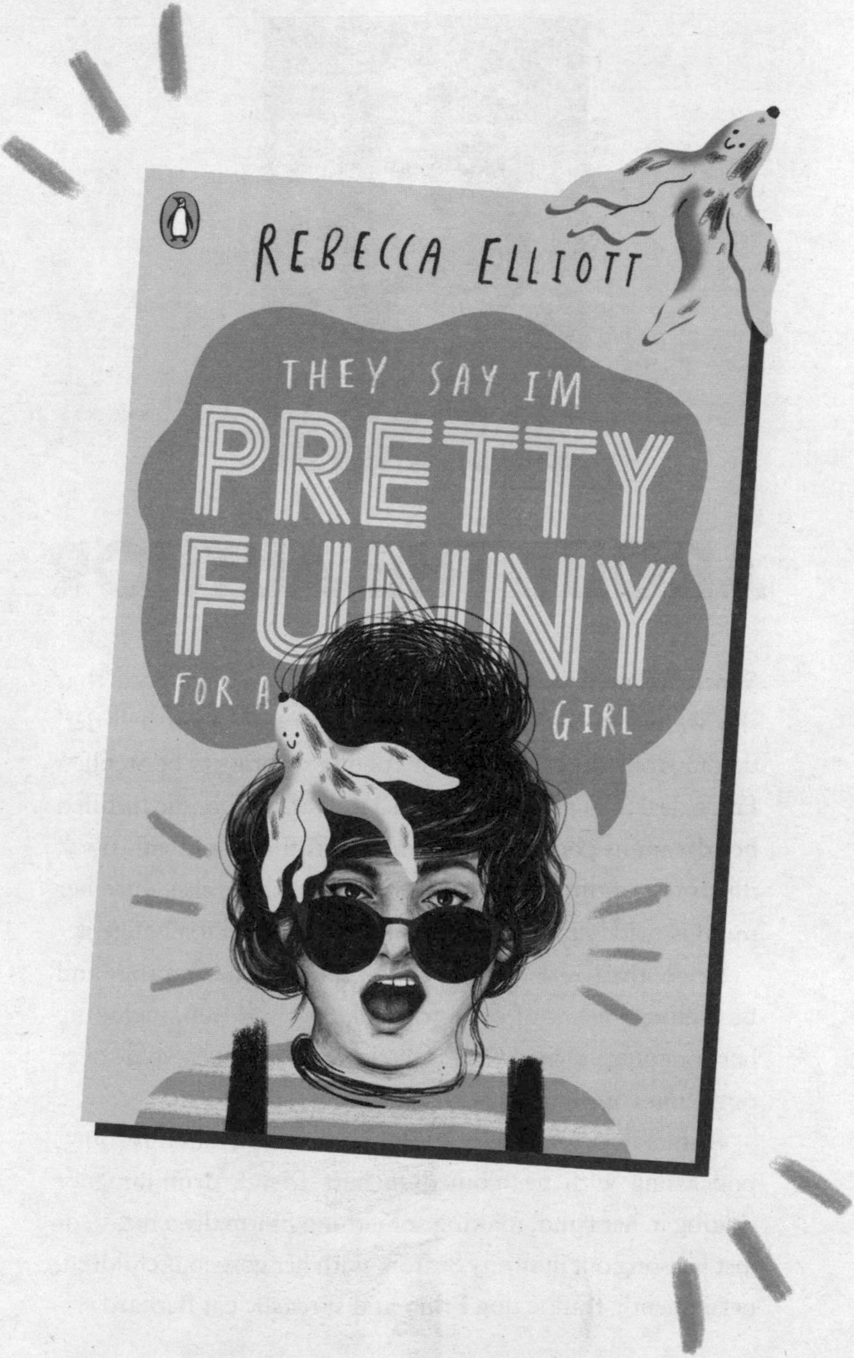
REBECCA ELLIOTT
THEY SAY I'M
PRETTY
FUNNY
FOR A
GIRL

© Tom Soper Photography

ABOUT THE AUTHOR

When Rebecca was six, she precociously pronounced that she wanted to be 'an artist and a writer'. After a 'brief' detour from this career plan involving wanting to be Stephen Fry, a degree in philosophy and a dull office job, she fulfilled her dream in 2001. She became a full-time children's book illustrator, ultimately proving that, if nothing else, once her mind is made up, she really can't be bothered to change it.

Since then she has become an award-winning and bestselling author of over 30 books for children, including her ongoing series Owl Diaries, which has sold over 6 million copies worldwide.

If she's not story-making, Rebecca can be found reading, podcasting with her comedian best friend, drumming or singing in her band, making something (normally a mess), or just hanging out in sunny Suffolk with her gorgeous children, permanently frantic dog Frida and sarcastic cat Bernard.